SHADES OF RESOLUTION

Distortion Series, Book 3

By Aimee McNeil

SHADES OF RESOLUTION

Copyright © 2017 by Aimee McNeil.
All rights reserved.
First Print Edition: January 2017

Limitless Publishing, LLC
Kailua, HI 96734
www.limitlesspublishing.com

Formatting: Limitless Publishing

ISBN-13: 978-1-68058-956-6
ISBN-10: 1-68058-956-3

DEDICATION

This is for me.
"Why?" you ask.
Because I wrote the damn thing…

Fine, it can be for you too…

This is for you and me.

CHAPTER ONE

Nate

The room spun as Nate pushed his exhausted body out of bed. He drug his feet over the coarse carpet, supporting himself against the wall as a wave of vertigo hit him. He leaned his head against his arm as he waited for the gripping feeling to subside. The liquor and drugs in his system were starting to fade and the beginning of an angry hangover was beginning to claw at his stomach. The smell of the dingy wall in dire need of cleaning did not do him any favors.

He looked up when the sound of voices began to infiltrate the fog in his head and he noticed he'd left the television on. For a moment he forgot where he was until his memories slowly allowed him access. Once Stephanie had been cleared at the hospital, they had brought her back to the motel to be with Lexie.

The thought of Stephanie and that horrid place made his insides turn and he bolted into the washroom. He barely made it to the toilet before he violently expelled the contents of his stomach. Nate turned on the sink and splashed water on his face. He grabbed the hand towel and dried himself off as he looked at his reflection. His eyes were red and dark circles hung heavy underneath. He looked exactly how he felt. When he turned off the water, the television grabbed his attention.

"...Belhaven is in a state of shock this morning when it was discovered that Mayor Terence Masten has a darker side than anyone could have imagined. A property that has been linked to Masten was found to have a young woman held prisoner..."

Nate pushed himself off the counter and walked into the main area to see the broadcast. Footage of the exterior of the house was on the screen. Crime scene tape was everywhere but he didn't need the footage to know how shocking the scene was. He had seen it for himself and the images still haunted him.

"It is known that Masten was on the property at the time authorities arrived and was arrested. The last we heard the woman is being treated for minor injuries. At this time we do not have all the details, but we do know the tale does not end there. Human remains found in shallow graves on the property indicate the situation is far more terrible than originally believed. The number of victims is still undetermined at this time. As the numbers climb, people are left wondering how they did not know their beloved Mayor was capable of such a horrific crime."

Nate hit the power button and stood staring at the

black screen for a moment, frozen with the reporter's words tumbling around in his throbbing head. He shoved the television off the entertainment unit and watched it crash to the floor. Ever since he saw Stephanie's tattoo and remembered hearing Masten call her by his mother's name, the realization carved away at him like a sharp knife. He couldn't stomach the truth of what this meant.

Nate spun around and walked over to his nightstand where his gun was sitting. He grabbed the handle and stalked back into the bathroom. He pulled the shower curtain back and stepped into the tub.

He dropped down into the tub and stared at the gun in his hands but all he could see was the lake house and that cage in the basement. He'd spent his whole life hating the mother who abandoned him and left him to a father who disowned him for a new family that wanted nothing to do with him. Hatred was so much easier to swallow than the pain of what was now presented to him. Instead of mourning his beautiful mother like he should have, he'd torn her memory down until he had erased her completely from his life.

Nate leaned his head back against the tile and wiped the tears from his face with the back of his shaking hand. He took a deep breath and slid the gun into his mouth. He didn't let himself think about what he was doing. He acted numbly, desperate to evade the pain as he pulled the trigger.

The sound of the empty click barely registered over his heartbeat filling his ears like rushing water.

"Jesus, Nate," Jackson blurted as he rushed into

the bathroom and pulled the gun from his hands. "You didn't think I would actually leave you alone with a loaded gun after how you acted yesterday."

Nate looked up at him as he dropped his hands in his lap. He couldn't even bring himself to respond. His mind was still digesting the fact that he was still alive.

Jackson grabbed him by the shoulders and hauled him out of the tub. Nate didn't resist as Jackson walked him out of the bathroom. "I can't believe you just did that. Don't pull that fucking shit again." Jackson led him toward the bed and guided him to the edge.

Nate sat numbly staring at the wall. The sound of a high pitched whistling filled his head and fogged his mind. His head felt too full, like it was ready to explode.

"...can you even hear me?" Jackson asked, leaning down in front of him. "Nate?" He slapped him lightly on the side of the face, which brought him back from being lost inside his head.

"Yeah," Nate responded lazily as he blinked his eyes and tried to focus. The outlines of his vision blurred.

"What the hell happened at the lake house?"

"Get my wallet." Nate waved languidly toward the nightstand.

Jackson looked over at the wallet and then back at Nate.

"Just get it. There's a picture tucked inside."

Jackson opened it up and pulled out the picture. He studied it for a moment before looking up at Nate. "Who's this?" Jackson asked in confusion.

"That's my mother. Remember how I told you she fucking left me when I was barely five years old and never came back?" Nate squeezed his eyes shut.

"Yeah."

"That tattoo on her neck…Stephanie's. It's identical to my mother's," Nate confessed as he took a deep breath and looked up at Jackson.

Realization dawned on Jackson's face. "It could just be a coincidence."

"Her name was Rose. That's what Masten called Stephanie."

"Nate…"

"I saw the news about there being other victims." Nate raked his hand down his face. "I can feel it, Jackson. I could feel it when I was there. I hated my mother my whole life for leaving me and now there could be a very horrible reason why she never came back. She deserved better from me," Nate sobbed.

Jackson dropped on the bed next to Nate without saying a word. Nate wasn't sure how much time passed as Jackson just sat beside him. One of the things he liked best about Jackson was that he knew the value of silence. He closed his eyes to take deep, even breaths as he came down from his adrenaline high and pain and exhaustion began to grip him again.

"You didn't hate her, Nate, or you wouldn't have carried her around with you all these years." Jackson held up the picture still in his hand. "I'm not gonna let you give up," Jackson said firmly.

"What now?" Nate asked, searching Jackson's eyes.

"Let's just start with you living another day and

we'll go from there. You have enough people trying to kill you. Let's not make it too easy for them."

"Fuck...where's that gun?" Nate moaned.

"I'm keeping it for now." Jackson gave him a pat on the shoulder with a pained smile. "Get yourself cleaned up. We need to take the girls back to Freyview."

"You still want me to come?" Nate asked.

"Yeah, we need you." Jackson tucked the picture back in Nate's wallet and set it back on the nightstand.

Nash rubbed his hands down his face and fell back on the bed. "It's so much easier to hate, isn't it?"

"Don't I fucking know it," Jackson sighed.

CHAPTER TWO

Jackson

Lexie and Stephanie were huddled in the backseat and had barely spoken a word during the drive. Once the detective in charge of the Masten case questioned Stephanie, they left the hospital in Millwood as soon as possible. Physically she was fine with only minor dehydration. It was what they could not see, the toll it had taken on her mentally that had everyone worried. It had become normal for her to stare blankly at nothing, tuning the world out around her. Jackson didn't know her well, but one thing was very clear. Stephanie was not the same person she was before she was taken. She barely spoke, and when she did, it was only to appease the questions of others with lifeless words. She was withdrawn and closed off. She looked like a girl who had accepted death and didn't know how to start living again. Jackson was intimately familiar with that feeling.

Beth's death had shocked everyone. It had

almost broken Lexie, but the return of Stephanie pulled her out of her own grief enough to focus her attention on her friend. The transformation from a state of complete despondency to doting friend was dramatic and too soon. While Jackson liked seeing Lexie functioning again, he knew she was just delaying the grief she needed experience to move on and heal. He knew eventually she would be worn down to the girl that lost her mother again and she would be overwhelmed with sorrow. When this happened, he planned to be by her side and help her through every step. Until then he needed to fix the crumbling world around them, starting with bringing Evan home.

After hours of shifting through the hospital's surveillance footage, Teddy was finally able to pin down the individual that had been in Beth's room before her death. Jackson wasn't surprised that the man was aware of the camera locations and avoided an identifying view of his face, but they all knew without a doubt who it was. As soon as Jackson saw the image of the man his lingering doubt about Rosh's involvement dissipated. His father's partner had betrayed them all and Jackson couldn't wait to shed light on him. He could still see the frame frozen on the screen, the only frame with a partial face. It wasn't enough to accuse Rosh, but it was enough to satisfy Jackson. He tightened his hands on the steering wheel.

As they drove into town, Jackson noticed posters pinned in store windows and on street posts. Pictures of Lexie, Beth, and Stephanie were displayed on each of them. The small town had been set into a state of panic when three of its own disappeared without explanation. The solemn mood thickened in the car. Even Teddy, sitting in the passenger's seat, didn't dare speak a word as they drove through the quiet streets.

Jackson had Dane take Nate to get him a good meal and a strong cup of coffee to get his focus back. He couldn't have Nate falling apart on him. He needed him strong to stay back and keep an eye on the girls while they went back to Belhaven. He didn't trust the officers who would be assigned to watch Lexie and Stephanie. Jackson needed someone he could rely on to give him eyes in Freyview so he could focus on what he needed to do. Jackson knew they were far from out of the woods. They were still in the middle of the storm without any sign of light on the other side, and Jackson needed to make sure they had hope that an end would come for all their sakes.

When Jackson pulled onto Stephanie's street, he finally broke the silence. "Remember the story. No one mentions John Stodden." Jackson glanced in the rear view mirror to see Lexie staring back at him. "The less people who know about his involvement, the better for us," Jackson continued. She nodded and pulled Stephanie closer to her side. Jackson brought the car to a stop in front of Stephanie's house and turned off the ignition.

The front door opened and a middle-aged woman with similar features to Stephanie walked down the steps, followed by two men Jackson assumed were her father and boyfriend. Jackson stepped out and rounded the car to open the rear door.

As soon as Stephanie stepped out of the car, the woman rushed to her and threw her arms around her neck. "Steph, baby," the woman cried. "I was so worried. I'm so glad you're safe."

When Lexie stepped out behind them, the woman gathered her up in their hug. "I'm so sorry, Lexie," she sobbed.

The older gentleman approached Jackson and offered his hand. "Thank you for bringing the girls back," he offered gratefully. "My name's Tom." He gave Jackson's hand a firm shake. "Her mother, Ruth, and this is Stephanie's boyfriend, Mike."

Jackson gave them a polite nod, noting that the boyfriend narrowed his eyes suspiciously. He obviously had reservations toward Jackson. He didn't blame him, Jackson was never one to give great first impressions, and after what they had just been through, his demeanour was less than welcoming. "There will be other officers coming shortly who will be posted outside for surveillance. We'll stay until they arrive."

"Is that necessary? Are the girls still at risk?" Tom asked.

"It's merely a precaution for peace of mind. The girls have been through a lot and we want them to feel safe." Jackson pulled a card out of his pocket and passed it to Tom.

"That sounds like a good idea," Tom agreed, looking at his wife and daughter. It was obvious the stress that had been plaguing Stephanie's family the last few weeks. It was written all over their faces and he knew they were eager to begin the healing process.

"If you don't mind, I would like to speak with Lexie privately," Jackson requested.

Tom looked at Lexie, who nodded to ease his concern.

"Of course," Tom said. He placed his hand on Lexie's shoulder. "Good to see you, sweetheart. Don't be long."

"I'll put on some tea." Ruth smiled at Lexie as she tucked Lexie's hair behind her ear.

Lexie watched Tom as he led Stephanie and her mother toward the house. Mike followed on their heels, throwing glances back at them like he was hesitant to leave her alone with him.

"Mike reminds me of Evan," Jackson said as he watched Mike close the front door.

"They *are* friends," Lexie offered quietly.

"That explains a lot," Jackson admitted, eliciting only the smallest of smiles from Lexie, but it was progress.

"Evan's not so bad," Lexie said sadly.

"Yeah, maybe, but don't tell him I said so," Jackson added.

Teddy was leaning against the car, and from the sound of it, he was playing a game on his phone. He was most likely not paying attention, but Jackson preferred to be out of earshot. He noticed the curtain moving in the front window of Stephanie's house, indicating he had more of an audience than he was comfortable with.

"Come here." Jackson took Lexie's hand and walked toward the side of the house for some privacy. He turned around and looked into her eyes. They were so full of turmoil it pained him to see her like this.

Jackson wasn't sure what Lexie needed from him. He didn't know how to console her and he was scared to do the wrong thing. She looked so fragile, but he knew how strong she really was, and it gave him some peace of mind.

"The thought of leaving you feels like the hardest thing I've ever had to do," Jackson confessed. "But I promised to bring Evan home to you, and that's what I'm going to do."

Lexie squeezed his hand in response and her eyes watered.

Jackson pulled her closer and placed a kiss on her forehead before wrapping his arms around her.

"I know how much it hurts. I still think of my mother every day," Jackson said sadly.

Lexie slipped her hands underneath his shirt so they were against his skin. The comfort it brought him was immeasurable. He could only hope it gave her a fraction of the solace it gave him.

"Promise me you'll come back," Lexie whispered against his chest. He could feel her tears saturate his shirt, making him squeeze her tighter.

"I promise," Jackson admitted. "There is no place I'd rather be."

Lexie retracted her hands and placed them on the sides of his face. Reaching up on her tip-toes, she placed her lips against his in a firm, emotionally driven kiss. When she pulled back, she searched his eyes and he hoped she could see how he felt, because there were no words.

"Make sure that you do," Lexie said before kissed him once more, this time gentle and quick before she spun around and headed toward the house.

It was the first time in his life that Jackson actually feared his mortality. He didn't want to push through life with his head down, paying no mind to the risks. He was terrified his past would now prevent him from having what he wanted. He no longer desired the dangers he waded through his entire life. He wanted to spend every minute with Lexie without having to look over his shoulder or fear for her safety. He wasn't sure if it was even possible, but it didn't stop him from hoping.

Jackson returned to the car and leaned against it, next to Teddy. He looked up at the house thoughtfully, thinking that Teddy was too consumed with his game to pay him any mind. He should have known better.

"A few months ago I would have bet my life that the world would freeze over before Jackson Finley fell in love. It's so trippy seeing you like this." Teddy laughed.

"Fuck you." Jackson shoved Teddy with his elbow and knocked him off balance.

"Oh…" Teddy said as he stumbled. "Shit," he said through his laughter. "I almost fell on my ass."

"That was the point." Jackson shook his head and couldn't help the smile that formed on his lips.

They both turned when a car pulled onto the street. Jackson instinctively placed his hand on his gun until it neared enough to see who was behind the wheel. "Fuck me sideways. This is the last thing we need right now," Jackson complained, pushing himself to his feet as the car pulled up in front of theirs.

Haffey swung her door open and stormed toward Jackson with fire in her dark brown eyes.

"Finley! What the fuck are you up to?" Haffey demanded. Her long hair was pulled tightly back into a ponytail, giving her a fierce look that accentuated her temper.

"Hello, Haffey, what are you doing in these parts? A little far from home, aren't you?" Teddy said casually.

"Piss off, Teddy," Haffey snapped.

"So spicy, I like it," Teddy fed her fervour.

Haffey rolled her eyes and came to stand in front of Jackson with her hands on her hips and leaned into his personal space.

"You and I both know those girls were in John Stodden's possession. When I can place you at that hotel, I will rip your ass to shreds."

"I know you like things kinky, but that's even pushing it for you," Jackson taunted.

"Oh my Jesus, fuck. How in hell does Giles put up with you assholes?"

"Calm down, Haffey. We have an audience," Jackson said, nodding toward the window.

Haffey glanced over and dropped her hands off her hips and straightened her posture. Haffey's partner opened his door and climbed out, tucking his phone into his pocket.

"Jackson, Teddy," Sieks acknowledged them, trying to keep his amused expression to himself.

"Hey man," Teddy greeted him.

"You can't talk to them now. They've been through too much," Jackson said.

"The hell I can't," Haffey bit off as she turned toward the house. Jackson grabbed her arm to stop her. "Get your hand off me."

Jackson released her and raised his hand in surrender. "Stephanie was already questioned by the officers investigating Masten and Lexie just lost her mother. They don't know where John is. I can tell you what you want to know."

"I told you to stay away from him, Jackson."

"I can't help it if he's the one coming after me. What do you want me to do, just let him kill me?"

"That's a start, yeah." Haffey nodded her head.

"It's not that easy to get rid of me, Haff." Jackson clenched his jaw.

"Don't I know it," Haffey agreed with an exaggerated sigh.

"You being here only raises flags. No one knows of Stodden's involvement in this case. It's best it stays that way for now," Jackson insisted.

"And why is that?" Haffey crossed her arms and tapped her foot.

Jackson glanced up at the house and saw Lexie and Mike in the window. "Let's not do this here." He placed a hand on her shoulder. Haffey looked up at the house and noticed their spectators.

Jackson nodded toward the car. "Let's go grab a coffee and talk," Jackson suggested.

Haffey narrowed her eyes. "You are gonna tell me what I want to know?"

Jackson raised his chin. "Let's go."

"Seiks, you stay here and watch that one," Haffey pointed at Teddy before she rounded her car.

Teddy raised his hands in question. "Why? I'm

the good one."

"I'll be back soon," Jackson told Teddy, who was looking at him with raised brows.

CHAPTER THREE

Lexie

"I don't like those guys," Mike said, looking out the front window as they watched Jackson and Teddy talk to a man and a woman who had joined them on the front lawn. They were both dressed in business attire. The woman was attractive with full curves and apparently a fiery temper as she swung her arms around when she addressed Jackson. The man that had gotten out of her car stood silently on the sidelines near Teddy.

"*Those guys* are the reason Stephanie and me made it home," Lexie said irritably.

Lexie could feel Mike's eyes on her as she watched the heated exchange between Jackson and the woman. An uneasy feeling filled her stomach as Jackson got in a car with her and drove off.

"Well, it looks like your little boyfriend is gonna get lucky now," Mike said with a smug smile.

Lexie turned toward Mike with a heavy scowl. "Why would you say that?" Lexie couldn't help the sliver of jealousy that pained the back of her throat. She tried to shove the feeling aside but it insisted on lingering, which only made her anger flare toward Mike.

Mike shrugged. "There's only one reason a woman gets that mad at a man. They're fucking."

"Shut your stupid face, Mike." Lexie shoved him away. He bumped into the side table and almost knocked over a lamp. Fortunately, Mike had good reflexes.

"Come on, Lexie. You can't seriously be into that guy? You barely know him and he looks more like a criminal than a cop. You were never one to lose your shit over a pretty face," Mike said with a shake of his head.

"It's none of your business, Mike."

"Something is going on here. You're not telling the whole truth." Mike squared his shoulders. "There's so many holes in your fucking story. When things start dying down, people are gonna start asking questions.

"I couldn't care less what you think, Mike. I know all about the holes in *your* story. You think I don't know it wasn't just strip clubs that you were sneaking around to go to." Lexie crossed her arms. "I know you're a cheating piece of crap. That's a good juicy story right there for our small town. No one will care about your suspicions when they find out what you've been up to."

Mike clenched his jaw and narrowed his eyes. "Where's Evan?"

"You already know he checked into a treatment facility. He needed help and you know that." Lexie tried to keep her voice down despite her anger. It was the cover story they were going with to appease Evan's family for now. It was the only story that made sense why no one could contact him. Unfortunately, no one could deny it was the place he should be.

Lexie could hear Stephanie's parents in the kitchen fixing them some food. Ruth had taken Stephanie up to her room to take a shower, leaving Lexie alone with Mike.

"You're lying," Mike accused.

"Leave me alone," Lexie said defiantly.

"Was it really a car crash that killed your mother?" Mike's words were like a slap in the face.

"Leave me *alone*," Lexie seethed as she leaned in close to make sure Mike knew he'd stepped over the line. She hated the lies but she knew they were necessary. She didn't want people to question her mother's honor if she was tied to John Stodden. Her mother kept this secret while she was alive and she wanted to make sure she respected it after.

He raised his hands and stepped back. "Okay, I'm sorry. I shouldn't have asked that."

She couldn't stand being in his company. She didn't have the energy to think about him and the fact that she hadn't been able to break the news to Stephanie about what Mike had really been up to. She was hoping Stephanie was going to end things with Mike and she wouldn't have to break her heart worse by telling her that he had slept around on her as well. She wanted to spare her friend the embarrassment.

She paused just outside the kitchen when she

heard Ruth and Tom talking in hushed voices. "The girls should be home with us. Not here."

"Stephanie wants to be here and we have to respect her wishes," Tom responded.

Ruth started crying. "My poor baby, she never spoke a word. Not one word, Tom."

"Come here," Tom said.

"And Lexie, her mother was all she had." Ruth sniffed. "How are we going to make things right? What are we going to do?"

"I think all we can do is be here for them. It's up to them to find their way through this," Tom said softly. Lexie had always adored Stephanie's father. He was always the voice of reason to Ruth's emotional outbursts and dramatic behavior. Lexie was surprised that Ruth was as calm as she was. She imagined they were both exhausted from the weeks of worry that they had been put through.

Lexie walked into the kitchen. Both Ruth and Tom looked up and acknowledged her. "Lexie," Ruth said, forcing a smile on her face and wiping her hair back from her face. "The water is almost boiled. Sit, darling." Ruth waved to the table.

Lexie dropped down in the chair and watched Ruth shuffle around the kitchen. Tom walked over to the table and sat down across from her.

"How are you holding up, sweetheart?" Tom asked, placing his hand over hers.

Lexie shrugged, she was worried if she tried to speak she would burst into tears.

"We can't even begin to imagine what you both have been through these last few weeks. When you're ready to talk about it, we'll be here."

"Thank you, Tom. I appreciate it," Lexie said.

"Here, child," Ruth said as she set a cup of tea in front of Lexie.

"Thank you," Lexie said as she wrapped her fingers around the hot cup.

"What can I get you to eat?" Ruth fussed.

"I'm good with just the tea for now," Lexie responded. The heat from the tea made her realize how cold she felt. Lexie brought it to her lips and wasn't surprised by the aroma of chamomile. Ruth had always told her it made everything better, and in that moment as she breathed it in, she wished it were true.

Lexie took a small sip and closed her eyes, trying to remember what she felt like the last time she had a cup of Ruth's tea. It felt like a lifetime ago, before life had taken a darker road. After Alex had died, Lexie closed herself off from a lot of people and barely ventured out into the world that had betrayed her. A part of her regretted pushing so many people away. She had missed Stephanie's quirky mother and the comforting presence of her father, who always found calm in every situation.

A bang overhead made them all look up at the ceiling. "I'll go check on her," Ruth said, wiping her hands off on the dish towel.

"Ruth?" Lexie called out as she stood up.

Ruth spun around and looked at Lexie.

"Can I please check on her?" Lexie asked.

Ruth paused for a moment before she nodded in understanding. "Oh…of course, dear," Ruth said, wiping her hands down the front of her blouse, smoothing out the fabric. "If you could get her to come down when she's done? You both should eat."

"Thanks, Ruth," Lexie said as she headed toward the stairs.

Lexie pushed herself up every step, she had so many wonderful memories in Stephanie's place, but the image of those dead men lying on the floor haunted her. Of all the times she had laughed to the point of tears, danced to ridiculous music, and ate cake for no good reason with Stephanie, only the tainted and horrible things came to mind because she was in a dark place.

Lexie closed her eyes, took a deep breath, and focused on the people still left in her life she held dear. They were what she cared most about in this world; the people who were still left to encourage her to want to live and laugh again. When she thought about happiness, her mother's face came to mind; the way she had always thrown her head back when she laughed. Her mother would spend hours in the garden, with her bare hands in the soil without any care to the state of her nails because she loved how it felt against her skin. She would also sometimes bring a book to the garden with her and just sit and read for hours until the smell of the earth permeated her clothes. Thoughts of her mother made her eyes sting with unshed tears.

Lexie grabbed hold of the railing and squeezed tightly. She held all her feelings and shoved them deep inside, turning her attention toward Stephanie, who needed her. Lexie knocked on Stephanie's door before she turned the knob and swung it open. Stephanie was still in the shower in the attached washroom. She could hear the water running but it did not drown out the sound of Stephanie's cries.

When she approached the door, she noticed it was open. She knocked and called out to Stephanie before she entered. She knew Stephanie had heard her because she grew very quiet. She walked into the steam-filled room and sat down on the closed lid of the toilet.

Lexie scrambled for something to say that wouldn't remind them of the pain they were suffering. "Remember when we let Tara Milton do our makeup for prom? We thought she was so fantastic because she had graduated the year before and was in beauty school. It was so exciting that she was willing to give us the time of day," Lexie said thoughtfully.

The water turned off but Stephanie didn't say a word.

"We looked like clown meets trashy hookers gone wild," Lexie continued, knowing Stephanie was listening. "Good thing Ruth came to the rescue. Although looking back now, my dress could have been better. What was I thinking?"

Stephanie pulled the curtain back to reveal she was sitting down hugging her knees to her chest. She looked so small and scared, it tore at Lexie's heart. Stephanie leaned her cheek against her knee and looked at Lexie. So much sadness clouded her normally bright eyes.

Lexie grabbed her robe off the back of the door and wrapped it around Stephanie's shoulders. She could feel her shiver through the thick terry cloth fabric despite the warm steam still circulating the room. Lexie grabbed a towel off the shelf and dried her hair before helping her out of the tub.

She picked up the comb off the counter and began untangling Stephanie's long curls before she turned the hairdryer on. Lexie needed the distraction from her thoughts and Stephanie needed to be taken care of while she struggled to find her words again. She ran her fingers through Stephanie's hair gently as the heat of the dryer began to dissipate Stephanie's chills.

"Alex said you were the most beautiful girl in the whole world that night," Stephanie said when Lexie flicked off the hairdryer and tucked it away in the drawer. Lexie spun around and looked at Stephanie, who was still staring at her folded hands in her lap.

"Alex also said I looked beautiful in the mornings too," Lexie said with a smile. "He had a way of stretching the truth." Lexie dropped down on the floor in front of Stephanie and grabbed her hands, looking into her eyes. "We are going to make it through this, Steph. I don't know how, but we will."

"It feels like a huge part of me was scooped out and something slithered in and filled the space. I don't feel like me anymore," Stephanie said as tears filled her eyes and spilled over.

"Look at me," Lexie said, tilting up her face with a gentle nudge under her chin. "I still see all of you in there. Broken maybe, but all pieces are accounted for."

Stephanie took a deep, shaky breath and twisted a ring around her finger.

"What's this?" Lexie asked. "She had noticed the ring before but it never seemed like a good time to ask."

Stephanie ran her finger over the surface of it. "I found it there...tucked in the mattress of..." Stephanie trailed off when her face twisted in pain as more tears ran down her cheeks. "I think it belonged to another girl," Stephanie whispered as she wiped her tears with the back of her other hand. "It made me feel less alone when I was there."

Lexie took her hand in hers and gave it a comforting squeeze.

"I know that I'm home and he's behind bars, but it's hard to let go of the fear. It feels like it is a part of me now," Stephanie said solemnly.

Lexie knew exactly what she meant because it was reflected in her eyes. She could only imagine what Stephanie had been through. She didn't want to push her to talk until she was ready.

"Let's not worry about anything other than eating your mother's delicious food and taking one day at a time. It sounds like a good start, right?" Lexie gave Stephanie's knee a gentle squeeze.

"Your mom..." Stephanie began.

Lexie's eyes watered. "It's too hard to think about right now."

"I understand," Stephanie said, placing her hand over Lexie's.

"Girls," Ruth called from the entrance of Stephanie's room. "The food is ready."

Lexie looked at Stephanie and smiled softly. Ruth always had to cook when she was stressed or worried. Lexie knew they would be well fed as they waded through their pain.

CHAPTER FOUR

Jackson

"When are you gonna tell us what you told Haffey?" Teddy asked from the passenger seat. He pulled a bottle of whiskey out of a paper bag and broke the seal.

"I told her what she needed to back off," Jackson admitted. The last thing he wanted to talk about was Haffey right now. That woman was ready to bite his head off but he managed to calm her down enough to have a reasonable conversation. Whether she liked it or not, his involvement in her case was no longer an option. He was on John Stodden's radar, and if Haffey wanted access to what he knew, then she would have to give up some control.

What he would never admit to them was that when he was sitting down with Haffey, he took the opportunity to give her the proper apology she deserved. Jackson's feelings for Lexie had given him a new perspective. How he had treated Haffey was inexcusable and he wished at the time he could

27

have seen the damage his actions would cause, but he couldn't see past his own veil of pain. He knew things would never go back to anything but tolerant between them, but it was better than being downwind of her wrath. At least now she was beginning to let go of the anger she was holding onto. It gave him some peace of mind.

"Do we have to worry about getting arrested?" Teddy raised his brow as he tipped the bottle to his lips. Teddy was disguised as the character he was playing in their plan. Jackson couldn't help but shake his head. His wig gave him long dark hair that brushed against his shoulders and thick framed glasses, giving him a much different look than what Jackson was used to. It also helped that Teddy hadn't shaved in the last few days. His disguise was believable enough to work.

"I didn't tell her that much," Jackson assured.

Teddy lowered his window as he swished the liquor around his mouth and then spat it out. Wiping his mouth with his fingers, he then rubbed them on his neck and down the front of his shirt before passing the bottle back to Dane.

"Do you think it was wise to leave Nate with the girls after what happened?" Dane asked. "He seemed quite shaken up."

"I don't know. I've been asking myself the same thing, but we didn't have much choice. He'll keep his head while we're gone because he knows we need him. He seemed insistent that we not worry."

"Let's hope," Teddy added.

Jackson glanced at the time. "Are you sure they're going to show, Dane? They're late."

"Yeah, maybe your girlfriends stood you up. Guess they didn't like you that much after all," Teddy teased.

"Relax, they'll be here," Dane replied confidently. "And technically, they'd be standing *you* up."

"Heads up," Jackson said, nodding toward the rear view mirror. Dane turned around and spotted the two girls from Max's apartment building heading toward their car.

"It's game time," Teddy said as he opened his door and climbed out.

Jackson started the engine and pulled away from the curb as soon as Teddy shut the door.

"That shrink chick called me," Dane said thoughtfully from the backseat.

Jackson looked up in his rear view mirror at the creased brow Dane wore. He had noticed that Dane had been quiet lately.

"And?" Jackson encouraged as he glanced at Teddy though the window. Teddy had thrown his arms over the girls' shoulders as he led them down the sidewalk. Jackson took a deep breath. Their plan was beginning to unfold. He turned the corner and left Teddy to do his part.

"She wants me to come in for a mandatory assessment," Dane said.

"By the department?" Jackson asked, wondering if it was just the standard protocol.

"Yeah," Dane replied, rubbing his cheek. "They want to make sure getting shot didn't mess with my head."

"What happened to old Dr. Millie?"

"She retired last month," Dane said, shaking his head. "I wouldn't give a shit if I had to go in and talk to *her*. I used to tell old Millie about the ball game that was on the night before and she would just nod her head and doodle on her paper. This new woman asks so many questions and it makes me so fucking uncomfortable." Dane leaned back in the seat with a sigh.

"And she's hot," Jackson added.

"Which makes it worse," Dane said, rubbing his hands down his face.

"Well, let's just concentrate on getting Evan out of this shithole alive or none of it will matter anyway," Jackson said with a chuckle.

"Yeah, true."

Jackson pulled up to an apartment building around the corner from Shimmy Shakers and parked the car in the nearly filled lot. The location was not discrect, but it would be quick access when they left the club. The evening had settled in light and energetic in the city of Belhaven. The warm air had many bodies on the streets. Even the rougher part of town was no exception.

Jackson's phone lit up in the console. He looked at the screen and saw Teddy's message.

"Black is in the club entertaining a small group of men that Teddy doesn't recognize. He said there's no sign of Freddie Krueger." Jackson smiled at the nickname he'd given Slash.

"Let's hope he's not here," Dane added.

"I don't think we'll be that lucky, but if you see the crazy fucker, shoot first and ask questions later. He's got a wicked hand throwing those blades,"

Jackson warned him.

"Got it," Dane confirmed.

"Ready?"

"Just a sec." Dane reached into his pocket and pulled out his bottle of pain medication. He popped the top and tipped the bottle up to his lips, and then chased the pills with the whiskey Teddy had given him.

"How's that side, anyway?"

"Much better. I don't think I'll need my meds much longer, but I figured its best, considering our situation."

"Maybe I should take some just in case," Jackson joked.

"If anything happens, just cover that pretty face of yours so your girlfriend will still like you." Dane laughed.

"What are you talking about? She likes me for my shining personality."

"Don't we all," Dane said sarcastically. "Let's go."

Jackson opened his door and pulled his hat low to shield his face from anyone who might recognize him. Dane was quiet as he closed his door and followed in Jackson's steps as they made their way toward the back of the club. Other than the distant sounds of the city, it was eerily quiet in the alley. A stray cat rummaged around a dumpster.

Jackson rounded the corner to the rear alley behind the club. It was mostly dark except for the small light over the emergency exit of the door

A homeless man flipped over on his makeshift cardboard bed when he noticed their approach. He

31

raised his head and watched them cautiously. "Hey there, why don't you go get yourself something to eat," Jackson suggested, passing him a folded bill.

The man's eyes fell to Jackson's hand and he got the hint. He pushed himself off the ground and grabbed the money with a grimy hand. He gave them both a quick nod before he limped off without a backward glance. That was a man who had lived on the streets long enough to know how to survive.

Jackson walked up the small staircase that led to the steel door. He leaned against the wall and knocked. After a short moment the door was opened by a man with a gun held against his chest. His eyes widened when Jackson grabbed hold of him and hauled him outside. Jackson twisted the man's gun out of his hand and tossed him to the ground. Dane grabbed for the door and shoved his knife into the latch before it could close. He tumbled to the ground and scrambled to get back on his feet. Jackson kicked him back down and stepped on the back of his neck. "Black is going to kill y—" the man threatened but Jackson pressed down on his throat with his boot before he aimed his gun at the man's head. The shot was deadened by the silencer but it still cast a dull echo from the surrounding brick walls.

Jackson drug the man's body off to the side and tossed a few garbage bags on him that were surrounding the dumpster. He headed back toward the stairs where Dane was waiting. Dane pried the door open and glanced inside. "Clear," he whispered before pulling it open to enter.

With their guns in hand, they headed in. Jackson

could feel the vibrations of the music in his feet as they quietly walked down the empty hall. When they neared the room Evan had been held in, they slipped inside. "Shit. They moved him." Jackson immediately noted the empty sofa where Evan had been the last time he was here. The handcuffs still dangled from the window bars.

"You looking for Country?" a woman asked who was looking at them through the reflection of her vanity mirror. She was dabbing makeup on the dark circles under her eyes.

"You mean Evan?" Jackson asked for clarification.

She shrugged her shoulders. "I only know him as Country. They took him to another room last night."

"Do you know where?"

"Nobody tells me anything," she said sourly as she leaned toward the mirror to apply a bright shade of red to her lips.

"Do me a favor and forget you saw us," Jackson requested.

"Done," she replied, locking eyes with him in the mirror. He noticed then the dark bruise she was trying to cover on the side of her face. Jackson nodded before he ducked back out into the hall.

When they heard approaching voices, Jackson grabbed the handle of the nearest room and they both ducked inside. Jackson was barely inside the room when he felt a sharp, piercing pain in his shoulder.

"Watch out, Dane," Jackson warned. "We have company."

Dane raised his gun as he too noticed who they'd

walked in on. They both looked across the room to see Slash standing up from his chair. He grabbed a woman who was scrambling to her feet and hauled her against him as a shield. She covered her own mouth like she was terrified she would make a sound as Slash held a blade to her neck. It looked like he had been using it on her clothes, by the state of her outfit.

Jackson looked at the small knife embedded in his shoulder. He grabbed the hilt and pulled it out, clenching his teeth against the pain. A thin line of blood began to run down the front of his shirt.

"I was just thinking how dull this evening was turning out to be." Slash's eyes flickered toward the woman in his hold with a displeased expression. "At least now I'll have a little fun," Slash said, giving her a squeeze that elicited a small terrified whimper.

"Yeah, we aren't interested in your type of fucked up fun," Jackson said disgustedly. Jackson looked around the small office. It was bare except for the old desk that Slash sat at other than a pile of boxes in the corner. "You must be upset that you get the shitty office. Guess you're not his favorite anymore."

"Something tells me you're not here to take Black up on his offer," Slash said, pursing his lips as he kept his face pressed against the back of her neck and out of a clear shot from Dane's gun.

"What gave it away?" Jackson asked sarcastically.

"I should have aimed a little more to the left then and I would have saved Black the trouble."

"I thought you were just losing your touch," Jackson baited.

Slash narrowed his eyes. "Pick up my phone, sweetheart," Slash cooed in the woman's ear.

The woman's frantic eyes darted around the surface of the desk.

"Right there," Slash moved his hand with the blade.

Dane took the opportunity and fired. Slash's hand exploded from impact as he stumbled backward. The woman screamed and twisted from his hold. She darted across the room and pressed herself against the far wall. She frantically rubbed her hands over herself, trying to confirm she wasn't hit as she noticed blood coating her. When she realized it wasn't her blood, she slowly slid to the floor and grabbed her knees.

Slash was looking at his mangled fingers with a sadistic expression on his face. He looked fascinated by the blood dripping from what remained of his fingers as he tried to flex his hand.

"I forgot to introduce you to Dane," Jackson said smugly.

"There's something about pain that is rather seductive, is there not?" Slash said as his eyes rolled up in his head. He sighed exaggeratedly as he looked up at Dane and Jackson, not even fazed by the fact that there were two guns aimed in his direction. His uninjured hand slowly moved toward his back.

"Don't move, you crazy masochist fuck," Jackson warned. "Where is Evan?"

"You won't leave here alive," Slash threatened.

"It's you who won't leave alive," Jackson replied before he shot Slash in the face. Blood sprayed against the back wall. The woman began to scream as she watched Slash's body fall against the desk. Dane quickly silenced her by placing his hand over her mouth.

"Be quiet. No one is going to hurt you," Dane assured her. She stared up at him with wide, frantic eyes.

Jackson walked over toward Slash's body and pulled the belt from his pants. "We have to tie her up and gag her. We can't risk her telling someone we're here," Jackson said as he ripped a piece of Slash's shirt off to be used as a gag.

"I won't say anything, I promise," she begged.

"Considering the company you keep, sweetheart, we're not inclined to trust you," Dane said apologetically as he took the belt from Jackson's hand.

Jackson was hoping their presence was still unheard from the cover of the music. They were prepared with silencers, but even still the sound would be recognizable if anyone was within hearing distance. Jackson pulled the door open and glanced down the hall, but from what he could see, everything still seemed business as usual.

Jackson pulled out his phone to text Teddy that Slash had been dealt with. Teddy's response was almost immediate to let him know that Black was still none the wiser they were there.

The woman seemed to calm considerably despite being tied. "You won't be here long." Dane made sure her chair was angled away from the bloody mess that Slash's body left.

"Ready?" Jackson asked Dane.

"Yeah, let's go."

CHAPTER FIVE

Jackson

With their guns readied, Jackson and Dane made their way back out into the hallway. Evan had to be in one of these rooms. He could only hope they found him before things went sideways. A man came out from the last door on the left. It took him a moment to realize Jackson and Dane were a threat, but by then it was too late. Dane had already pulled the trigger and the man's body dropped to the floor with a gurgling sound. Unfortunately, he was not alone, and another man began sending bullets blindly down the hall as he hid behind the corner. Jackson and Dane narrowly missed getting hit as they dove into an open door.

When Jackson heard the man reloading his gun, he darted the rest of the way down the hall, keeping low as Dane covered him. Dropping to the ground, he angled his arm around the corner and shot the man before he was able to ready his gun. Jackson knew they needed to act quickly because someone would have heard the man's crazed gunfire.

Jackson pushed off the ground and aimed his gun into the room the men had exited but lowered it when he realized no more of Black's men were inside. He was relieved to see Cherry with her hands raised, and Evan sprawled out on the sofa. She dropped her hands when Jackson lowered his gun and her spark flared back to life behind her heavily painted eyes.

Evan was barely conscious, and from what Jackson could see of his half-closed eyes, they were heavily bloodshot.

"Jacks..." Evan slurred. "Where have you been?" he drew out slowly.

"So much for keeping him clean." Jackson waved toward Evan.

Jackson watched Cherry's fiery personality erupt. "I have to work. It's not my fault that most of these dimwits working here don't understand when I say to watch him." Cherry placed her hands on her hips. "Besides, the poor child is a train wreck."

"Don't I know it," Jackson agreed.

"Friendly visit, huh?" Cherry raised her brow as Dane dragged the bodies into the room. "Black is gonna flip his shit when he finds out you came into his place and started shooting shit up. He's probably gonna show up any second."

Once the bodies were inside, Dane closed the door. "There's no way that went unnoticed," Dane said with a shake of his head. "We need an exit plan in a hurry." Dane aimed his gun toward the door, knowing they would have company any minute.

Jackson walked over toward Evan "Get up," he

demanded. "We need to move."

Evan tried to push off the sofa and stumbled.

"Fucking great," Jackson cursed as he pulled his buzzing phone from his pocket.

"Get the fuck out!" Teddy yelled on the other end before the line went dead.

The sound of the door crashing open caused Cherry to dive behind a chair. "Oh shit," she hollered.

Dane shot the man who came barreling through the door but his partner managed to get a shot off that grazed Jackson's arm before he dropped to the ground on top of his friend.

"Fucking great." Jackson looked down at the blood seeping down his arm.

"Sorry, man, he came in shooting."

"It's just a scratch. We need to move." Jackson turned toward Cherry "You like working here?"

"Fuck no," Cherry said, crossing her arms.

"Good, I need you to get help us get Evan out of here." He tossed Cherry the keys. "If things go to shit, I need you to take him to the address in Freyview that's in the glovebox. We're parked in the lot at the end of the block. We'll cover you. Just worry about getting his sorry ass to the car."

"How do you not know I won't just steal your car?" Cherry said, looking at the keys.

"You won't," Jackson threatened. "Besides, you really want to stay on this sinking ship?"

"Fuck it," Cherry said as she grabbed Evan's arm and pulled him to his feet. "Let's get out of here, Country. Cherry needs a change of scenery, anyway."

"Jackson," Dane called in warning as he looked to see if the hall was clear.

"Stay close," Jackson told Cherry before they filed out of the room. Jackson and Dane fired on Black's men as they poured out of the club. They were responding to the noise without knowing the threat, making it easy to pick them off.

"In here," Cherry called. "The window is an easy drop to the back and we can get to the parking lot quicker." Dane and Jackson backed in behind her as they held cover. As soon as they were inside, Jackson closed the door and Dane pushed the desk over to barricade it.

Cherry leaned Evan against the wall before she pried the window open.

"Easy drop, you say?" Jackson questioned the rather high altitude from the alley below.

"Shit, they moved the dumpster," Cherry complained.

A large bang on the other side of the door had them picking up the pace. "Dane, you go first," Jackson said, waving him toward the open window.

"I'll stay in case they get through this door," Dane said, just as someone started shooting through it. They all ducked as one of the bullets came clean through and lodged in the wall beside them.

"Go," Jackson demanded. "I need your help to catch Evan when I pass him down."

Dane tucked his gun in the back of his pants and grabbed the window ledge. "Don't try any of your stupid heroics, Jacks. You come down with us," he warned before lowering himself down. Jackson ducked as more bullets fired through the door and someone began throwing weight against it. "Yeah, yeah, just go already."

Dane dropped down, giving a muffled curse as he landed. Jackson looked down to check on Dane.

"I'm good," he said, waving for Jackson to lower someone down.

"Let's go," Jackson told Cherry, who was more than eager. She lifted her heel adorned feet through the window and began to lower herself down as Jackson held onto her hand. "Don't kill Dane with those fucking spikes for shoes you have on."

"You obviously don't have good taste," Cherry said under her breath. Once Jackson lowered her as much as he could, Dane eased her drop.

Jackson grabbed hold of Evan, who was barely able to support his own weight. "Move, shithead, before you get us both killed," Jackson ordered. He helped Evan lift his legs and shimmy out of the window just as the door banged loudly and the desk scraped along the floor. Evan was barely out of the window before Jackson felt the barrel of a gun pressed against his neck.

"Don't move."

"Fuck," Jackson breathed angrily. He let go of Evan and kicked back as he grabbed for the gun and twisted it away from the man holding him hostage. When he turned, he noticed the other armed men entering the room and his survival instinct kicked in with a fury. Jackson managed to move fast enough to catch his attacker off guard. Using him as a shield, Jackson used the man's gun to shoot the men filling the room. Gunfire rang out as they responded to Jackson's attack. He could feel the man in his arms jerk with every bullet he received until the body grew heavy and Jackson could no longer hold him with one arm.

When the last man dropped and the gun Jackson was firing ran out of ammunition, he heard a familiar laugh from the hallway.

"I should have known you would pull some shit like this, Jackson," Black announced as he entered the room with his gun aimed at him, unfazed by the dead men around his feet. Jackson tossed the empty gun to the floor.

"It's a pity, Jackson. I didn't want to have to kill you," Black said as he raised his gun.

Jackson stared at the barrel of Black's weapon and the first thing that came to mind was the gut tearing awareness that he would never see Lexie again. The fear of this fact had his heart racing as he faced his last moment. It was not the fact that John Stodden was still alive, or that his father's murderer was still free, but the realization that he was in love with Lexie Wilder. Her very existence had forever changed him and made him capable of love. The fact that he would never be able to tell her how he felt was the most devastating thought of all.

"You seem disappointed, like you actually thought you would get away with this," Black said with a shake of his head.

"I did," Jackson confessed with a frown.

"Slash will be sorry he missed this." A sly smile curled the edges of his thin lips.

"Slash won't be anything at all, because he's dead." Jackson raised his brow.

Black's eyes narrowed as he stared down the

barrel of his gun at Jackson. He was completely unaware that the tide was about to change.

"Don't move," Teddy said as he pressed his gun against the back of Black's head.

"It's about time," Jackson breathed out in relief.

"Yeah, well, there are a lot of distractions out there. Can you blame a guy?" Teddy pressed the gun harder against Black's head. "Drop the gun," he ordered.

"Why the fuck would I do that?" Black asked angrily.

"Because I'll let you live," Teddy responded. "And you will let Jacks and I walk out of here."

"I can't do that," Black refused, tightening his grip on his gun.

Jackson watched Black's eyes flicker back toward Teddy when he spoke. He only needed a second to grab the gun he'd noticed next to his foot that one of the men had dropped.

"It's your only option to get out of this alive," Teddy insisted.

Shouting and heavy footsteps sounded down the hall. Black ducked, bringing his elbow up into Teddy's side. Black grabbed onto Teddy's gun and wrestled for control. Jackson took the opportunity to make his move. He grabbed the gun off the floor and shot without hesitation.

The seconds seemed to slow as Jackson watched Black realize that he had been shot. Blood began to pool out of his right eye and nose as he stared blankly at Teddy. His grip slackened enough for Teddy to wield his gun around and take out the three men that charged into the room.

Black's body swayed and then collapsed onto his knees and Jackson looked up at Teddy standing behind him.

"That could have gone a little better." Teddy tilted his head as he looked at Black's body.

"No, it's about right. There was no way I was leaving while Black was alive," Jackson said, tucking the gun in the back of his pants. "Let's go." Jackson rushed toward the window and kicked his legs out before shuffling down. The jolt of the drop was welcomed after almost meeting his demise only seconds before. He welcomed the pain that was beginning to register in his body.

Teddy was just seconds behind him as he landed on his feet. The sound of sirens began to filter through the constant hum of the city.

"Move," Dane ordered them as he started jogging ahead of them. Cherry and Evan were already gone.

"You're bleeding," Teddy nodded toward Jackson's side and shoulder.

"Nothing to worry about." Jackson was in good condition considering that he was stabbed and grazed by a few bullets. He knew for a fact he could be much worse.

As they came out of the narrow alley Cherry was behind the wheel of Jackson's car and pulling up toward them. "Get in," she shouted as she reached across the passenger's seat and opened the door for Jackson. Dane and Teddy piled in the back, shoving Evan off to the side with a groan of protest.

As soon as their feet left the pavement, Cherry threw the car in drive and sped out of the parking lot. "Jesus, where did you learn to drive?" Jackson asked, grabbing the door handle.

"I used to drag race." Cherry flashed a smile.

"You're full of secrets, aren't you?" Jackson raised his brows.

"Fucking right I am, sweetheart." Cherry laughed.

Jackson's ears felt like they were underwater as the sound of rushing waves echoed in his head. He opened the glove box and pulled out his headset. He quickly unwound the cord to place the buds in his ears when he realized the wave of torment was not crashing in on him. He looked down at the player and didn't move. It was the first time he welcomed the silence after bloodshed. Normally he would be desperate to drown his head in the familiar sounds of the music on his player—instead his heart swam with relief. His hands shook and his body thrummed with encrgy, but the only thing he could concentrate on was relief, true and pure. He was grateful to be alive.

CHAPTER SIX

Stephanie

A quiet shuffling sound pulled Stephanie from a restless sleep. Her mind was trying to sort between dream and reality when suddenly her heart was sent pulsing frantically. She couldn't remember where she was. Unable to determine if she was still behind the bars, she jolted up, pushing the blankets off her that had tangled around her sweat-soaked body. Her eyes took a moment to focus on the soft cream color of her walls and the pale blue pattern of her sheet before she released a sign of relief. She was home, but still the reprieve only penetrated so far. She was still heavily drenched in a sickening feeling that refused to leave. She wondered if her mind would ever truly be free of the fear that still clung to her memories.

Stephanie pushed the knotted dark curls from her eyes and glanced around her room. The late morning sun was filtering in through her curtains. Even though she had gone to bed relatively early, she still felt exhausted from waking up so often through the night to a restless mind. Movement in the corner of her eye pulled her attention. A scream tore through her throat when she noticed someone standing at the foot of her bed.

It was only a matter of seconds before a rush of footsteps thundered up the steps and Lexie came barrelling in the room.

"Steph—" Lexie gasped as her eyes fell on Stephanie and then Nate standing at the foot of her bed with his hands raised in surrender.

"I'm sorry. I need to talk to Stephanie and that asshole boyfriend of hers won't let me in the house," Nate said defensively.

"So you break in?" Lexie asked in disbelief.

"Yeah," he answered with raised brows. "How else would I get in?"

"Next time try calling me, Nate." Lexie pulled her phone out of her pocket and waved it in his face. "You're lucky her parents stepped out for a bit or they would probably have you arrested. Why are you even here? Aren't you supposed to be with Jackson and them?"

"Jacks wanted me to stay behind to make sure the officers were keeping an eye on you two."

"Obviously not if you snuck in Steph's bedroom." Lexie placed her hands on her hips.

"Hence the reason he made me stay." Nate raised his brow.

"What the fuck!" Mike hollered as he came into Stephanie's room. "I told you to leave!" Mike tried to push past Lexie but she held her ground as she pushed back.

48

"Stop, Mike, he's here protecting us," Lexie said.

"The fuck he is. I don't trust him." Mike narrowed his eyes and practically frothed at the mouth as he glared at Nate. "Get the fuck out of Stephanie's room."

"I want to talk to her. It's important," Nate said, standing his ground. He was obviously not feeling guilty enough about barging in Stephanie's room and causing a scene to drop his attempt to speak to her.

"Cool it, Mike." Lexie shoved back at him.

"Stop," Stephanie said quietly. Her hand was still clamped against her chest, trying to calm her racing heart. Her voice went unheard over the commotion Mike was making. Stephanie reached down deep inside her and pulled all the strength she had. "Stop!" She surprised herself how demanding her voice actually sounded.

Everyone turned toward her. "Leave, Mike," Stephanie said, quieter this time. She didn't have to force her words now that everyone's attention was on her.

"No, I'm not going anywhere while this fucktard is in your room." Mike shook his head as he clenched his jaw angrily.

"You don't have a choice," Stephanie answered. "I'm telling you to go calm down. Nate is a friend of Jackson's and I trust him." Stephanie listened to his accentuated breathing as he tried to contain his anger. "Go." Stephanie nodded toward the door.

Mike looked taken back by her demand he leave and the crease in his brow deepened.

"I'll be right outside if you need me," Lexie said

before shoving Mike toward the door. Despite Mike's anger, he finally let Lexie guide him out of the room, but not before throwing Nate one last heated glare.

"Don't try anything!" Mike threatened. Stephanie knew Mike was barely holding himself together. He seemed reeled too tight since she had gotten home and his insecurity about their relationship had her turning in the other direction. She knew he was looking for signs that things were good with them, but she didn't have it in her to give him comfort when she couldn't even console herself.

Mike was never the most considerate of people, and it never really bothered her too much before because she was never in a situation where she really needed him to be. Right now the fact that he couldn't see past his own face made a bitter taste form in her mouth. He seemed to have no concept of what she needed. She was seeing the truth of who he was without the veil of lust that had once drawn her to him.

Every time he looked at her she could tell he was impatiently searching for the old version of her. What he couldn't understand is that there was no going back, and she wasn't sure what that meant for their relationship. The only thing she could see was an end, but she wasn't strong enough right now to shoulder the weight of a breakup, she just needed a little more time to find her feet to stand on.

Lexie cast her a gentle smile as she left the room. She knew Lexie was being strong for her despite her own mourning; she could see the sadness in her eyes. Just like she knew that's what Lexie saw when she looked at her. They clung to each other like two broken pieces, desperately trying to make the other feel better when they couldn't even do it for themselves. They both had so much to talk about but they were still dealing with the shock of each other's pain, so quiet consolation was what they both relied on for now.

Every time she thought about the fact that Lexie's mother was gone, it carved away at what was left of her. She would be Lexie's family and she had no intention of letting her down.

Stephanie looked up at Nate. His sandy blond hair waved out in different directions. His big brown eyes looked back at her under his raised brows that gave him a youthful look despite being a man. A scar ran across his jawline that carved through his unshaven face and she was surprised the thought that he looked adorable twisted into her muddled brain.

"What do you want, Nate?" Stephanie said, pushing up to lean against the headboard. She pulled the blankets up tight around her.

"Can I sit?" He pointed toward the end of the bed.

"Yes, of course."

Nate very slowly came around the foot of the bed and sat on the edge like he was terrified she was made of glass, and if he moved too suddenly she would break. "Your boyfriend is a douche," Nate said, looking up at her. "He was out on the front step looking at porn on his phone while you are in here..." Nate trailed off. "Sorry, it's not my place to fuckin' say nothin'."

Stephanie sighed. "Is that what you wanted to talk about?" She wasn't surprised that Nate's words didn't elicit an emotional response from her, reaffirming the fact that she needed to tell Mike it was over. She didn't want the illusion of love anymore. She knew how precious life was and she only wanted to be surrounded by what was real. She needed something solid to hold onto when she wasn't her best.

"No." Nate shook his head. He was nervous; she could tell by the way he picked at her bedding. "I know this isn't a good time..." Nate trailed off. Now that he was closer she could see he was visibly upset.

"It's all right, Nate. I know it's important, otherwise you wouldn't have broken into my room." Stephanie tried to smile encouragingly but it wouldn't form on her face. She wondered if she would ever be able to smile again.

"That night when we found you and you told me that Masten put that tattoo on you. Do you know why he did?" Nate looked at her with so much pain in his eyes it made her chest hurt to look at him.

Stephanie touched her neck where the rose was. Tears filled her eyes as she looked back at him. "I don't know...why are you asking me this?" Stephanie whispered as the tears escaped her and ran down her cheeks.

Nate dropped his gaze and looked around the room as he took a deep breath. He grew too quiet and it scared her.

"Why are you asking?" Stephanie demanded, a

little harsher this time.

Nate reached over his shoulder and pulled his shirt over his head. Stephanie was confused as she pulled her blankets up to her neck. It wasn't until he stood up and turned toward her that she understood what he was doing. Nate was covered in tattoos that extended the lengths of his arms and the majority of his back, but his chest was bare except for a lone tattoo that was placed over his heart. It was the exact same rose that was tattooed on her neck.

Stephanie gasped and placed her hand over her mouth. "I don't understand."

She pushed her blankets off, unconcerned by the fact that she wore only her underwear and a thin tank top. She walked up to him, staring at his chest. She could feel the scowl of confusion form upon her brow as she took in the details. It was not a new tattoo. This had been placed on his heart for a long time.

Without thinking, she touched the petals of the rose and traced the lines. "It looks the same," Stephanie said in disbelief.

"It is the same," Nate confirmed.

Stephanie looked up into his dark brown eyes. "How can it be?" she whispered.

"My mother went missing when I was only five years old." Nate pulled a wallet out of his back pocket and flipped it open. He pulled out a photograph and held it up for Stephanie to see.

With shaky hands, Stephanie took the picture. A young woman was smiling back at her with the exact same tattoo on her neck. "What was her name?"

"Rose."

A sob escaped Stephanie before she could cover her mouth. "Oh my god," she cried. "He called me Rose. You think she was one of the other girls?"

Nate nodded his head and bit his lip nervously.

"Is this why you have been acting so strange around me?" Stephanie asked quietly.

Stephanie looked up into Nate's tear-filled eyes. "I need to know what happened to her. I need to know what she went through," he whispered.

Stephanie passed back the photo and wiped her eyes. She took a deep, shaky breath to collect herself. "If she is the same Rose, then I think in his own twisted way, he loved her. He told me he did. I wish I could tell you she didn't suffer, but I can't…I can't…" Stephanie trailed off in tears.

She wasn't expecting Nate to wrap his arms around her, but the feeling of comfort it gave her was beyond anything she could imagine. His warm body and strong arms made her feel safe.

"We don't need to talk about it anymore. I'm sorry," Nate said, stroking her hair.

She clung to him, wrapping her arms around him she pulled him closer, seeking all the relief he could give her as she cried against his chest.

She wasn't sure how much time had passed when he leaned down and picked her up to carry her to the bed. He set her down gently and Stephanie finally relaxed her hold as he stepped back. She hadn't known Nate very well until now, but she felt a strange connection to him with his admission. She patted the spot beside her on the bed. "Please stay with me," she requested quietly.

His eyes danced around, she could tell he noticed her state of dress and was trying to be polite in not staring.

"Please," she insisted. Nate nodded his head and sat down tentatively next to her. "Where did you get all the scars?" she asked, looking at the marks that covered his skin. He had a long scar that carved from his shoulder down toward his chest, and small narrow scars on his left side, and a few across his stomach.

"I grew up on the streets. Most are tokens of my childhood, so to speak, and the rest are me being in the wrong place at the wrong time."

"This one looks like it was bad," Stephanie whispered as she touched his shoulder. She could feel him shaking under her touch. "Are you all right? You're shaking."

"You make me really nervous," Nate confessed.

"Me? Why?"

"I...can you pull the blanket up over yourself? I can't think around you. This isn't right...I shouldn't have come...I need to go." Nate moved to stand but Stephanie grabbed his arm.

"Do you have to?"

"My heart is racing so fast and I am really bad at filtering what I say, Stephanie. I don't want to scare you."

"You don't scare me," Stephanie assured him.

"Good." Nate nodded and took a deep breath. "Next time I promise to wait until you're dressed before I drop in on you, and I do admit, I should have used the door."

Stephanie could feel a strange feeling bubble up

in her chest. She didn't recognize it first.

"What?" Nate asked nervously, noticing her expression.

A small laugh escaped her and she placed her hand against her chest, savoring the feeling that came over her. The feeling of warmth penetrated the fog inside enough to warm her slightly. "I'm actually thinking I should thank you for breaking in."

"Yeah?" Nate looked over at her, his shoulders visibly relaxing.

"Yeah."

Nate leaned back against her headboard and looked up at the ceiling. He grew quiet for a moment, and Stephanie could tell he was thinking about his mother. "I keep listening to the news, wondering if they found her with all the other women he buried in his backyard." Nate wiped his eyes with the back of his hand. "Being here with you, knowing you survived him, makes me feel better."

Stephanie took a deep breath before she spoke. "I heard the news too. My parents listen to it when they think I'm asleep. I heard they found the remains of fifteen women, and it makes me think about how close I became to being the sixteenth." Stephanie leaned against Nate's shoulder tentatively, unsure of what was acceptable between them. At first he tensed, but when she felt him begin to relax, she did as well. "Even though he's behind bars, I'm still terrified he's gonna come after me. Sometimes when I wake up, for the first few seconds it feels like I'm still there…inside those bars," Stephanie whispered.

"You're never going back there," Nate assured her as placed his hand cautiously on top of hers. They both grew quiet, each lost in their own turmoil of thoughts and taking comfort in each other's presence until Nate finally broke the silence.

"I still remember the day she disappeared. I don't remember much else back then, but that day is so clear. I can remember her waking me up with a big smile on her face and she told me she had a secret that she wanted to tell me before anyone else found out.

"I remember feeling so special and excited as she brought me out to the kitchen to a big plate of chocolate chip pancakes. They were my favorite. That's when she told me I was going to be a big brother." Nate stopped talking and closed his eyes.

"I'm so sorry."

"I have never had chocolate chip pancakes since that day," he confessed sadly. "But I can still remember how good they tasted."

Stephanie wanted to tell him that Masten had made reference to the fact that Rose had been pregnant, but she thought it would only make his pain worse. She didn't want to think about what that monster would have done with a defenseless baby. She prayed it was not subjected to his cruelty.

CHAPTER SEVEN

Lexie

Lexie pressed her ear to Stephanie's door. She could hear Stephanie and Nate's muffled voices and it gave her relief knowing that Stephanie was talking. Lexie knew that every word she spoke would alleviate some of the built-up emotions she was struggling with. Stephanie had barely spoken since she returned. Knowing that she felt comfortable with Nate brought Lexie peace of mind. Lexie placed her hand gently on the door and smiled softly before quietly stepping away. She didn't want to disturb them.

She ran her fingers through her hair and then down the front of the oversized shirt she had found in Stephanie's drawer that morning. She recognized it immediately as one of the tie-dyed shirts Stephanie and she had made when they were younger.

They had made a huge mess with the dyes. The cabinets by the sink had a blue tint for years until it eventually faded to a dull cast that could be played off as a trick of the light from the window. The thought of her mother's face when she walked in on them made her eyes well with tears. They hadn't exactly asked permission before beginning the process, but her mother was never a stickler for rules. Lexie remembered how the look of shock on her mother's face faded to a big grin before she kicked off her muddy boots from the garden, turned up the music, and helped them finish the shirts. Their fingernails were blue for weeks afterward, but Lexie loved her shirt until it had worn so thin it wasn't wearable anymore. Luckily, Stephanie preserved hers, because wearing it was exactly what she needed right now.

As soon as Lexie started down the steps, she could see Mike standing at the bottom with his arms crossed and his jaw clenched. Lexie inwardly cringed as she approached him.

"If you honestly think something inappropriate is happening in her room, you need to have your head examined," Lexie said with a shake of her head.

"What the fuck am I supposed to believe when a guy crawls in her window?" Mike seethed. "I'm the one that's supposed to be with her."

Lexie rubbed her forehead and sighed. "Listen, Mike, Stephanie has barely eaten. She barely sleeps with all the nightmares. Just relax; nothing is going to happen that should cause you any worry. She has been through hell and back. The last thing she needs right now is a jealous boyfriend."

"What exactly happened to her?"

Lexie looked at his rounded shoulders and his

scruffy hair and her anger dissipated. She had no right to be judgemental. Mike had been here since Stephanie had returned, trying to be supportive, even though he was focusing on all the wrong things. She had voiced her concerns long ago, but she had to respect Stephanie's decision to have Mike in her life.

"I don't know," Lexie said honestly. "I can only assume at this point."

"What do you mean, you don't know? She tells you everything." Mike narrowed his eyes in disbelief.

"She's not ready to tell me. Maybe she won't ever be. I'm just making sure that I'm here for her. That's all I can do and so can you," Lexie said.

"I didn't sleep with anyone else," Mike admitted as he ran his hand through his hair.

"It's not me you have to convince, Mike. When Stephanie's ready to face the issues between the two of you, it will be her decision."

"Does she think I slept with someone else? Is that why she's pushing me away?" Mike asked as he scratched the back of his neck.

"I didn't tell her what I heard. That's one of the things you can bring up when it's time to face it. Until then, you just have to be patient and wait for her to let you know when she's ready."

"When will that be?" Mike asked impatiently.

Lexie squeezed her eyes shut. "It's a miracle that she's home with us. Can you please just get over yourself?" Lexie bit off. She couldn't hold her tongue anymore. She and Mike had always bumped heads, but Evan and Stephanie had always been there to buffer the situation. Lexie was worn too thin to deal with Mike. She didn't wear the same rose-colored glasses as her friends did when they looked at him.

"Fuck you, Lexie." Mike stepped closer and pushed his face closer to hers. "I'm not just gonna sit here while some idiot is in *my* fucking bedroom with *my* fucking girlfriend."

"It's not your bedroom. She kicked you out long ago, remember?" Lexie leaned in to show that he couldn't intimidate her. "Maybe it's best if you left."

"You probably have been talking shit about me." Mike narrowed his eyes in contempt.

"Believe me, you didn't need any help creating a case against yourself," Lexie seethed. "How much have you drank? I can smell it on your breath."

"I don't know why Evan and Alex ever saw more than just a good fuck when they looked at you. Maybe Evan would still be alive—" Mike's words dropped off when Lexie slapped him across the face. Even he was smart enough to know that he had gone too far.

Lexie wasn't surprised by what he had said. Mike was always one to take low blows and she couldn't deny this one carved deep into her fragile remains.

"What the hell is wrong with you?" Lexie shoved him. "You need to leave *now*." Lexie was surprised she could keep her voice contained—she was ready to explode. "Leave," she repeated as she pointed toward the door.

"Lex...I..." Mike started.

"Please don't." Lexie held up her hand. She couldn't listen to one more word from his lips.

For a few intolerable moments he continued to stare at her like he was contemplating what to say, but thankfully, he spun around and headed toward the door.

After Mike slipped out, she felt the relief as it melted her tense shoulders. She couldn't believe she just had that conversation with Mike. Until now, she didn't think she could like him any less than she already had, but he had proven her wrong. She could only hope that Stephanie would eventually see his true colors.

Lexie walked into the kitchen, thankful for the opportunity to make herself a cup of tea without Ruth or Tom looking at her like she was about to fall apart. She had heard them leave for church earlier while she was still curled up in bed with Stephanie.

Lexie wanted to be close to Stephanie when she woke up through the night, terrified that she was still trapped inside those dark cell walls. Lexie wanted to be the one to soothe her back to sleep and remind her that she was safe. It didn't matter how many times Stephanie woke, sleep seldom found Lexie, and she was grateful to have the distraction from her own haunting thoughts. The only thing she wasn't sure of was how safe they actually were with John Stodden still out there. Lexie didn't know if he would still come after her now that her mother was gone. She wrapped her hands around her stomach and tried to ease the ache that pulled at her insides.

Lexie picked up the kettle off the stove. The sun

was shining in the window and it felt warm upon her skin as she turned on the water. She closed her eyes and took a deep breath. She wished she could turn her mind off and enjoy the moment, but it was no use. All the little things she used to take pleasure in seemed to be lacking and dull.

Lexie looked down at her hands that shook with all the emotion that fueled her blood. She pulled her phone out of her pocket and looked down at the screen. She fought against the urge to call Jackson. She wanted to hear his voice. She wanted him to tell her that he was coming back to her and he was bringing Evan home, but she couldn't bring herself to dial his number. The worst case scenarios kept circling through her mind. She hadn't heard from Jackson since he had left. He had promised he would come back with Evan and she needed to hold onto that.

She tucked her phone away and turned off the water. She picked up the kettle and it slipped from her hand, splashing water over the side of the sink. She leaned against the counter, grabbing the edge until her fingers turned white. She watched the water spread out over the counter.

She should have stayed with her mother at the hospital. She knew if she had, that man would not have been able to slip into her room unnoticed. She needed to accept the truth that sat heavy in her stomach. She was tired of making mistakes that hurt the ones she loved. She wondered if she had been awake when it happened, and if she had called out to Lexie to help her. She prayed her mother's last moments hadn't been full of fear.

"I'm so sorry I wasn't there, Mom," Lexie cried as she wiped her face with her hands. She couldn't fall apart now. She needed to be strong as she took deep, soothing breaths.

Lexie noticed an envelope sitting on the kitchen counter and it immediately sobered her from her emotions. It was the envelope John had given her with her name written on the front. Her stomach sank to the floor. She walked over to the table where her purse still hung on the back of the chair where she had left it. She unzipped it and frantically searched inside, where she had tucked it. Any hope that her mind was playing tricks on her vanished.

She spun around in confusion before she walked back to the envelope and picked it up. She wasn't sure who would have gone through her purse and taken it out. It didn't look like it was tampered with as she flipped it over in her hands.

Lexie ran her finger over the seal. She didn't want to spend the rest of her life staring at it and wondering what it would tell her. Lexie walked toward the table and dropped herself down in a chair.

Lexie took a deep breath before she tore open the envelope and pulled out the paper inside. She looked at the words typed on the page, trying to force her brain to register the information. The words seemed to blur in front of her eyes.

Lexie heard the front door open and Tom and Ruth's voices floated down the hallway toward her. She couldn't bring herself to face them right now. Holding the paper tightly in her hand, she grabbed her purse and walked toward the back door. She slipped out just as she heard footsteps approach the kitchen.

She couldn't force herself to stay in those walls anymore or she would be physically sick. She needed to talk to the one person she knew would listen. She was confident she was leaving Stephanie in good hands. If she was honest with herself, she knew Stephanie was safer without her anyway. She had found herself in a temporary lull, but she knew that it was bound to change. She had made too big of a splash lately not to have a ripple effect.

Lexie took a deep, calming breath of fresh air as she looked up at Stephanie's bedroom window before she slipped through the broken fence in the backyard. She couldn't shake off the sense of doom that nipped at her heels. She prayed that she would be able to slip away unnoticed. She needed to be alone right now.

CHAPTER EIGHT

Jackson

"Is all this shit actually gonna help?" Jackson complained as Cherry grabbed items off the shelf and dumped them into the small grocery basket Jackson was holding.

"This isn't my first rodeo. This method is tried and true, baby."

"Can we just hurry up?" Jackson sighed.

Cherry tapped Jackson on the side of the face. "You're adorable when you're all stressed out, you know that, Duke?" she teased.

"Why do you keep calling me that?" Jackson asked with a scowl.

Cherry tilted her head with a mock frown. "It suits you."

The basket got increasingly heavy with the water, grapefruit juice, and sports drink she added.

"Is that it?" Jackson asked impatiently.

"Almost," Cherry said, pursing her red lips and skimming the aisle with medication. She grabbed a handful of boxes of various drugs and tossed them in on top of the other stuff, then grabbed a bag of black licorice. "That." She pointed at the licorice on top of the basket. "Is for me," she declared like it was non-negotiable. "And I also need some red wine."

"Yeah, yeah." Jackson raised the basket. "Are we done now?"

"That should cover it," Cherry said. Jackson followed as Cherry led them toward the cashier of the convenience store. Her heels clicked loudly against the floor as she walked with an exaggerated sway of her hips.

Cherry was proving to be a vital part in getting Evan back home in one piece. Cherry had packed her bags and insisted on leaving town with Jackson, knowing that if any of Black's men survived, they would not be kind to her since she was involved in Evan's escape. From what Jackson could gather, Black had been holding something over her head and she was thankful to be free of him.

Jackson was grateful Cherry insisted she come along to Freyview and help Evan work through his withdrawal. She and Evan had formed a friendship, and she was genuinely concerned for his safety. Besides, the three of them had no clue how to get Evan back on his feet, and would've most likely wrung his neck before they got him home. Jackson knew Lexie and Stephanie were certainly in no shape for the task, being as they were barely holding their heads up themselves.

"Why don't you put your eyes back in your head and ring us through," Cherry demanded when the man behind the cash register openly gawked at Cherry's over-the-top appearance.

"Whatever, freak," the cashier mumbled before grabbing the basket Jackson had set on the counter. He tallied up the total before dropping everything in bags.

Cherry stepped back and waved Jackson forward when the cashier gave them the total.

"I'm just here as a pretty face. You're mister money bags," Cherry declared, flicking her wrist.

The cashier scoffed.

"Oh honey, don't get all frustrated because I make your dick hard. Who would blame you?"

"Fuck you," the cashier spat angrily. "People like you make me sick."

"People like me?" Cherry stepped forward but Jackson intervened.

"He's not worth it, Cherry," Jackson warned. He threw some bills down on the counter.

"Put your dog on a leash," the cashier said as he grabbed the cash off the counter and hit a few numbers on his register. He shoved the money inside the drawer while discreetly sliding a few bills into his pocket before grabbing Jackson's change and handing it to him.

Jackson allowed the coins to slip through his fingers. They hit the counter and rolled off, landing on the floor near the cashier's feet.

"Oh shit, sorry, man," Jackson apologized. When the man leaned over to pick them up, Jackson reached over and grabbed the man by the back of the head and smashed his face down on the counter.

The man screamed in pain as he shuffled back,

grabbing his face. "What the fuck!"

Jackson grabbed the bags off the counter and headed toward the door.

"I'm calling the police," he shouted after them.

"Good idea. I'll be sure to tell them about the money you're skimming from the register," Jackson challenged.

The man immediately ended his string of cursing and quieted, the look of guilt painted on his features as he held his bloody nose. "Get the fuck out of here." He pointed toward the door.

"Thought so," Jackson said.

Cherry raised her brow when Jackson made eye contact. A satisfied smile played on her lips.

"Look at you, Duke, defending my honor. This is the beginning of a wonderful friendship." Cherry pushed the door open for them as they headed out of the store.

Evan was fading fast and Jackson hoped that Cherry's plan was going to work to clean him up. Jackson was anxious to get back to Freyview—to Lexie.

They had stayed at a hotel the night before. Evan was in need of a shower and something substantial in his stomach. It had been almost a week of one high to the next for him, and the effects of it were about to show their true colors. He had already begun to break out in cold sweats. It was only a matter of time before he snowballed, and this time he was not feeding the habit. Evan was going cold-turkey this time whether he wanted to or not.

When they returned to the car, Evan was lying down in the backseat. Teddy and Dane were arguing about something Teddy had up on his phone. They both stopped and perked up when Jackson and Cherry neared.

"Got what you need?" Teddy asked, pushing off the front of Jackson's car.

"I fucking hope so," Jackson said.

No one questioned his call to allow Cherry to accompany them home. They all knew she would be at risk if she stayed in Belhaven, and they couldn't leave her behind knowing she would have a target on her back for what she had done for them. Cherry insisted on picking up her car that morning before leaving. Jackson immediately suspected that Cherry lived between her car and the club by the amount of belongings she had already packed in the trunk. Her eagerness to flee filled in the rest of the blanks for his suspicions. It was only the details that were left to be discovered.

"Teddy and Dane, you take Cherry's car." Jackson nodded toward her red '69 Camaro.

"I'm driving!" Teddy blurted.

"Oh, come on," Dane complained.

"Are you serious?" Cherry glared at Jackson. "Do you know how much money I put into my baby? That was my grandaddy's car. The one person in my entire family that didn't disown me, and you're just gonna let these clowns drive it." Cherry's hands were placed firmly on her hips.

"I need you to ride with me and help Evan," Jackson insisted.

Jackson had barely spoken the words before Evan stumbled out of the backseat and threw up, barely missing Cherry's shoes.

"Oh Jesus fuck." Cherry darted away. "Give me those fucking bags." Cherry walked over to Jackson and grabbed the bags from his hand. She rummaged around inside and pulled out a bottle of water and a box of something she must have thought would help. Evan looked horrible, and Jackson wasn't looking forward to the rest of the ride back to Freyview.

Cherry slapped the water into Evan's hands and tore open the box and popped out a few pills before holding them out for Evan. "Swallow these, Country," she ordered. Evan didn't argue as he took them and shoved them in his mouth.

"If you so much as put a scratch on my car I will claw your eyes out, Teddy," Cherry threatened as she rummaged through her purse and pulled out her keys.

"Don't worry, I believe you," Teddy confirmed as he held his hands up for them.

Cherry looked down at her keys sadly before she tossed them. "Why do I get the overwhelming sense that something bad is going to happen?" Cherry asked when Teddy flashed her a smile.

"What could possibly go wrong?" Teddy winked.

"Oh god. Is he for real?" Cherry looked at Jackson.

"I don't know what he is." Jackson shook his head. "Let's go. Evan, get your sick ass in the car."

Evan moaned in response as he propped himself against the car, clutching his stomach.

Jackson slid behind the wheel and waited while Evan crawled pitifully back into the backseat. He didn't even bother trying to sit up as he sprawled out along the entire width of the back. His coloring was various shades of grey and spoke greatly of the misery that was beginning to claim him. They all knew he was just starting to scratch the surface of what lay ahead.

Cherry shut the back door and slipped in the passenger's seat. "Do you mind if I smoke? It calms me down."

Jackson gave her a nod as he pulled out of the parking lot. Once Cherry lit her cigarette, she sighed in contentment and melted into her seat. "Do you want one?" she offered.

"No, my life is at risk enough as it is. I don't need anything else to build a case against me," Jackson declined.

"I believe that," Cherry said with a smile. She leaned closer to her open window to cut down on the smoke in the car.

"You all right?" Jackson asked when he watched Cherry get lost as she watched the scenery go by. Cherry had not been quiet once since he met her, it seemed out of character.

"I've been dealing with shitheads like that..." Cherry nodded back toward the direction of the store, "...for as long as I can remember. I just need a moment."

"Our world is full of arrogant shitheads," Jackson said, glancing between Cherry and the road. "I usually just assume everyone is a piece of shit until they prove me wrong."

"Look at you, Mr. Optimistic. Sounds like you had a colorful childhood too." Cherry frowned before taking a long drag and tossing the rest of the cigarette out the window. "Sadly, out of all of the fucked up things that people have said to me, my family has said worse."

Jackson could tell Cherry was struggling with inner torment. It was one thing they had in common. They both had a hard outer shell but the inside was a mess.

"How did you get caught up with Black, anyway?" Jackson asked curiously.

"My sister called me up one night out of the blue. I hadn't spoken to her in over five years at that point, so I knew she was in trouble. She had asked me to meet her at her place and I went without thinking better of it. When I arrived, she was long gone, and Black's men were there waiting. She had stolen money from Black and took off. She had set me up to take the fall for her. Black was all too happy for me to work off my sisters debt. It wasn't long before I found out why. Black had certain fetishes that I was forced to play a part in. My sister knew and she fucking threw me under the bus. Black took everything from me and I never heard from my sister again. I have nothing but my fucking car." Cherry glanced in the side view mirror at Teddy and Dane in her car.

"I promise your car will be fine," Jackson assured her.

Cherry pulled a compact and lipstick out of her purse. She powdered her nose before touching up her lips. "Let's just say I'm not sorry that sick fuck is dead."

"Let's just say I'm not sorry I killed him,"

73

Jackson said with a smile.

"Thank fuck for that." Cherry slapped her thighs.

Jackson's phone rang and he picked it up from the console. Nate's name lit up the screen.

"Yeah?"

"Lexie's gone," Nate said in a rush.

"What the fuck do you mean, gone?" Jackson said angrily. Fear coiled around him.

"I mean she's not here. She must have just left. There's no sign that anyone else was here. The fucking cops outside said they didn't see anything and they're useless as fuck. I just turned my back for a second, Jacks. I didn't know she would leave. I already checked her apartment and her mother's house."

"Goddammit," Jackson cursed.

"I found an opened envelope on the floor with her name on it, but no letter or anything else. Does that mean anything to you?"

"Yeah, we're on our way," Jackson said before disconnecting the call.

Evan sat up and grabbed one of the bags by his feet and dumped out the contents before he threw up in the bag.

"What's wrong?" Cherry asked Jackson after wrinkling her nose at Evan.

"Hopefully nothing," Jackson said, speeding up. "Where would Lexie go if she was upset about something, Evan?" Jackson hated that Evan knew Lexie better than he did.

"Her mother's?" Evan suggested. "What's going on?"

"She's not there. Where else?"

Evan was quiet for a moment before he spoke up. "I know where she is."

CHAPTER NINE

Lexie

Taking a deep breath of fresh air, Lexie let the heat of the day soak into her skin. The sun shone brightly overhead, broken only by the brief shadow of a passing bird. Being here always gave her a sense of peace, and now more than ever, she needed it. Her eyes skimmed over the endless rows of headstones, all marked with names of people who had come and gone. All of them left their own mark before they returned to the earth.

She and Alex used to come here on occasion and wonder who the people were that were written on the intricate memorials. They would take turns coming up with wild and beautiful stories about their lives. She never imagined how soon he would become one of them and she would be visiting him. When she saw his name carved into stone, she didn't have to imagine anything. She already knew the exceptional person he had been. The familiar ache filled her stomach when she thought of him.

"Hi babe." Lexie smiled sadly. "I know it's been awhile. I'm really sorry." Lexie dropped her purse and knelt down in front of his marker. She ran her fingers over the letters in his name and took a deep, shaky breath. "So much has happened I don't even know if I understand it all. I really need you right now."

Lexie sat down and leaned back against the cool stone. She rubbed her thighs and looked up at the sky, suddenly feeling a chill despite the sun. "Mom died." Tears started running down her face. "She's gone." Lexie wiped her cheeks with the back of her hand.

"I remember when you said everything happens for a reason. I'm trying to hold onto that, but it's so hard when the people you love keep leaving." Lexie tilted her head up to the sky. "I'm starting to think you were full of crap," Lexie said affectionately. "There is no reason good enough to justify both you and Mom being taken before you were able to grow old and grumpy. Remember when you said you were going to get us a tandem wheelchair when we were too old to walk everywhere? I thought you were so ridiculous and it made me fall in love with you more."

Lexie reached in her purse and pulled out the letter. "I have a horrible secret, Alex," Lexie whispered. "One that might have made even you see me differently." Lexie ran her fingers over the paper, willing herself the strength to unfold it.

"I'm glad my mother never knew for sure. I would have been terrified to see the look in her eyes when she realized what I am. I think in her heart she was convinced I was really the daughter of the man she loved. I wish I could've been." Lexie closed her eyes and listened to the gentle breeze rustling the leaves in the nearby trees.

"I have another confession to make, as if that one wasn't enough...I know." Lexie smiled sadly. She could almost hear Alex now. He always knew how to make her smile even when she was sad.

"I met someone...I didn't mean to. I was scared at first, but it didn't change how I felt about you. You know I will always love you. The space in here..." Lexie touched her heart. "It just got bigger somehow. I think I'm falling in love with him. It's not the same as when I was with you. It's different, but just as beautiful in its own way. I don't deserve to feel this way again. I know that, but I do, it's what I have been holding onto since Mom died. It's the only thing that has kept me strong enough for Stephanie." Lexie gently traced Alex's name in the cool stone.

"I'm scared what will happen when Jackson finds out I am a piece of the man he hates. How will he not see John Stodden when he looks in my eyes? I don't know how to survive it."

Lexie laid down on the grass, spreading her hand out to feel the soft blades through her fingers as she continued to tell Alex everything that happened without leaving out a single detail. She needed to tell someone before the weight of everything crushed her. Although some things were hard to put into words, she needed Alex to hear it all. She didn't want to keep any secrets from him. "John Stodden is still out there somewhere. Maybe I should run like my mother did. Leave everything behind. At least then I know the people left in my life will be safe. I don't know what to do."

Lying here on Alex's grave was the closest she could get to him. "Thank you for listening, Alex. I wish you could give me some of your great advice. I could really use it right now," Lexie whispered as she closed her eyes. She was so incredibly tired, and talking to Alex made her feel like she could breathe again. It was peaceful here with him, just like it was when he was alive. Lexie wasn't sure how much time had passed when she felt something brush her shoulder. She opened her eyes and looked up at the shadow cast over her. She hadn't even realized she had fallen asleep. For one brief moment she thought she was looking up at Alex until the differences started to register.

"Hey beautiful," Evan said.

"Evan!" Lexie gasped as she pushed off the ground and threw herself into his arms. "I was so worried about you."

Evan whimpered as she squeezed him tight. "Please be gentle. I'm not feeling the greatest."

"What's wrong?" Lexie stepped back and looked him over.

Evan had a pained expression on his face. "I fucked up. I was doing good. Jackson and the guys were helping me kick this and...well, I'm trying to get clean again, but it's kicking the shit out of me. I'll be fine soon."

"I missed you. I'm so happy you're back." Lexie squeezed his hand.

"Not as happy as I am to be home."

"How did you know where I was?" Lexie asked.

Evan just tilted his head in disbelief.

"Silly question, I guess." Lexie smiled. "Is Jackson mad?" Lexie looked past Evan to see Jackson standing just off the path with a woman in a very short shirt and towering heels. She couldn't help the jealousy that spiked through her stomach at the sight of them standing together, but she immediately stomped on it. She had no room for frivolous emotions.

Looking at Jackson now suddenly made her feel like a mess inside. She didn't want to tell him what the letter had said because she was terrified what it would mean to him. He had a way of reading her that suddenly made her terrified to look him in the eye.

"Naw, just worried," Evan eased her concerns. He held his hand to his stomach and Lexie noted his discomfort and his pale complexion.

"Who's the girl?" Lexie asked quietly.

Lexie looked over at Evan when he didn't answer. A sly smile curled up the edges of his dry lips. "Are you jealous?"

"No, of course not," Lexie said defensively. "Just curious."

Evan wrapped his arm around her and leaned on her a little more than he probably intended. "Her name is Cherry, and don't worry, she's not Jackson's type. She helped us out and Jackson brought her with us because it wasn't safe to leave her behind." Evan attempted a smile, but it turned into more of a cringe. "You'll like her."

Lexie nodded and tried to smile, but being next

to Evan was making her emotional.

"I'm so sorry, Lexie. I should have been with you." Evan rubbed her back.

"It hurts so bad. I miss her so much." Lexie leaned into his side.

"Here," Evan said, curling his arm around her and pulling her closer. She felt so much relief knowing Evan was home.

"Evan?" Lexie pulled back when she noticed his body tensing up. She could tell he wasn't well.

"We need to go, Lexie. I would feel bad if I threw up on someone's grave." Evan covered his mouth and took a deep, soothing breath.

"Sure. Can you just give me a second?" Lexie requested.

"Of course," Evan said. He leaned down and placed his hand on Alex's gravestone. "I love you, brother. I miss your sorry ass every fucking day."

Lexie saw his eyes water before he turned away to head toward Jackson and Cherry. Lexie reached in her purse and pulled out one of the bottles of nail polish she still had in her purse. She wrapped her fingers around one and squeezed it tightly in her hand.

"I love you forever, Alex," Lexie whispered before she set the bottle down next to the gravestone. "And I will never forget the sacrifice you made for me."

Lexie caught up to Evan and wrapped his arm over her shoulder to help support him. "I can't go home like this, Lexie. I was hoping I could crash with you at your apartment."

"Yeah, of course, but I think we would be more

comfortable at Mom's place."

"Are you sure?"

"I need to feel close to her right now," Lexie insisted. "And there is far more room there than my tiny little apartment. You can't go home anyway because your parents think you're in rehab."

Evan looked up at her with a raised brow.

"We needed to tell them something other than you can't be contacted because you're being held prisoner by a criminal threatening to kill you. It was the most believable story, anyway," Lexie defended.

Evan just offered her a sad smile.

Lexie look up into the intense gaze of Jackson as they neared. Those beautiful dark eyes were locked on her and the emotion that took center stage was shame. She wanted more than anything to wrap her arms around him and press her lips to his but she didn't have the right to be that person for him anymore. She couldn't pretend because the hope she had held onto by not knowing was gone. She couldn't carry on selfishly and deceive him. She knew she would have to tell him because it would only be a matter of time before he discovered it for himself. She feared the moment he looked upon her with hatred. She knew without a doubt it could break her.

Lexie looked at Cherry when she rubbed her hands together excitedly. "And I thought this little town was going to be boring," Cherry said.

Lexie couldn't help but smile. "Hello, I'm Lexie." She could feel Jackson's eyes on her but she couldn't bring herself to acknowledge him. The truth hung heavy over her head and she was nervous he could see it just by looking at her.

Cherry was a surprise, to say the least. It wasn't until she was close that Lexie could see the subtle indications that Cherry was not your average girl. Her underlying masculine qualities were discreet, but still very much a part of who she was.

"Oh, I know who you are. I'm Cherry." Cherry held out her hand. "Between Country's loose lips and Duke's brooding, I knew there was going to be a pretty face to go with this story."

Evan sprinted away from them to a row of bushes just off the path and threw up. He clutched his knees as he took deep breaths. "I'm good," he mumbled with a wave before he continued to expel the entire contents of his stomach.

"Country and Duke?" Lexie asked with a smile.

"They earned themselves some nick names along the way," Cherry responded. "Stories for another time." She winked.

"It's nice to meet you, Cherry," Lexie said over the sound of Evan's heaving. "Circumstances could be better."

"Nonsense, life is full of ugly with a few bits of beautiful thrown in. I learned to roll with it long ago. Come on, doll, Jackson can help Country to the car."

"Lexie?" Jackson questioned.

Lexie looked up at Jackson. He looked uncertain as he waited for her to say something. She felt bad giving him the cold shoulder. She felt a force inside her pull toward him. She was aware of him on every level, and denying it seemed to go against nature.

She needed to find a way to put some distance between them until she could think properly and figure out how to approach it. "We should get Evan to my mother's place." It felt like the best option to approach this slowly.

CHAPTER TEN

Jackson

Other than stolen glances, Lexie seemed to be avoiding Jackson. She was so quiet on the drive and Jackson couldn't find the words that seemed appropriate. Cherry sat beside him, throwing curious glances his way. He knew she could feel the tension rolling off him and he was grateful that for once she remained quiet. Evan was lying down in the backseat with his head in Lexie's lap. Jackson glanced back at her and noticed she was running her fingers through Evan's hair. Jackson hated the fact she was touching him. He hated how easy they were with each other. He would never admit the fact that he was jealous of Evan, not even to himself as he shoved the very thought deep inside.

Whatever was going through Lexie's head that was keeping her distant from him, he wanted her to be able to talk to him. He couldn't take her silence for long because it was terrifying.

Jackson pulled up to a stop in front of Lexie's

apartment. "That's Molly's car," she said, sitting up straighter. Evan pushed himself up and leaned against the seat with a moan of discomfort.

"Who's Molly?" Jackson asked.

"My mom's best friend. She works at the diner," Lexie said sadly as she grabbed the handle of the door. "I'll be as quick as I can." Lexie patted Evan on the shoulder gently before she stepped out of the car.

"I'm gonna help Lexie," Jackson said, opening his door.

"Um hmm." Cherry raised her brow.

Teddy and Dane pulled up behind Jackson in Cherry's car. "Lexie is just grabbing some things," Jackson called to them.

He followed Lexie up the stairs toward her apartment. Unbeknownst to Lexie, Jackson had already been in her apartment and knew exactly where it was. A lot had changed since then. He would never have thought things would have turned out this way.

When they got to the top of the staircase, a woman with fiery red hair was headed toward them. "Lexie!" she called out. "I heard you were back and I've been trying to find you. You weren't answering your phone. I have been out of my mind." The woman grabbed Lexie up in her arms. She looked up at Jackson, just noticing him for the first time. "Who's this?"

Lexie brushed her hair back from her face as she pulled away from Molly's tight embrace. "Molly, this is Jackson," Lexie introduced nervously.

Jackson looked at Lexie for a moment, trying to

read her face. "Her boyfriend. Nice to meet you, Molly."

"You as well. I wish it could be under better circumstances, but I'm so glad to see that she has someone to help her through this painful time," Molly said, taking Jackson's hand.

"Sorry about not answering my phone, Molly. I've been getting a lot of calls about Mom and I'm not ready to face it all yet," Lexie confessed. Jackson could feel her pain because it reached deep inside him and became his own.

"Let me take care of it, sweetheart. You don't worry about a thing. You've been through enough. Your mother always did so much for me, it's the least I could do," Molly said, placing her hand against her chest. Tears welled in her eyes. "I can make all the arrangements." Molly gently placed her hands on Lexie's shoulders.

"I'm going to be staying at Mom's," Lexie said quietly.

"Okay, dear." Molly leaned in and kissed her gently on the cheek. "You call me if you need anything. I'll stop by with some of your favorite pie later."

"Take care of her," Molly said to Jackson as she walked past him. She placed her hand on his arm. "She needs your strength."

"Yes, ma'am," Jackson said. Molly seemed like a very genuine person and Jackson appreciated the fact that Lexie had people like her in her life. He could tell Lexie cared for her.

Lexie watched Molly disappear down the stairs before she continued to her door. "This is a small town, Jackson. You can't tell people things like that or it will become front page news.

"That I'm your boyfriend?"

Lexie nodded as she slid the key into the lock.

"Are you worried people are gonna judge you for moving on? Or is it that you don't want people to know?"

Lexie didn't answer as she swung the door open and walked inside hesitantly. Jackson knew it was the first time she had been home since before she had been taken and her mother's death. Her view of the world was different now and she was probably realizing how different it would feel.

"I actually like the way it sounds. I've never been someone's boyfriend before…" Jackson trailed off when he noticed how terrified she looked.

"Lexie, what's wrong?"

"I think someone has been here," Lexie whispered.

Jackson looked around the main area and made sure the window were secure. Nothing raised any flags. He pulled out his gun and kicked the bathroom door open to make sure it was clear before he walked into the bedroom Lexie had set up as a studio. Everything looked to be in order to him.

"No one's here, Lexie." Jackson tucked his gun away.

"Some of my pictures have been moved," Lexie said, walking into the main living area. She picked up one of the frames sitting on a small table beside her sofa.

"This was in my studio," Lexie said, holding it

up. "And this…" Lexie looked down at a picture of her and her mother. Jackson wasn't sure if it was the aftermath of what she had been through or if her fears were legitimate. He would never put it past John to play games with someone's head. She picked the picture up and ran her finger over the glass. "Do you think John will leave me alone now that she's gone?" Lexie asked sadly.

"I'm going to stop him, Lexie," Jackson assured her.

"I can't shake the feeling I'm being watched." Lexie set the picture back down on the table. "He told me that he owns me."

"Listen, Lexie." Jackson placed his hand on her shoulder and turned her toward him. "I'm here. I promise to do whatever I can to keep you safe." Jackson leaned his forehead against hers and pulled her close. "John will never own you."

"Too many people have been hurt because of me."

"Because of John, not you. Don't blame yourself for any of this. You are innocent," Jackson insisted.

Lexie tried to pull away but Jackson grabbed hold of her waist. "Don't push me away, please."

Lexie placed her hands on either side of Jackson's face and he could feel himself want to melt in her hold. She gently pressed her lips against his and he savored the taste of her, not wanting the moment to end. He wanted more, he was desperate for her affections, especially now, but he knew he had to follow her lead. He had never given someone control over him before and he was not used to feeling vulnerable…though on some levels he found it empowering to give part of himself to her, becoming something bigger than himself. He would do anything to protect her. He had a purpose that now gave him hope.

"I'll go get my things," she whispered as she dropped her hands and stepped back. She had built a wall between them. He could feel it and he wanted to find a way to knock it down.

Lexie only took a moment to pack a bag and she was ready to leave. She walked over to the table and picked up the picture of her and her mother, tucking it inside her purse.

He could tell she was anxious to get out of her apartment. She felt unsettled since she walked in and noticed things seemed different. Jackson gave one last look around before he shut the door behind them. Jackson knew he would do whatever it took to make her feel safe again. No one should feel fear in the place they call home. He knew too well how devastating it could be.

Evan was sitting on the sidewalk next to the car when they exited the building. His head was between his knees as he took long, deep breaths. "Thank god," Cherry said when she noticed them. "We need to get him somewhere soon. He's about ready to fall apart."

"I thought that stuff you got was gonna help? He doesn't look any better than when we weaned him," Jackson asked.

"Yeah, when he's in bed. He can't be up walking around and shit." Cherry waved her hands in exasperation. "He needs to be sleeping."

"Let's go." Jackson waved toward Teddy and

Dane.

Jackson's phone started buzzing in his pocket. He pulled it out and noticed an unknown caller.

"Hello?"

"Jackson, it's Giles. I'm calling from a secure line. My phones were tapped."

"Shit." Jackson rubbed his hand down his face. "Rosh. How much does he know?"

"He knows we suspect him of his involvement. Though, the tape is not enough to convict him. Any judge is gonna throw it out because there's no way to prove it was him."

"Where's Rosh now?" Jackson asked.

"No one has seen him since yesterday. I sent a couple of officers to his place this morning and they said it looked like he left in a hurry. I'd say he knows what Mary had on him and he's lying low for now. Any idea where Mary would have stashed the evidence?"

"No." Jackson sighed. "I'll call on this number when I have something."

"Good…Jackson?"

"Yeah."

"Be careful how close you get to that girl. This might not end well for anyone," Giles said solemnly.

"Too late, Giles." Jackson ended the call.

CHAPTER ELEVEN

Lexie

When Jackson pulled up in front of her mother's house, Lexie didn't move. She saw her grey Honda Civic parked in the driveway and remembered when she had parked there. It was just when everything was beginning to fall out beneath her. Her mother was still alive then. It was the first time being here knowing that her mother would never be again. It made her body feel heavy and her heart swell with emotion until it felt as if it would burst. She felt as if she could cry for the rest of her life and it would not lesson the pain of loss.

Jackson opened her door for her and she looked up at the grey sky that reflected her thoughts. The air was heavy with moisture, ready to start falling to the dry earth. Jackson held out his hand and Lexie looked up into his face. She wished she could throw herself into his arms and forever stay in his embrace where she would be safe, but she needed to stand on her own feet. She needed to face what had become her life. Hiding would not change the fact that John Stodden was her father or the doom she felt inside. Her life was forever thrown off course and she had no idea what direction she was headed.

When Lexie approached the door, she noticed yellow tape across it from when the police investigated the break-in. Lexie ripped it off and hastily threw it aside. Walking inside was just as painful as she imagined it would be. John's men had torn everything apart. All of her mother's belongings were scattered on the floor. Lexie covered her mouth with a gasp as she looked at all the things her mother loved strewn around carelessly.

"It looks like they really wanted to find what your mother had hidden," Jackson said despondently.

"Shit, sorry, Lexie," Teddy said, walking behind them, supporting Evan.

Lexie walked over toward the kitchen island. Broken dishes crunched under her shoes as she set her purse on the counter.

"Bring Evan into the guest room," Lexie said, waving for Teddy to follow her. She headed toward the hall off the living area to the bedroom. Other than the furniture, the room had mainly been bare, so it looked better than the rest of the house. Lexie straightened the sheets for Evan to lie down. She grabbed the bathroom garbage bin that had been lying in the hall and set it beside Evan's bed.

Evan collapsed on the bed and Lexie pulled the sheets up over him. He was shaking now as chills began to rack his body.

"Dr. Cherry is coming!" Cherry called out as she came into the room with a bag in her hand. She smiled brightly at Lexie. "I'll get him comfortable enough to sleep in no time."

"What's all this?" Lexie asked when Cherry began taking out the contents of the bag and setting it on the night stand.

"It's a do-it-yourself weaning kit, doll. It's gonna get him through the next couple of days without him wishing he was dead."

"I wish I was dead now," Evan mumbled into the pillow.

Cherry shrugged. "Well, you get what you pay for."

"Thank you for your help, Cherry. Evan told me you took a risk helping them. I just wanted to let you know I appreciate it," Lexie said sincerely. She walked up to Cherry and wrapped her arms around her.

"Oh," Cherry replied. She seemed taken back by Lexie's show of appreciation. "Of course." Cherry patted her arm. "I'm not used to having people hug me. Maybe you could throw in an insult so I don't think the world is ending."

Lexie laughed and shook her head.

"Okay, fine, I'll just take some wine. This girl needs it after taking care of this big baby," Cherry said.

"Sure, I'll see what I can find," Lexie said with a smile.

When Lexie walked into the main area, Jackson was sweeping the broken dishes into a pile on the kitchen floor. The ones that had survived where piled up on the counter. He had already righted most of the furniture in the living room and replaced the chairs around the dining table.

"I didn't know where the dishes go," Jackson said. "None of the dishes look the same to put together."

Lexie laughed half-heartedly. "Mom didn't like sets. I don't think anything actually does match."

"That explains it," Jackson said as he bent down to pick up another plate and set it on the stack he made.

Lexie reached down and picked up a wooden carving her mother had kept on the mantle and placed it back into position. "Thank you, Jackson, but you really don't have to clean up."

She could hear him stop moving. She knew he was watching her as she stood staring at the piece of wood like it would bring her mother back.

"I want to help," he insisted. "It's the least I could do."

"Where are Teddy and Dane?" She looked up at him and knew he was trying to read her.

"I sent them to pick up some food." Jackson set the broom against the counter and walked toward her. She fought the urge to open her arms and seek his comfort. When he stopped, he was so close to her, she could feel the heat of him against her back. She found herself leaning back; wanting to close the distance.

"I'm here for you." Jackson wrapped his arms around her stomach and Lexie didn't resist anymore.

Jackson gave her a gentle kiss on the side of the

neck and Lexie sighed in contentment. She didn't realize how much she needed this, but the truth clawed at her and wouldn't let her completely submit.

"Jackson, I need to tell you something." Lexie turned around in his embrace, taking his hands in hers and giving them a gentle squeeze before she let them go and looked up into his dark, tormented eyes. He already knew what she had to say was important; she could see it in his expression. Lexie noticed a bandage peeking out from under his sleeve. "What happened?"

"It's just a scratch," Jackson dismissed. "What do you want to tell me?"

"The baby is finally down and Momma needs her wine," Cherry said as she sauntered down the hallway, coming to a standstill when she noticed Lexie and Jackson's serious expressions.

"Coming right up, Cherry," Lexie said, forcing a smile. She took the opportunity to flee the difficult conversation with Jackson.

"Lexie," Jackson said as he reached for her. He wasn't as inclined to drop the conversation.

"I could really use a glass of wine myself," Lexie said as she walked into the kitchen and stood on her tip-toes to open the cabinet over the fridge.

"Here," Jackson was suddenly behind her. He placed a hand on her lower back and his heat scorched through her clothing. His height easily allowed him to reach one of the bottles. He leaned down so he was only a breath away. He was only inches away and his heady scent filled her nose and made her body ache for him. "This conversation is not over, Lexie. We need to talk," he whispered.

Lexie could only bring herself to nod as she accepted the wine he held out for her.

Luckily a half a dozen wine glasses still remained intact on the shelf as Lexie set three out and filled the glasses.

"It's already looking a lot better in here. We should have it cleaned up in no time," Cherry said optimistically.

Lexie pushed a glass toward Jackson. He seemed reluctant as he picked it up and smelled the contents.

"Don't tell me that you drink whiskey straight but don't like the taste of wine?" Lexie asked in disbelief.

"I've never tried wine before," Jackson answered honestly.

"He's a bit of a barbarian," Cherry said as she rolled her eyes and Lexie laughed.

Lexie set Cherry's glass in front of her before joining her at the table.

"I, on the other hand, enjoy the finer things in life." Cherry raised her glass. "If life gives you shit, drink wine." Cherry raised her glass.

"Cheers to that." Lexie clinked her glass to Cherry's.

Jackson pulled up the chair next to Lexie, sitting close enough that their legs touched under the table. "Cheers," he said before tipping the glass to his lips and downing half the glass.

"Well?" Cherry asked.

Jackson shrugged with a frown. "I guess."

Jackson's lack of appreciation for wine had

Cherry raising her brow. "Well, we still have time to fix you," she said, giving his hand a pat.

It wasn't long before Teddy and Dane returned with armloads of grocery bags.

"Pop tarts?" Lexie questioned as she picked up a box of strawberry flavored treats with icing and sprinkles on top. "Do people actually eat these?"

"Yes, of course," Teddy said defensively. He grabbed the box and cradled it lovingly to his chest. "She doesn't know what she's talking about, baby

"Oh god." Cherry shook her head. "What the fuck is all this?" Opening the bags, Cherry pulled out microwave dinners, frozen pizzas, boxes of macaroni and cheese. "Gummy bears?" She held up a bag in disbelief. "How are you still alive if this is how you idiots eat?"

"I like to believe I'm invincible," Teddy said with a smirk.

"Dear god," Cherry said with a shake of her head. "We ain't eating this shit. Baby doll, I'll whip us up something that actually has some nutritional value. May I?" Cherry looked at Lexie and waved toward the kitchen.

"Please do. Whatever you can find, feel free to use," Lexie offered.

Lexie refilled her glass and returned to the mess at her feet. Jackson and Dane took to work as well while Cherry and Teddy continued to playfully argue in the kitchen. Lexie picked up her mother's music player and set it back on the hutch. It looked to be undamaged as she turned the power on and hit play. Her mother hadn't changed her playlist since Lexie had made it for her five years ago.

Lexie closed her eyes and listened to the song start to play, "Wonderful Tonight" by Eric Clapton. She closed her eyes and tried to remember when last she had heard this song. The last time she listened to it she was standing in the kitchen with her mother and they both had sung along as they washed dishes. She could still hear her mother's off tune voice faintly in her memory.

By the time wonderful smells began filtering from the kitchen, the main area had been straightened up. It had sustained the most damage of any area of the house and she was grateful it was back in order. A lot of her mother's things were unsalvageable, but enough remained that the space still felt the same.

Lexie stood back and observed their hard work. "What would've I done without you guys?" Lexie said appreciatively. "Thank you."

"I'll take payment in kisses," Teddy piped up. He was tying the last of the garbage bags when Dane walked in the back door.

"Hit him for me, Dane," Jackson said from across the room.

Dane backhanded Teddy on the face as he grabbed the garbage bag from his hand.

"Hey now," Teddy said, placing his hand on his cheek. "You didn't even know what the reason was."

"Do I need one?" Dane smirked.

"Apparently not," Teddy sulked.

"Supper is ready, children," Cherry called from the kitchen.

With the exception of Evan, who was in a drug-

99

induced sleep, they had a delicious meal thanks to Cherry, who showcased her talent in the kitchen. Cherry had an ability of making the light shine in the darkest of places. Lexie couldn't help but be drawn to her. She wasn't sure exactly how she got pulled into this whole mess, but Lexie was grateful she was with them.

The group of them sat down at the table and Lexie couldn't help but smile as they all carried on. Nothing about any one of their situations were ideal; they had all dealt with tragedy in one form or another, but here they were sitting down to a fabulous meal.

Cherry had rifled through the cabinets, freezer, and her mother's herb garden, and came up with the most delicious pasta dish Lexie had ever eaten. Lexie couldn't remember the last time she laughed so hard; her face hurt.

Lexie grew quiet and it didn't go unnoticed as everyone's attention was drawn to her. "Everything all right?" Jackson asked, bumping her shoulder.

"I was just thinking how much my mother would have loved to be here sitting at this table and getting to know all of you. Though, she probably would've insisted on cooking and it wouldn't have been anything near as good as this. She had a habit of burning everything," Lexie said thoughtfully. "She loved people who were outside the box."

"Is that a nice way to say we're weird?" Dane asked playfully.

Lexie laughed. "There is nothing wrong with weird. My mother always used to say normal is boring."

"Well then, she would have loved me," Cherry said. "It don't get more outside the box than me. Most people can't get past the fact that they don't know what's between my legs. It boggles their fucking minds."

"What do you have going on there, anyway?" Teddy asked curiously.

"Ha. Haven't you figured out by now that girls like their secrets? Let's just say it's more impressive than yours." Cherry smiled mischievously and everyone laughed.

Teddy's phone began to ring and they all quieted as he looked at the screen. "It's Giles," he said before picking up the call. "Yeah."

They all remained quiet as Teddy spoke on the phone.

"Giles needs me to look into something for him. Dane and I are gonna stay at a hotel so I can set up my office."

"Why don't you use my apartment? There's a desk in my studio."

"You sure?" Teddy asked.

"Positive," Lexie insisted.

"Nate called earlier. He's bringing Stephanie here. He said she needs a break from her parents."

"I was wondering how long it would take." Lexie smiled knowingly.

CHAPTER TWELVE

Jackson

The house was quiet as Jackson ascended the stairs. Stephanie had arrived earlier when they were wrapping up dinner. She looked much better than when he had seen her last. The dull cast to her eyes had begun to dissipate. Jackson could see how deep the ties ran between Lexie and Stephanie when they were together. They found a perfect balance between each other and it allowed them to draw strength when they needed it.

Stephanie joined them for a glass of wine before she curled up on the sofa and fell asleep. Her parents had been hovering too much and she needed to be out from underneath them for a little while. She knew they meant well, but she felt like she was disappointing them by not being able to step back into her old shoes. She had told them she tried to force it for their benefit but Jackson could tell it had exhausted her.

When Evan woke up, Cherry saluted everyone

and grabbed a new bottle of wine off the counter. She claimed she needed it to get through the night, and no one argued. The house was quiet now other than the sound of the shower running upstairs. Nate had left with Teddy and Dane to head to Lexie's apartment.

Jackson wanted to finish the conversation with Lexie from earlier. It had been on his mind all night and not knowing was grating on him. His mind had been cycling through possibilities because he remembered the look in her eyes before they were interrupted. The only thing he knew for certain was that she didn't think he would like what she was going to tell him.

Jackson glanced in the first room off the stairs and assumed it was Lexie's mother's room. It was still untouched from when it was pulled apart, but Lexie refused to let anyone enter it. She wanted to clean that room herself when she was ready.

When Jackson walked into the other room he couldn't help but smile. Groupings of pictures covered the walls. He knew Lexie had taken every one by simply glancing at them. She had a way of capturing the world that was uniquely hers.

The bed was covered in throw pillows, just like the bed in her apartment; all different colors and patterns. The bed itself looked like a piece of art. He was glad that Lexie's room didn't sustain much damage. He hadn't seen it before it was straightened, but he imagined it couldn't have looked much different. Jackson sat down on her bed and leaned back against the pillows. He tucked his hands behind his head and looked up at the ceiling.

It was covered in what looked a mural made from pieces of magazine cut-outs. All of the colors organized into a beautiful picture of ocean waves, fading into a starry night. It was absolutely breathtaking. Jackson closed his eyes and took a deep breath. The sound of the running water lulled him and he took a moment to rest his tired eyes.

Jackson woke to the sound of shuffling. He opened one eye and saw Lexie standing near him, looking over the camera in front of her face. "I didn't mean to wake you," she whispered.

"No, it's good," Jackson said, rubbing his hands down over his face. "I was waiting to talk to you." He propped himself up on his elbows and noticed that Lexie was dressed in only a towel. Her skin was still damp and glowed from the lamp light. Her wet hair was combed back from her face and hung down her back. He never thought she looked as beautiful as she did then; so raw and captivating. He wanted to be her everything because she had become his.

Lexie set her camera down on her nightstand. She walked closer until her leg bumped into his. "It's strange seeing you on my bed."

Jackson started to push off the mattress when Lexie stopped him, pressing against his chest until he submitted and dropped back down. "Don't get up," Lexie insisted. "Until today, the part of my life with you in it was strange and unknown. Now, you're in the house I grew up in. I'm just surprised how natural it seems."

"That's good?" Jackson asked. The way she was looking at him started to heat his blood.

104

Lexie grabbed onto Jackson's belt and pulled it from the loop and began to unfasten it.

Jackson placed his hand over hers. "We need to talk first, Lexie." Jackson tried to sound convincing but the fire she was stirring was beginning to roar to life.

"I don't want to talk and I don't want to think right now. I just want to be with you." The tone of Lexie's voice was like throwing fuel on a fire. She pulled his pants down to expose him. His body was ready for whatever she had in mind. He could feel every muscle coiling tight in anticipation.

She pulled the towel free of her body and dropped it on the ground. Jackson stopped breathing as he looked at her curves, the dips and lines that he knew would feel like heaven under his fingers, and pressed against his body. He didn't know he could contain so much feeling as it swam through him, full and demanding.

She dropped to her knees and ran her hands up his legs. His body pulsed in expectation, his heart thrummed so loud he could hear nothing else. She grabbed hold of his erection with a firm grasp. The air he had been holding onto rushed from him as she began pulling pleasures from deep within him. Her tongue felt warm as she explored him. It was hard for him to remain still as she pleasured him, his animalistic nature threatened to break free of its cage.

Jackson's heart felt like it was going to explode as pleasure filled him like flashes of lightning, igniting his entire body. As her strokes became more frenzied and her mouth moaned greedily, he almost lost himself. Jackson grabbed for Lexie's shoulder and pulled her up against him. He concentrated on slowing his breathing and clearing his mind.

Her body tensed against his as his erection throbbed painfully against her stomach, angry that he denied himself release. "Don't move," Jackson whispered as he clung to her. Her body began to melt into him and he couldn't believe how satisfying it was to have her bare flesh against his. It filled him with euphoria more potent than any drug.

With her body straddling his he leaned back and brushed the hair from her face. Leaning his head against hers, he looked into her expectant eyes. "What's wrong?" she asked.

"I'm twenty-seven," Jackson said.

"What?"

"I want you to know about me," Jackson said before he pressed his lips softly to hers and brushed her hair back from her face. She nodded, not breaking their eye contact.

"When I was young, I couldn't understand why my father gave his life for his job and left me and my mother alone. I hated the fact that my mother didn't love me. I became a bitter, angry person with no purpose. I hurt many people and did things that I will never forgive myself for. Giles was the reason I got off the streets and put me on a path that I could focus all my hatred on a single goal. Until I meet you, my sole purpose in life was to solve the case my father died for; avenge his death, and bring down the man that was at the helm of it all, John Stodden." Jackson placed his hand against her cheek.

"I didn't think I was capable of feeling anything else but hatred. You changed everything. At first I was angry with you. I hated the distraction, but before I knew it, my world had changed and I was seeing everything for the first time. I realized I was capable of more." Jackson ran his thumb over Lexie's bottom lip. "I'm in love with you, Lexie."

Lexie's eyes watered. The light glistened off them and he pulled her closer, but she began pushing against him.

She shook her head gently. "No, don't say that."

"Why? It's the truth," Jackson asked, releasing his hold on her as she pushed herself off him. She continued to shake her head as tears ran down her cheeks. She began frantically wiping her face. "You can't," she said, her voice was becoming frantic. "You can't love me."

Jackson stood up and pulled his pants back into place. "I can and I do, Lexie." He tried not to let anger slip into his voice. "You don't need to love me back."

"You only think you do. You'll change your mind when you know the truth," Lexie confessed as she turned her back. The pain on her face was breaking him. He stepped closer, wanting to comfort her. He ran his fingers down her arm in a gentle stroke.

"What truth?"

"I'm John's daughter," Lexie gasped and covered her face.

"Lexie…" Jackson wrapped his fingers around her arm and turned her toward him. He pulled her hands from her face and tilted her chin up so she could look into his eyes. "I have always believed you were his daughter. From the first time I laid eyes on you."

"What?"

"I know exactly who you are," Jackson confirmed.

"Why don't you hate me?"

"To be honest, I tried that at first, but it was a sad attempt at best. You have become what's most important to me. That's why I can't bring myself to leave you."

"Then don't," Lexie whispered.

Jackson crushed his lips to hers, tasting the salt of her tears and the divine flavor that was uniquely her. Jackson grabbed her waist and lifted her against him. She wrapped her legs around him as they deepened the kiss. Their actions became emotionally driven as they desperately clung to one another. Lexie ran her fingers through his hair and grabbed tight. He moaned in her mouth as she rubbed her body against his. The pleasure he felt was beyond him and he felt possessed as he laid her on the bed.

Jackson tossed the mound of pillows onto the floor and shoved his pants down. He wanted nothing between them as he lowered himself against her.

"I never had a home, Lexie. I never felt like I belonged anywhere but I want to belong here," Jackson said against her neck as he pressed himself against her entrance.

"You do." Lexie made a beautiful sound deep in

her chest as he rubbed against her. Her back arched off the mattress as she grabbed his shirt. He pushed off the bed and reached over his shoulder and hauled it over his head; discarding it on the floor.

Lexie gasped when she looked at his chest. "What happened?"

Jackson looked down at the injuries he had sustained when they had rescued Evan. He had been grazed by a few bullets and was covered in scratches. Dark bruising had formed on his ribs, but he didn't feel any pain. Truth be told; they were relatively tame compared to injuries he had sustained over the years. He had plenty of scars to prove it.

"Hazards of the job," Jackson quickly discarded. "They don't even hurt."

Jackson grabbed her hand that was gently touching his bruised ribs and brought it to his lips, kissing it. "The only thing I feel is you." Jackson looked up at Lexie with a sly smile. "And you feel amazing." The worried crease in her brow quickly melted with her smile.

Jackson braced himself on either side of her as he looked upon her. He wanted to remember every detail of this moment when he would make love to her. He slid his length into her until he filled her completely. He leaned down and kissed her face and she gave a gentle moan of satisfaction. Jackson moved slowly at first: in and out in languid thrusts. He was slowly kneading her pleasure, building it until he ripened it enough just so that she would feel the bliss that currently blurred the edges of his vision and set his body on fire.

Reaching up, Lexie grabbed the bars of her headboard and met each thrust as she demanded him to move faster. Her body writhed and her breasts bounced with each push. Jackson held her hips firm against him as to not break their connection. He ran his hand down her leg before placing it over his shoulder. Jackson could no longer separate himself from the pleasure he felt as his body was completely victim to it. He grabbed onto the edge, refusing to fall until Lexie joined him. He used his thumb to milk her with each thrust as he rubbed her swollen sex until her body began to jerk against him. He could feel the trembling of her legs as she came undone for him. A beautiful whimper left her lips. Jackson let go and it hit him like a crashing wave.

CHAPTER THIRTEEN

Lexie

Heavy drops fell from the grey sky and splattered on the windshield. It was the perfect weather for the representation of Lexie's loss. She ran her finger over the smooth surface of her mother's urn as she clutched it in her lap. The small ceramic jar contained all that was left of the beautiful person she was. A whole lifetime reduced to ashes in a pretty jar.

Lexie was so grateful to Molly for taking care of the details, she felt like she wasn't even in control of herself as she floated through the day. She had always known her mother wanted to be cremated. She had always said that when she died she didn't want her bones to be buried in the ground out of fear that she would be forever tied to them. She wanted to be set free. Lexie always laughed at her mother's strange belief, but now she felt a sense of peace that she had her wish.

Holding the jar now, she didn't feel her mother's

presence. What was in the jar felt like only ash; nothing more. Her mother was no longer bound to the restrictions of her life. Lexie looked out the window and wondered where her mother's soul was. She hoped that she was a gentle breeze that softly caressed a bed of flowers, absorbing their aroma. Drifting free from one place to the next, wherever the sun led her; free as a bird. That was what she wished for her mother, to never feel worry or pain again.

Jackson reached over from the driver's side of the car and placed his hand on her leg. The touch was so gentle but it offered immense comfort. Lexie placed her hand on top of his. He grabbed hold of her fingers and gave them an affectionate squeeze.

When they pulled up in front of the diner, Lexie looked up at the sign. It looked exactly the same but felt so strange. She suddenly felt like a stranger in her own life. Lexie took a deep, shaky breath and leaned back against the seat. Molly decided it was the best place to hold the wake. They had the facilities to handle the food preparation and the seating. Lexie thought it was perfect because her mother spent most of her time within the walls of the diner. She loved this place. There was a sign placed out front stating that it was closed to the public for a private service.

"Do you want me to keep the guys out here? We don't have to go in if you think its best," Jackson offered. "Keep you from having to explain to everyone who we are."

"Are you kidding? The only thing that will keep the questions contained is the fact that most people will be scared to ask with you there." Lexie grinned softly. "I'm sure the whole town has been talking about you."

Stephanie reached up from the backseat and placed her hand on Lexie's shoulder. "Ready?" she asked.

Lexie turned around to see Stephanie and Cherry quietly watching her. "I need you all with me," Lexie said.

Lexie watched Jackson walk around the car and open the door for her. She wished circumstances were different so she could appreciate how stunning he looked. His dark hair was swept back, accentuating his pronounced cheekbones and a jaw that put others to shame. Jackson opened the door and held out his hand for her.

Lexie looked at it and up at him, trying to will her body to stand up.

"Take as long as you need, Lexie," Jackson said.

Lexie looked up and noticed Molly standing in the open door, waving toward them.

"Cherry and I can buy you some time," Stephanie suggested, grabbing Cherry's arm as they huddled under a red polka-dot umbrella.

"We have it covered, doll," Cherry agreed before they both walked off. Evan, Teddy, Dane, and Nate walked toward them. They had traveled in a different car and had just arrived.

"We'll be in shortly," Jackson said as they all looked at Lexie.

"Lexie?" Evan questioned. He looked like a new person after the harsh few days he'd suffered. Thanks to Cherry, Evan was well enough to attend today. He still had a long road ahead of him, but at least he was on the right path. He finally broke the news to his parents that he hadn't made it to rehab. They made him promise he would go and he gladly accepted. He wanted to get his life back on track and Lexie was proud of him. The mischievous twinkle had returned to his eyes and his color was much improved. Now that the physically taxing part of the process had come to an end, the hardest part would be dealing with the reason he'd become an addict in the first place. This was a part of the process that could not be handled in a matter of days. Evan's road was long but he would not be alone.

"I'm fine." She nodded. "Just need a second."

"Do you want me to stay with you?" Evan asked.

"No, go ahead. Molly said she would make extra apple pie, but it won't last long."

Evan glanced back and forth between Jackson and Lexie. "Okay, I'll save you a piece."

Lexie watched Evan throw her one last look before he swung the door open and walked inside. She knew everyone was waiting for her. She knew they would all have questions about why she and her mother had taken off without a word and then weeks later her mother ended up in a fatal car crash. Even Evan and Stephanie's story was altered to keep people away from the truth.

Lexie hated the lies but she knew it was necessary. She was nervous that she would let something slip and expose the truth they were all carefully trying to remain hidden—at least for now.

"I used to spend so much time here as a child,"

Lexie said thoughtfully, looking up at the sign. "I would fall asleep in one of the booths when Mom worked late and not even wake up when she carried me to the car. It was just me and her for so long. I don't know how to live without her." Lexie teared up as she looked down at the urn.

Jackson crouched down and took Lexie's hand. "She'll always be with you, just in a different way."

"How'd you do it?" Lexie asked. She knew he had lost his mother but he didn't talk about it much. "How'd you deal with the loss of your parents?"

"I don't really know how to answer that for you. Eventually the rawness of it faded but it's still a big part of me. It changed me."

Lexie placed her hand against her heart. "Like a scar?"

"Yeah," Jackson agreed.

Lexie sighed and thought about the beautiful scar her mother left on her heart. She grabbed hold of Jackson's hand and brought it to her face, leaning into his touch. She needed the comfort that only he could provide. Jackson pressed his lips against her forehead. The simple gesture seemed so full of emotion it reached inside her and filled her heart. She never imagined the seed planted when they had met would grow roots so deep and intricately woven. She no longer knew where she ended and he began.

"Thank you for staying with me," Lexie said.

Jackson wove his fingers in hers and helped her out of the car. "Where else would I be?" he replied and they both broke out in a smile.

"I can think of a few places," Lexie replied,

looking up into the sky. The heavy drops fell onto her face and they felt refreshing. She had always loved the rain and how it cleansed everything. Even the air was fresher. Lexie closed her eyes for a moment to collect herself before she had to face all of the people that would remind her that her mother was forever gone. When Lexie looked at Jackson, he offered her a warm smile. The look in his eyes made her want to melt.

"Sorry, I'm making you stand here in the rain," Lexie said.

"I like the rain," Jackson assured her.

"Me too. We should probably get inside, though. Evan's good intentions always go out the window when food is involved. I could really use a big slice of apple pie right now."

"Evan is not allowed anywhere near your pie," Jackson joked.

Lexie laughed nervously as they approached the door. "This will be so painful." Lexie squeezed his hand for strength.

"You got this," Jackson said as he swung the door open.

Lexie took a deep breath and walked inside, holding her mother's urn in one hand while clinging to Jackson with the other. The interior was packed with familiar faces. Everyone turned toward her as she entered. She managed a small smile before Molly gathered her up in her arms. "Sweet Lexie," she said, holding her tight.

"Don't make me cry, Molly," Lexie warned softly.

"I know, I know, I'm sorry." Molly dabbed her

eyes with a tissue that had been balled tightly in her hand. "Hello again, Jackson," Molly offered with a gentle touch on his arm. "Come with me. There's a table set up over here." Molly led her through the crowd of people that all acknowledged her as she passed.

The table had a white lace table cloth and was covered with beautiful pictures of her mother surrounded by white candles.

"This is beautiful, Molly," Lexie said, placing the urn in the center. She picked up one of the pictures of her mother and smiled. Lexie remembered the day it was taken. She'd gone to the beach with Molly and her mother and spent the day looking for shells. "Thank you so much for doing this," Lexie said gratefully.

"You're welcome, sweetheart. Your mom deserved the best." Molly straightened the edge of the tablecloth thoughtfully before turning toward Lexie. "I know this is not the place for business talk but soon we need to discuss the fact that this…" Molly waved around the diner, "…is yours now. I have to admit that for the mean time we have this place covered, but none of us are qualified to run this place like she did."

Lexie hadn't even thought of it until now. She had been too distracted with the loss of her mother to consider what it meant. "Yes, of course."

Molly smiled and took her hands in hers. "She loved this place, didn't she?" Molly said.

"Yes, she did."

"We're all here for you, Lexie," Molly said.

"Thank you, Molly, I really appreciate it."

"It's good to see Stephanie and Evan looking well. The three of you have seen so much pain."

Lexie placed her hand on Molly's arm. "We find strength in each other."

"Yes, you always have, haven't you," Molly said thoughtfully. "You have very interesting additions to your group, if you don't mind me saying."

Lexie looked over at Jackson, who was watching her from across the room, next to the rest of them. They really stood out in the crowd.

"Interesting is a good way to describe them." Lexie grinned. "They've become very close to my heart."

"Let's get you all fed before everyone starts to talk your ear off."

Molly served them up a piece of warm apple pie with a large helping of ice cream. Once Teddy took a bite, he was asking Molly to marry him. Molly turned as red as her hair and absolutely loved the attention.

Lexie lost track of how many people she had spoken to. There were so many people in the small town that stopped in to offer their condolences over the course of the afternoon. It wasn't long before she was emotionally exhausted from the ups and downs of revisiting old memories.

When the kitchen staff became overwhelmed, Cherry grabbed an apron and stepped in. No one knew quite what to make of her at first as she began directing people around the kitchen to better utilize the space and their efforts. Before long, the kitchen was running smoothly and everyone was warming up to Cherry. Lexie soon learned that Cherry's

Shades of Resolution

talent for cooking extended toward managing a kitchen as well. She was a natural as she worked her way around the space. Molly was grateful for the help with the extra rush of customers. Her big personality seemed very compatible with the other staff and she quickly earned their respect. There were a few ignorant customers that mumbled under their breath, but Lexie knew their small town had its backwards people who would never change.

Lexie shook her head and smiled when a few of the local single girls moved in on the fresh meat. Poor Dane, Teddy, and Jackson didn't know what they were in for when the women came with their claws sharpened. The small town options were slim and they didn't realize that these women didn't waste any time before they were about ready to brawl each other for the front of the line.

Though she had to give the guys credit, they certainly knew how to handle themselves around women. Jackson had the alpha-male persona, Teddy was the charmer, Dane was the tortured soul, and Nate had a boy-next-door thing going on. They were like a romance novel come to life.

Lexie spun around in her chair when the front door swung open and rattled on its hinges from the force. Mike came sauntering in with his shirt mis-buttoned and his tie hanging from his neck. His bloodshot eyes narrowed when they fell on Stephanie sitting beside Nate on the bar stools.

"Oh shit," Stephanie mumbled under her breath. "This won't be good."

Lexie hopped off her stool and approached Mike. Most people noticed his entrance and the sight of

119

him brought most conversations to a standstill.

"Mike," Lexie acknowledged when she came to stand a few feet from him. She could smell the liquor on his breath.

"Lexie." He tilted his head and raked his eyes over her. "You look fuckable. What do you say?"

Jackson tried to step around Lexie but she held her hand up. Jackson looked ready to start swinging and this was the last place she was going to let a fight break out.

"It's best if you leave, Mike," Lexie demanded.

"I got this, honey." Molly swooped in and grabbed Mike by the arm. "Let's go outside to talk," she said before waving to one of the other waitresses. "Package up a piece of pie for Mikey, will you, dear?"

Mike didn't put up much of a fight as Molly led him outside. He looked like he was barely able to walk in a straight line. Lexie watched through the window as Molly spoke to him. She had a way with people that made them put their guard down. Lexie was grateful she stepped in because she had no patience for Mike right now.

Luckily he didn't return inside the diner. One of the men attending offered to take him home and he went without a scene. Lexie watched him stumble into the truck and then drive away. She felt her shoulders drop with relief. Mike always had a temper on him that got him into trouble. He was unpredictable, especially when alcohol was in the mix. He obviously wasn't taking the break up with Stephanie very well. She had a sinking suspicion that this was not the end of it.

CHAPTER FOURTEEN

John

"It's healing nicely," Dr. Collins said as he removed the bandage on John's side.

"Good." John was sitting on the edge of the bed; a cigar in one hand and a drink in the other. He placed the cigar in his mouth and paid no mind to the fact that the smoke seemed to bother the doctor. Dr. Collins waved the cloud from his face before tossing the soiled bandages into the garbage can.

"How's the pain?" the doctor asked, pushing his glasses up his nose with his forearm.

"Don't notice much, to be honest," John answered with a casual frown.

"Well, I suppose the liquor helps with the pain management," the doctor said with a raised brow.

"I suppose it does," John said defiantly as he tipped the glass to his lips. The doctor had recommended he not drink while in recovery but John never did pay attention to things that did not suit his desires.

Dr. Collins had been John's personal physician for years and John knew he appreciated his paycheck and would not risk falling on John's bad side. Everyone close to John knew that they didn't want to cross into such waters or bad fortune would find them.

A knock on the door captured their attention. Rayner walked in, his expression subdued. "Rosh is here to see you, boss," he said.

"Good." John drained his glass before setting it down. He stood up and grabbed his shirt from the back of a chair.

"I'm not done with your new dressings," Dr. Collins complained, throwing his hands up in frustration.

John ignored the doctor and stalked out of the room, following Rayner. He was anxious for word on Mary and Lexie. Having to lay low meant he was cut off from most of his sources of information for the time being. He hated being confined and unable to conduct business as usual.

The club was coming along nicely. The construction had a few setbacks, but now the finishing touches were near completion. The smell of paint filled the interior as the workers were finishing the black trim in the hallways that led to the private rooms. Most of the furniture had been delivered and the bar was being stocked for the soft opening for the preferred customers.

Rayner led him down the hallway toward the offices, tucked away from the main area. Rosh was seated in one of the armchairs when he walked into the room. He looked a bit unraveled, indicating that

Rosh was about to deliver unwanted news. John nodded for Rayner to leave them in privacy before he swung the door shut.

"Let's have it," John demanded without offering any pleasantries.

"Wherever Mary had stashed the information, I know for certain it hasn't fallen into the wrong hands. Maybe she had gotten rid of it. If either departments Belhaven or Westford had a lead about the information, I would know about it."

John narrowed his eyes suspiciously. "What of Mary?" John had been angry with himself for injuring her. Shooting her had merely been a reflex, one he wished he had not been forced to do.

Rosh loosened his tie around his neck. "She didn't make it," Rosh confessed, clearly uncomfortable with delivering the news.

John could feel every muscle in his body tighten. "What do you mean she didn't make it?"

"Complications," Rosh said, unbuttoning the top of his shirt to loosen his collar. "I'm sorry, John. As soon as I found out where she had been taken, I went to find out her condition. She was already gone when I arrived."

"Leave me," John demanded.

"We need to talk about Masten. How do we know he won't say anything? It's only a matter of time before the connection is made."

"Leave!" John withdrew his gun and shoved it in Rosh's face. He watched the sheen of sweat break out across the man's forehead as he pressed it into Rosh's cheek. "I said to fucking leave me."

Rosh stumbled backwards and knocked a chair

over before he grabbed the door handle. He left without another word, leaving John in much needed solitude.

John had convinced himself that the wound had not been fatal. He had shot countless people over the years and knew a fatal shot when he took one, but this completely blindsided him. He wasn't expecting Rosh to deliver the news his Mary was dead. Rage boiled hot in his stomach. He had only just gotten her back. She was supposed to be here with him. She wasn't supposed to leave his side again. He had killed her.

John hit a box off the desk that was sitting in the middle of the room. The contents scattered over the floor. A vase shattered, spraying glass amongst the litter of paper and picture frames.

It wasn't enough to satisfy his need to destroy something. He wanted to leave nothing untouched. John grabbed the desk chair and swung it at the desk. The large piece of furniture scraped along the floor with the impact. Over and over he swung until the chair was destroyed and fell apart in his hands.

John looked down at the blood coating his fingers, his outburst had torn his flesh and left his hands bleeding but he felt no pain. He had opened the wound on his stomach. The blood began to soak through his white shirt and yet he felt nothing but a deep, dark anger that consumed him from the inside out.

John opened the door and noticed Rayner on the other side. He stepped back as John exited the room. "Send someone in to clean up the mess," John said as he walked past.

"Yes, boss."

John headed back to his room. The doctor had left while he was gone and the room was now empty. John needed to be alone. He loosened his tie and pulled it free before he opened the closet and hung it up with his other ties, making sure it was hanging properly before he closed the doors. John glanced at the full length mirror and untucked his shirt. Lifting it up, he took a look at his wound. The bleeding looked like it had stopped.

The sound of a phone ringing in the bathroom reminded him that Rebecca was here. He heard her answer her phone and her shrill laughter following as she conversed with whoever was on the other end of the line.

John opened the bathroom door, letting it swing until it hit the wall. He stood in the doorframe and looked at Rebecca in the tub filled with bubbles. The entire room smelled like a mixture of flowers from whatever scented product she had filled the tub with.

"I'm gonna have to call ya back," Rebecca said to whoever she was talking to. She hit end and set the phone down on the edge of the tub. "Do you need me?" Rebecca asked slowly. She wrapped her arms around herself as she waited for his answer. She had grown to fear him as of late. The only thing he sought her for was to relieve his frustrations, and this proved to be beyond her limits. Her skin showed his handiwork as she clung to herself. He could see the fear in her eyes.

John didn't respond as he walked into the washroom, his eyes never leaving hers. Everything about her now reminded him that he had put up with her because she had been the closest thing he had to Mary. Then for a brief moment in time he had Mary back, and Rebecca faded into the background. Now he saw her again. Now she was all he could see, and she was a sad substitute for what he really wanted.

John sat down on the edge of the tub and gently ran his fingers along the skin of her arm.

"What happened to your hands?" she asked hesitantly.

"Shhh…" John said as he dipped his hand under the surface of the water. He welcomed the sting as his blood mixed with the water and swirled on the surface. He continued to gently stroke her tense body until her nervousness began to melt away as she leaned back and allowed him to caress her wet skin, opening herself to him. She closed her eyes and began to pant under his touch.

John curled his fingers around her neck with his other hand. He applied gentle pressure as she continued to enjoy his caress until her eyes opened in panic. His fingers tightened until they burned.

She tried to gasp for breath as she clawed at his hand, struggling against him. Water splashed wildly from the tub as she frantically tried to gain leverage to resist him. John slowly pushed her down under the water, watching her eyes saturate with fear. She realized this was her last moment and he watched her face twist in panic.

He could feel the water soak his clothing. The hot water immediately began to cool against his skin as his clothes clung to him. Rebecca's thrashing began to wane as he thought about what suit he would wear. When her body grew still he released her and watched her body float lifelessly in the frothy water.

John stood up and unbuttoned his shirt. He slid it off his arms and threw it in the garbage can. He whistled a tune that suddenly came to mind as he dried his hands and face off on a towel. He was trying to remember where he had heard the song. The name of it eluded him.

John opened his closet and selected a new shirt and dark grey suit. Once he was dressed in clean, dry clothes, he straightened his tie in the mirror and picked up his phone.

He dialed a number and waited as the phone began to ring.

"Hello?" a familiar voice answered.

"I need some help on the inside." John didn't waste time getting into the thick of it.

"John, I was wondering when I'd hear from you. What do you need?"

"I have a problem I need taken care of," John said bluntly. "I want to make sure Terence Masten doesn't decide to open his mouth."

"I'll let you know when it's done."

"Good," John said before hitting end and tucking his phone into his pocket. Running his hands down the front of his suit, he double checked his appearance in the mirror. He straightened a stray hair on his head before leaving the room with the mysterious tune still on his lips.

CHAPTER FIFTEEN

Lexie

"You're going back?" Lexie asked.

Stephanie stared at her hands that were clenched tightly on the table. "I know it seems strange, but if there's a possibility that something good can come of this whole situation, I need to," Stephanie confessed.

Lexie placed her hand on top of Stephanie's. "What do you think you'll find by going back to Belhaven?"

Stephanie's gaze flickered up toward Nate. He looked a bit uncomfortable as he leaned against the counter, seemingly unsure how this conversation was going to play out.

"Nate was contacted this morning by the managing officer of the case, Jordon Carlton. It was confirmed that his mother was one of the victims," Stephanie said sadly as she glanced at Nate.

Lexie swung around to look at Nate. "What?"

Jackson looked over his coffee cup as he sipped

the hot liquid and Evan leaned against the table looking ready to fall asleep. "Why do I seem to be the only one surprised by this?" Lexie asked in disbelief.

"I didn't know. I'm just too tired to show any emotion right now," Evan admitted. He sat at the end of the table nursing his coffee and a box of cookies. "Sorry to hear, man."

"Thanks." Nate nodded.

"Nate's coming with me," Stephanie continued.

"So am I," Lexie insisted.

Jackson stepped forward and set his mug on the table. "Bad idea, Lexie. You would be making it too easy for Stodden if you go waltzing back to Belhaven."

"I can't let her go back without me. I'm the reason she got caught up in this in the first place," Lexie said defensively.

"It's not your fault…" Stephanie started.

"Yes, it is," Lexie jumped in. "It *is* my fault."

Stephanie grabbed Lexie's hand. "I watched you suffer since Alex died because you blamed yourself for his death. I'm not gonna let you do it again. Everything that happened was because of John Stodden. He's the one to blame for all of the shit that happened to me, you, your mom…not you."

Lexie's felt her shoulders drop at the mention of her mother.

"She's right, Lexie," Jackson agreed. "There's only one person to blame for all this shit."

Lexie looked up into Jackson's insistent gaze. Over the last few days they had both searched every square inch of her mother's house, trying to find the evidence she claimed to have. Their hours of searching gave them nothing. There was no sign that her mother was hiding anything. She did not own a safety deposit box, she had not hidden away a mysterious key. Her diary mentioned nothing in regards to the evidence. Lexie was at a loss and she knew time was running out.

As much as she wanted to believe Stodden was done with her, Jackson insisted that he was only waiting for the right time to make his move.

"What do you think you'll accomplish by going back? I don't understand," Lexie asked.

"This ring that I found…" Stephanie twisted it around her finger. "I want to be able to return it to the woman's family. What if this is a wedding band? I want her husband to have the piece of her she left behind." Stephanie wiped her eyes as they filled with tears. "I want to give them the answers I can."

Lexie nodded her head. She couldn't argue against that when she herself would want to do the same. She knew how much solace that ring had given Stephanie when she needed it.

"Officer Carlton said he would help me find out who the ring belongs to."

"I'll keep her safe," Nate added.

Lexie nodded to Nate. "Good." She trusted him and knew he would keep his word. She spread her hands on the top of the table and looked at them thoughtfully. She didn't want to meet Jackson's gaze because she knew he wasn't going to like what she was about to say. "I've already decided I'm going back to Belhaven too. John won't be expecting me to go back. What if we can use that to our advantage?" Lexie looked at Jackson. "Why can't we be the ones to make the first move? I don't want to be a sitting duck anymore."

Jackson began shaking his head. "No."

"If Stodden knows I'm there…"

"Absolutely not. We're not using you as bait," Jackson said firmly.

"Why not? You said no matter where I am, he'll find me. I don't want to draw this out anymore. I want this to be over."

"I can go after him myself. You don't need to be involved," Jackson insisted.

"Jackson's right. He knows what he's doing, Lexie. You don't need to be involved if you don't have to. You just lost your mother," Evan added.

Lexie narrowed her eyes. "Yes, I did just lose my mother but now I feel like kicking some ass and taking what's left of my life back from that bastard." Lexie turned her anger toward Jackson. "You should understand more than anyone."

"Lexie…" Jackson started.

"Don't." Lexie held up her hand. "Don't you dare try to treat me like a delicate flower in need of protection. I don't want to be sheltered. I'm stronger than you think I am and I won't let anyone tell me to sit this out." Lexie threw accusatory looks toward Evan and Jackson.

"No," Jackson said. He clenched his jaw tightly and looked Lexie in the eye.

"It's my choice. I hate him as much as you. He's the reason my mother is dead and the reason Stephanie was hurt." Lexie stood up and shoved her chair back.

"You're gonna get yourself killed," Jackson said, refusing to budge.

"I may be the only one who can get close to him. He wanted me to know he's my father. That has to mean something. What if he believes I want to get to know him?" Lexie was determined to make Jackson understand that she needed to be a part of this fight. "I could earn his trust."

"I said no," Jackson raised his voice. Lexie and Jackson locked eyes, neither one of them refusing to submit.

"Lexie…" Evan started.

"Shut up, Evan," Lexie bit off as her eyes remained on Jackson's. She refused to be the first to break eye contact. Jackson was clenching his teeth so hard she wondered if they were about to crack.

"I need something stronger than this shit." Jackson waved toward his cup before he walked out of the kitchen, opened the front door, and slammed it behind him.

"Well, that went well," Stephanie said, staring at the door.

Lexie dropped back in her seat with an exaggerated sigh.

"He's right though, Lexie, you don't need to put yourself at risk again. Jackson is trained for this sort of thing…you're not," Stephanie said quietly.

Lexie looked at her and then Evan's displeased expression. "I'm not scared to die for this," Lexie admitted.

"Oh Jesus," Evan said in a rush.

"I can't hide. That's what my mother did and

look where it got her," Lexie added.

"Then I guess I'm coming too," Evan said.

"No way," Lexie and Stephanie both said in unison.

"You're going to that rehab facility your parents booked you into. You have your own battles, Evan. You have to start taking care of yourself," Lexie insisted.

"How can I go, knowing you're there?" Evan asked as he shook his head.

"You can and you will. Don't get me wrong; I have every intention of being here when you're released. When I was being held by John, I promised myself I was done being a victim. I can't live like that anymore. This is something I have to do, and I need you both to understand this."

Stephanie threw her arms around Lexie.

"There is no going back to before, is there?" Stephanie whispered. "I wish we could be carefree again. I would give anything to lie in the grass and look up into the sky like we used to. Talk about the lives ahead of us like they were going to be a perfect fairy-tale."

"Life was perfect then, I will never forget it." Lexie squeezed her back tightly.

***

Lexie looked out the front window as she watched Stephanie and Nate drive away. She gave one last wave as they drove out of sight. She had said her goodbyes and she needed to believe Stephanie would be all right without her. At first when Stephanie mentioned she wanted to go back to Belhaven, her initial response was fear, but now that she had time to think about it, she understood how it would help Stephanie heal. Even though Stephanie was planning to go to Belhaven as well, they were headed in different directions. Stephanie would still be far from any fallout from what she was attempting to accomplish.

It made knowing that she would be confronting John easier because she knew both Stephanie and Evan would be out of harm's way.

Evan walked up beside Lexie and pushed the curtains aside. Jackson was sitting on the front step. He hadn't moved since he had walked out. He had his earbuds in as he stared off into the distance.

"The only reason Jackson let me tag along the first time was because he made me promise that once he got you back from John, I would keep you far away from him," Evan confessed thoughtfully.

"From Jackson?" Lexie asked and Evan nodded.

"I was more than happy to agree. I hated him. I thought he was the worst person to be in your life." Evan released the curtain and dropped down in the armchair close to him. Lexie glanced at Jackson before she turned toward Evan. "Not to mention I was jealous because of the way you looked at him."

"Evan…"

"Let me finish," Evan stopped her. "I don't think he was expecting you. I don't think he knew at the time what you would become to him. I don't think I could keep you away from him if I tried now. The more time I spend with him, I realize he might be the best person in your life. He's fierce, he knows how to fight, he fears nothing but losing you. He looks at you and I know that he would tear down the entire world if he needed to—for you. I can't believe I'm going to admit this, but I think even Alex would approve." Evan ran his hands down his face.

Lexie shook her head with a smile. "Wow, what happened to my Evan?"

"I don't fucking know. Did I just trip you out?" Evan asked.

"A little," Lexie admitted. "But I could get used to this new side of you."

"You should go talk to him," Evan encouraged.

"Yeah, I know."

"Do you know when Cherry is supposed to get back?" Evan asked, rubbing his stomach.

"She was planning on staying at the diner until after the supper rush. She'll be at least a couple more hours." Lexie glanced at the clock on the wall. Cherry had taken a liking to the diner and found a very comfortable place among the employees. Molly was grateful for the help since one of the girls had recently had to leave to attend school full time. Cherry's management skills were exactly what the diner needed. Lexie was grateful, because at this point in her life she couldn't run a business. Cherry was more than happy to step in and had more than enough experience to make the transition easy.

"She promised to bring me back some pie. I'm gonna take a nap till she gets back." Evan wandered off down the hall.

CHAPTER SIXTEEN

Terence Masten

"Christina Mayfield, Clara Montgomery, Rachael Clayton, and Rose Holzman were all at the Obelisk club within days of their disappearance." Haffey leaned against the table, spreading pictures of the women out in front of Masten. "I know this was not a coincidence. I'm sure if I keep digging into the rest of your victims, I will also find connections." His eyes were drawn to each one of them. He knew them all intimately, but there was one face that stood out more than the rest...Rose Holzman. He couldn't resist the urge as he raised his shackled wrists and touched the photograph. He could remember every detail about her as he closed his eyes and relished the memories he had.

"I want to know John Stodden's involvement. I know you didn't abduct these women without help. I want details and confirmation and I'm sure we could find a way to take the death penalty off the table."

Terence looked up into Detective Haffey's dark eyes. "What do I care? I have nothing left to live for."

"You have a wife and a son," Haffey offered.

"My wife can't the stand the sight of me, and my son, well…let's just say she made sure he felt the same. I can't even begin to imagine what they think of me now," Masten said as he ran his fingers along the outline of Rose's photograph.

"It looks like the men in here don't like you much, either," Haffey pointed toward his face. It was true that since he had arrived he had been targeted. The bruises on his face and the cut on his brow confirmed it. His high profile case had gotten a lot of attention and many of the guards had very strong opinions on the matter.

"Seems so," Masten replied flatly.

"You were the mayor for years; don't you have some small part of you left that wants to do something good for your city?" Haffey pleaded, placing her hands on the table in front of him.

Masten looked up into the dark, seductive eyes of the detective. She was desperate; he could smell it. She wanted to find the weak link in the chain to bring down John Stodden. A part of him wanted to hand over the bastard that allowed those men to take what was his. He had finally found his Rose again and she was taken away from him. John had promised him that no one would come looking for those women on his doorstep.

"I've always hated this fucking town," Masten responded without feeling.

Detective Haffey slid a pad of paper and pen in

front of him. "Everyone has a price, what's yours?"

A knock on the door visibly irritated Detective Haffey. She grabbed the handle and opened the door just a crack. Terence couldn't see who it was, but he could tell she wasn't happy.

"I said no interruptions," Haffey said, displeased.

Masten couldn't hear the voice on the other side of the door as he picked up the pen and began writing his demand on the paper.

"On whose authority?" Haffey spat angrily. *"God dammit."*

The door swung open and two guards came in to collect him. "Let's go." Masten dropped the pen and watched Haffey lean over the table and grab the notepad. She read his conditions before she looked over the paper with narrowed eyes.

Terrance chuckled before he was led from the room. "See you soon," he called back over his shoulder.

His shackles rattled as he moved, both his wrists and ankles bound. He was led down the long hallway of beige painted concrete blocks toward the holding cells. So many scratches and marks had chipped away at the paint from years of abuse. He could hear the rise in voices of the inmates as they drew nearer, like the hum of a beehive. At this time they would all be collected in the common area, waiting to be herded outside for a brief reprieve in the fresh air.

Masten's mind was filled with thoughts of Rose. If he breathed in deep, he could still smell her sweet scent when he would press his face against her hair. He knew she was scared of the dark by the way she would tremble. She didn't like being held behind bars and she had pleaded to be free of her cell, but it was too dangerous—someone might have seen her. He wondered if he would have granted her the ability to feel the sunlight against her skin, would she have run from him in the end?

He knew she had grown to love him as he did her. She had confessed her feelings for him. If he would have had more time, maybe things would have been different. He was robbed of the only happiness he had known.

Now it was only anger that sizzled deep in his stomach. He had nothing else left because it was all stripped away from him.

When his shackles were removed and he was directed to join the others, he hung back from the crowd of judgmental eyes that followed his every movement. He hadn't spoken a word to anyone since he had been locked away with them. They were all common thieves, scum of the very city he had tried to wean them from over his stay in office. He would not pretend to be one of them.

Normally he was kept separate from the others, but today was different. He didn't bother to question why he was now being herded into the crowd, because he wanted to feel the sun. He hadn't had the opportunity to be outside since he arrived. He wanted to know what it would have felt like for his Rose to have been able to have the luxury after months in the dark.

He hung back, waiting for the others to walk down the hall and through the exit doors until he approached. He could feel the warmth of the sun long before he actually stepped out the door. Long chain link fences guided them down a path until it opened into a courtyard. Many of the inmates had already spread out over the grass when he stepped out on the gravel.

The sun felt hot and revitalizing on his cooled skin. He tilted his face up and smiled. He should have given this to her. He should have brought Rose out into the sun where they could have enjoyed this glory together. He knew she would have smiled. He would have loved to see her face aglow by the sun.

Terence continued down the path, avoiding eye contact with anyone lingering along the fence. He knew how delicate these situations could be. Someone bumped into him while he walked past.

Masten was annoyed to be disrupted from his peaceful thoughts of Rose but he kept his mouth shut. He wasn't about to begin any trouble. Someone else bumped into his other side, but this time he noticed a raw sting from the impact. Terence looked down and noticed blood on his shirt. The bright red color spread across the fabric as he watched in strange disbelief. His finger caught in a hole in his shirt where the blood had originated. They had stabbed him. The two puncture wounds began to thrum with pain as the saturation of blood connected on the front of his shirt. A few men began to gather around him, none of them with any mercy upon their faces. His initial flee response quickly dissipated when he noticed he was surrounded. Masten realized that this was his final moment. There was no escape from the death that loomed over his head.

He closed his eyes and tilted his face up to the sun. "I'm coming, Rose," he said as he felt a sharp stab into his stomach and another in his neck. Terrance dropped to his knees as weakness swept through his body. He could hear the whistles of the guards faintly in the distance, but they were too far away. He did not fear his death because he knew his love was waiting on the other side.

CHAPTER SEVENTEEN

Lexie

Lexie opened the front door and walked out on the step. She noticed Jackson's shoulders tense despite the fact that he had his earbuds in. She couldn't understand how he could pay attention to anything else with the music playing so loud as she sat down beside him. Her instinct was to lean into him, but she wasn't sure if he would accept her touch. He seemed so angry.

Lexie pressed the pause button on the iPod clenched in his hand. He pulled the ear pieces out and looked at her. His eyes looked so dark and stormy; she didn't know how to begin to calm the emotions that shone through.

"Will you come with me? I want to show you something." Lexie stood up and held out her hand. He looked at her for a moment before he accepted it. Lexie was relieved with her small triumph. She led him toward the garden shed in the backyard.

The door was already open as she neared. She

hadn't thought about it until now that the men would have searched it. She opened the door and noticed most of her mother's gardening supplies scattered on the ground.

Lexie picked up a shovel and placed it back against the wall. "It was neater than this before…but not much," Lexie admitted with a sad smile. "Mom loved to garden."

Jackson remained quiet as Lexie watched him right a few pots.

"Come this way," Lexie said as she walked over toward a wooden ladder that led to a loft overhead. "This was my place up here," Lexie said as she started climbing up.

"Should I be nervous?" Jackson asked. His lighter mood made her stomach spin happily.

"Maybe." She smiled down at him as she watched him grab the ladder and start climbing up behind her.

It had been so long since Lexie had set foot up here. She was only a girl then and life was still full of magic. The paint on the slanted ceiling had faded over the years but it was still there. Lexie ran her fingers over the flowers and stars she had painted to make the space more beautiful.

"Wow, it looks like a rainbow threw up in here," Jackson said when he looked at the bright colors, set aglow by the small window placed just before the ceiling peaked. The space was not tall enough for Jackson to stand up in. It was always small but now it looked tiny as Jackson crouched down.

Lexie couldn't help but laugh. "I used to hang out here all the time when I was little. I forgot that the space might be a little small for a full sized man."

"So this was Lexie, the girl, huh?" Jackson ran his fingers over the painted boards.

"Yeah, I used to pretend I was a princess with a magic unicorn. Of course there was always the prince." Lexie pointed to the corner where a crude drawing of a man and a horse stood in the corner, standing a total of three feet; the perfect size for her little castle.

"White pants, blond hair and a horse. I obviously don't fit the description of your prince." Jackson raised his brow.

"No, you are definitely unexpected," Lexie confessed.

"Was this Alex for you?" Jackson asked. His question surprised her but she could understand his curiosity.

"This guy's name was Charming, and he was too perfect to be real. He was the fantasy of a little girl before she understood the world. I loved Alex, but he was just as human as me and you."

"That makes me feel a little bit better," Jackson joked.

"I much prefer real and imperfect," she confessed.

"That goal seems much more attainable," Jackson responded.

Lexie grabbed a blanket that had been tossed in the corner. She gentle shook it off and laid it out. Something heavy tucked inside the blanket made a loud thud when it hit the floor boards. "It's a little dusty," Lexie said, waving her hands. She lifted the blanket to see what had made the noise. She wrapped her fingers around the black ball.

"I forgot about this." Lexie looked at the magic eight ball she had tucked away long ago. Lexie gave it a shake and looked at the answer that floated into the window display.

"*Signs point to yes,*" Jackson read over her shoulder. "What did you ask?"

"If you were still mad at me," Lexie confessed.

Jackson looked into her eyes. "I'm not mad; I'm scared you're going to get hurt, Lexie."

"Nothing about this situation is safe, Jackson. You know that better than anyone. Whether I go or stay, I'm in danger," Lexie reasoned.

Jackson took the ball out of her hand and shook it. Lexie leaned in and looked at the answer—*reply hazy, try again.*

"What did you ask?" Lexie asked curiously.

"If you were going to take your shirt off now." Jackson's full lips turned up and Lexie felt like melting.

She shook her head with a laugh before lying down on the blanket and looking up at the ceiling like she used to. "It doesn't look the same in here anymore. I suppose it's lost some of its magic after everything that happened."

Jackson climbed down beside her, looking up at the artwork. "I like it."

Lexie glanced over at Jackson and wondered what was going on in his beautiful head. Lexie turned on her side and ran her fingers along his arm. When she looked up, he was watching her quietly.

Jackson shook the ball again, this time more

vigorously.

"What are you doing with that?" Lexie asked, watching as he tilted it toward himself to view the answer.

"Trying to get the answer I want," Jackson answered with a frown. It read—*ask again later*.

"That's not how it works. What do you want an answer for?"

Jackson dropped his hands with the eight ball and held it against his stomach with a sigh.

"When you're with me...do you wish I were him—Alex," Jackson asked thoughtfully. "I know you still love him. I just want to know if you're with me for me or because you miss him?"

Lexie had been so wrapped up in her own feelings she'd never considered how Jackson would feel about her confessions of love for her late boyfriend. She liked that Jackson was opening up to her. It made her think about things that had been running through her mind as of late. Things that she knew she needed to shed some light on for both their sakes.

"When Alex was alive, life was safe and predictable. His love was gentle, sweet, and thoughtful, but there were also the things that I tucked away when he died. I only wanted to remember the good times with him. Nothing else mattered after that...until now. With you there is danger, rawness, heat, and fire. You make my head spin with emotions I didn't know I was capable of. Despite all the chaos of what is me and you, I have never liked myself better. There always feels like there is too much space between us, even when you're inside me," Lexie confessed.

Jackson grabbed hold of her hand and pulled her closer. His hands felt warm and his touch ignited her.

"When I'm with you, everything else fades away and I feel whole again. Until I met you, I would have given anything to turn the clock back, but now..." Lexie paused and looked into Jackson's searching eyes. He was drinking in her every word. "A part of my heart will always love Alex, but when I'm with you, you have all of me and nothing less, I promise you."

Jackson tossed the ball aside and placed his arms on either side of Lexie, leaning over her. "Your answer is much better than that stupid ball."

Lexie laughed. "In fairness, that would be a lot of words to fit on a small triangle."

His smile could have lit the world. Jackson had such strong, captivating features. Anyone who looked at him could see that, but the more she got to know who he was, the more she could see the beauty of his strength within. He was absolutely breathtaking in every way.

Lexie placed her hands on either side of his face. "I want to move forward, but I can't until I put all this behind me," Lexie admitted honestly.

Jackson brushed Lexie's hair away from her face.

"This is all so new to me. This is the first time in my life that I remember being scared since being a kid."

"Don't worry, I'll protect you," Lexie whispered as a smile took over her face.

Jackson chuckled and shook his head. "You are something else," he said before pressing his lips against hers. Lexie grabbed hold of his shoulders and refused to let him go. This was exactly what she needed right now. She wanted to be loved by Jackson, to feel him close to her.

Lexie ran her fingers through his hair, along his shoulders, and down his back as he pleasured her mouth. She couldn't get enough of him. She wanted to completely possess this raw, intense man.

Jackson's fingers grazed the sensitive flesh of her stomach as he grabbed her waist and pulled her closer against his body. Every nerve ending came alive and spun with delirium. It became a frenzied rush to remove their clothes. The moment her body moulded against his, flesh to flesh, she wished this moment could last forever.

Every kiss, every caress felt like it was directly linked to her sex, pooling hot and deep inside her. Unrestrained moans and gasps flowed from her as Jackson spread her legs and massaged her wet center. Lexie couldn't feel the floor beneath her. She was combusting from the inside out and her senses went completely numb to the outside world as she was immersed in Jackson.

His rough chin left a delightful burn against her skin as he kissed her. His mouth devoured her lips, neck, and breasts as his fingers plunged inside her, stroking her insides and milking her of pleasure. All of her nerve endings set off like fireworks throughout her entire body as she exploded from his touch.

Lexie completely melted into the floor like a

puddle, unable to move or form a coherent thought.

"Are you still with me?" Jackson whispered against her neck.

"Ummm…" Lexie managed.

His kisses became gentle again as he kissed her cheek and her lips, savoring the skin of her neck as he ran his fingers over the sensitized flesh of her breasts. His attention to her nipples made her inner pool begin to heat again.

"What are you doing to me?" Lexie gasped. Jackson took her mouth, and wrapping his arms around her, he lifted her off the ground and into his lap so she was straddling his waist. Jackson squeezed his eyes shut and held his breath as he pushed inside of her, his hands holding her still for a moment. "Go gentle on me, baby. I want this to last long as possible," Jackson said, opening his eyes and looking deep into hers.

Lexie ran her hands over her breasts and fondled them as she watched the heavy rise and fall of Jackson's chest. His eyes never left her breasts as she molded them into taut peaks. Lexie took control of her pleasure, feeling empowered by his rapt attention. His entire body was coiled tight beneath her and she used it to her advantage.

Lexie ran her hand down her stomach and began stroking her pleasure bead, still swollen and wet. She began rocking her hips and the sensation of his hard length rubbing her inner walls quickly brought her back toward the climb to pleasure. She could feel her wetness seeping out of her, dripping heavily with desire as he watched her every movement.

Jackson began matching her thrusts as he

grabbed her hips and moved with her. Lexie could feel her legs tremble as she neared the top of her climb to release. Jackson pushed off the floor and wrapped his arms around her, flipping her over onto her back. He took her breast in his mouth as he thrust hard and inside her swollen center, causing heat to rush through her body and push her over the edge. Lexie screamed out as Jackson forced himself deep inside her. His body trembled as she clung to him. He buried his face in her neck and gently kissed her as Lexie waited for clarity to find her again. She wanted to stay like this, Jackson's arms wrapped around her and their bodies both sated.

Jackson rolled onto his back and pulled Lexie against his chest. They were both quiet for a few moments, savoring what had just transpired between them.

"I think I made your little prince very jealous," Jackson said, placing a kiss on Lexie's forehead.

Lexie smiled and raised her head enough to see her drawing on the wall.

"I think you just blew his mind." Lexie laughed.

CHAPTER EIGHTEEN

John

"You can't keep pulling this shit, John," Brian Crothers argued. "Detective Haffey is already crawling up my ass trying to find a reason to shut us down. Our clientele will not be happy knowing we have authorities sniffing around. This whole business is dependent upon discretion. Now, we have to dispose of a body. *Jesus Christ.*"

"I'm taking care of it," John replied, looking at Brian through a cloud of smoke. John always respected Brian's eye for business and the care he took in his personal appearance. The man reminded him of a younger version of himself...though sometimes Brian needed a reminder of who he was dealing with.

"How?" Brian asked, picking up the decanter of whiskey and pouring himself a glass from the tray on the edge of John's desk. Brian had partnered with John over a year ago to establish the exclusive club, Bitter Sweet. John had learned a long time ago of the fortune to be earned in drugs and tailoring to the sexual tastes of rich men. This company was to give them the platform in which to distribute to a specific clientele. "The city is already in an uproar after what happened with the mayor. Everyone is out for blood. That detective is just itching to find a connection between you and Masten."

"I think you need to calm the fuck down," John said, placing his cigar in the ash tray. "Leave this side of the business for me to handle."

Brian ran his fingers through his hair and looked at John before he dropped his hands. "It's a hard thing to ignore, John. This business can come to a stop before it's even open at this rate."

"Your lack of confidence is insulting," John challenged.

"I mean no disrespect, but you have to understand my worry," Brian offered. Brian took a generous drink.

John pursed his lips thoughtfully. "After tonight you won't have to worry about the detective."

"What do you have planned?" Brian asked suspiciously.

"Like I said, leave these things to me to deal with. As for the dead body, it's being taken care of as we speak. Rayner and Jacobs are very discreet. As far as you're concerned, it's business as usual."

"Won't Rebecca be missed?" Brian drained his glass with an exaggerated swallow and set it down on the tray.

"She's already forgotten," John assured him.

Brian nodded his head. "I have a shitload of things to do to get this place ready. I need you to look these over." Brian slid a file of papers across the desk in front of John. "I will leave this in your capable hands."

"Please send in Rosh." John waved his hand toward the door.

John looked around his new office. Now that the paintings were hung and everything was in its place, he could appreciate the overall feel of the space. The entire club offered an old world feel with ornate trim and deep, rich colors on the wall. It was the perfect backdrop for the atmosphere they were creating. John rubbed his forehead where a dull headache refused to subside. Thoughts of Mary had plagued him and kept him awake at night. Knowing she was dead and gone forever made so much anger furl tightly inside him. He found himself seeking out excessive drink and release with countless women, but nothing alleviated his mood. The effects of sleepless nights were beginning to wear on him.

John barely had a drink poured when Rosh came into the room. "John," Rosh acknowledged, closing the door behind him. Rosh had been under his wing for years, but John never put much faith in men with gambling addictions. When it came down to it, the man was not in control of himself, and therefore John knew that his value had its limits. His respected position among law enforcement had been his saving grace all these years but now that has been tainted.

"Having you here does not do either of us any favors," John began. "It will only be a matter of time before someone recognizes you."

"Giles suspects my involvement with you. It's best for me to stay away from Westford for the time being until things are dealt with," Rosh insisted.

'I'm not suggesting you go back to Westford. I have a job for you. Flint has not shown his face since the ambush at the hotel. He's not answering my calls, and from Lexie's admission, I have a feeling that he knows I will not look favorably upon him if he does turn up," John said.

"You want me to track him down?" Rosh asked.

"Yes, and I believe you should start looking in Freyview." John set his glass down on the desk. "I'm sending Rayner and Jacobs with you."

"What do we do when we find him?" Rosh questioned.

"Flint has been by my side for many years. I think it would be best if he was brought back so we can talk about what he did." They both knew what this meant. It was understood that John wanted to deal with Flint's betrayal first hand.

"If Flint is after Lexie, then Jackson won't be far. What do you want me to do with him?" Rosh asked hesitantly. John knew that Rosh had history with Jackson, being he was his father's partner. His knowledge and ability to get close to Jackson might prove useful. Jackson, like his father, was a thorn in his side that he could not wait to get rid of.

"I want him dead."

Rosh nodded in understanding. He was always willing to do what John requested, he was a man that carried the burden of addiction, and this made him pliable. Rosh's debt was more than one man could pay in a lifetime, and this meant that John owned him. Rosh would never be a free man again for the rest of his lifetime.

"I will leave for Freyview then," Rosh said, walking toward the door.

"I want Lexie brought back to me," John added. "She's to be unharmed."

"Of course."

"I will be expecting you to keep me informed."

When Rosh opened the door, Rogers was standing on the other side. He nodded toward Rosh as he passed him and stepped into the room.

"We're ready for you, boss," Rogers said.

"Good," John said as he followed Rogers out of the room.

John unlocked and pushed open the door leading to the basement stairwell. Most of the storage items were kept on this level, as well as some of the high end liquor. They passed a few crates on their way toward the few rooms that were located in the far corner of the lower level. John opened the door and walked into the room. This unused area was already proving to be most useful for certain business exchanges. It even had an exit to the rear of the building, which led to a stairwell into the alleyway, making it easier for John's people to come and go without entering the main part of the club.

With no windows, the only lighting came from the stark fluorescent bulbs overhead. The room was anything but comfortable, but it was perfect for what John's intentions were.

Rogers led him toward the center of the room, where a man was bound to a chair. His head hung forward, his dark hair matted with blood that dripped down his face and splattered on his shirt. Rogers grabbed the man by the hair and hauled his face up for John to view.

The man's left eye was swollen shut and several cuts covered his face. He didn't respond to Rogers' touch. He was unconscious and his breath indicated the stress his body was under. John studied his men's handiwork and was pleased with the result.

Rayner was standing behind the man, wiping his hands off on a rag. "Find Jacobs and get ready to leave. Rosh will fill you in on the details," John ordered.

"Yes sir." Rayner tossed the rag aside, pulled off his ski mask, and started for the door.

"Rayner?" John called after him. "Keep an eye on Rosh," he said in warning.

Rayner nodded and closed the door behind him. Rayner was aware that John had his reservations about trusting Rosh.

John turned his attention back to their prisoner and narrowed his eyes. A mixture of saliva and blood dripped from his mouth as he made a small whimpering sound.

"I think if we do anymore you will not be able to recognize him," Rogers added.

"No, this is good," John confirmed. He walked over toward a makeshift table created from a couple of wooden crates and grabbed the camera. John turned on the power and looked through the lens. Having the camera in his hand reminded him of Lexie. He wanted to bring her back to him. She was all he had left of Mary now.

"This was the message I was going for," John

confirmed.

John passed the camera to Rogers before loosening his tie and pulling it from his collar. He rolled up his sleeves, pulled on a pair of gloves, and picked up a black ski mask.

Once John's identity was disguised, Rogers hit record on the camera. John picked up a pair of wire snips sitting among an assortment of tools. Turning his attention back to their captive, he tilted his chin up so his head flopped backward. A low moan rumbled from his chest as he started to come to. John ran the snips along his cheek. His victim opened his eyes slightly and started to make a pained sound from the back of his throat that quickly turned into pleas. John watched a tear drip from his eye and mingle with the blood upon his cheek.

"Please...no..." The man's voice was barely recognizable as he forced it through his swollen throat, tears now streamed down his face.

John shoved a rag into the man's mouth and placed a piece of duct tape over it to muffle the man's screams that he knew would soon follow. The man was so weak from his torture he couldn't resist as John gagged him.

John dropped his gaze toward the man's hand that was taped to the arms of the chairs. His fingers tightened their hold, turning white. John pried his little finger off the arm rest and placed the wire cutters around the flesh, squeezing tightly.

A muffled scream tore through his throat as he jerked so violently that the chair scraped along the floor. John didn't stop until the cutters pushed through the entirety of his finger and severed it from his hand. Blood poured down the arm of the chair and splattered on the floor as the man cried out in agony.

John held up the dismembered finger for the camera before tossing it along with the snips onto the table. Rogers stopped recording and set the camera down.

"What do you want me to do with him now?" Rogers asked over the cries that echoed in the room.

"Wait till dark and take him to Trent Baker's place. He can keep him there until anything changes," John said. "Bandage up his hand so he doesn't get blood everywhere and clean this place up."

John turned toward his victim. "I'm sure you can understand that we can't have your sister stirring up shit," John said as he tapped him on the side of the cheek. "She needs to learn a lesson if she is going to be a detective in this town." John pulled off the gloves and threw them on the table. He noticed blood on his arm and grabbed the rag off the table to wipe it off. "Keep him gagged until he stops making noise."

John took the camera from Rogers and headed back toward his office. He didn't want to waste any time getting the footage into the right hands. John smiled to himself, it hadn't taken him long to find what he needed to make sure Detective Haffey would not interfere with his business again.

CHAPTER NINETEEN

Jackson

Opening his eyes, Jackson stared up at the ceiling of Lexie's dark bedroom. His mind raced from his dream that danced too close to danger. He placed his hands over his face and took a deep breath. He knew it was just a dream, but he couldn't shake off the lingering emotions. Normally whiskey and sleeping pills would ensure a dreamless night, but he couldn't risk it now. He needed a clear mind for what lay ahead. Fear of failing to keep Lexie safe plagued him and there were too many unknowns to put his mind at ease.

There was a reason Stodden had secured his position. He was a man who calculated every move and knew how to work the angle. Jackson needed to be smarter to stay a step ahead. He had exhausted all his informants and he knew the time was near where he needed to act on what he knew. It was nowhere near a perfect plan but Jackson had gone with much less before.

The reason Lexie's plan bothered him so much was because it would have been what he would have insisted upon if it was anyone else but he didn't want to put Lexie in that position again. He couldn't stand the thought of putting her in danger. Stodden was unpredictable and he did not trust that Lexie would be safe with him even though they shared the same blood. Jackson knew he was wasting too much time trying to come up with a solution. Their window of advantage was already closing.

He was terrified to loosen his hold on Lexie. He had lost too much in this lifetime that the fear of losing her was enough to bring him to his knees. She had become his everything, the very heart beating in his chest.

Jackson reached for Lexie but she was no longer in bed. He pushed himself up and glanced around the empty room. The lingering panic from his dream tightened its grip. Jackson soundlessly climbed out of bed and pulled on his jeans. He grabbed his gun off the nightstand; a habit from years of living in danger.

Jackson stepped out into the hall. The bathroom light was not on and there was no sign of Lexie as he headed toward the stairs. The darkness of the house was heavy and ominous as Jackson kept his gun in front of him. He could not shake the feelings from his dream that had played a similar scenario. His head was reeling with fear.

When he neared the top of the stairs he noticed a silhouette in Lexie's mother's room. Jackson lowered his gun and came to stand in the doorway.

Lexie was standing against the window with her hands pressed against the glass. Lexie glanced over at him when she noticed him.

"You scared me when I woke up and you were gone," Jackson said as he tucked the gun in the back of his pants.

"I couldn't sleep," Lexie said as she looked back out at the dark property.

Jackson walked up behind her and wrapped his arms around her waist. He loved how she melted into his arms, like she needed him as much as he needed her.

"I think I remember something," Lexie whispered as she wrapped her arms around his and squeezed tightly.

Jackson placed a kiss on the top of her head, enjoying the peace of having her in his arms after the panic of his waking without her in bed. "What's that?"

"When I was young, I remember waking up from a bad dream and coming into my mother's room to crawl in bed with her. I did that often when I was little. She would always wrap her arms around me and hold me until I feel asleep." Lexie took a deep breath before she continued. "She wasn't in bed. When I looked out the window I saw her down there." Lexie pointed toward a bed of flowers. "She was digging in the dirt in the middle of the night. I remember being scared, like I was seeing something I shouldn't, so I crawled in bed and waited for her to come in.

"I can still remember when she finally came to bed. She pulled me close and wrapped us tightly in the covers. She thought I was asleep, but I was waiting for her. She smelled like fresh soil and it lulled me to sleep.

"The next morning when she made breakfast she told me we were going to buy some flowers and start a garden. It was the beginning of her love of gardening."

Jackson stayed quiet as she visited the memory of her mother. "I think she buried something there. What if it's what we're looking for?" Lexie spun around in his arms. "I think we should dig it up."

"I'll go get a shovel," Jackson replied without hesitation.

***

The moon was full as it cast substantial light down upon the ground, making the use of flashlights unnecessary. Jackson had been digging for the better part of an hour. Lexie couldn't remember exactly where her mother had been that night; only the general area. After carefully transplanting some of the plants Lexie wanted to salvage, he began digging. Lexie waited beside him with her arms wrapped around herself, feeling the chill despite the oversized sweater she wore.

Jackson could tell she was on edge, every sound in the distance made her nervous. "I think I just heard something," Lexie said anxiously.

Jackson stopped moving and listened. The only sounds he heard were the normal sounds one would hear in nature. "I don't hear anything," Jackson said, looking at Lexie.

"It might be just the breeze, or over my overactive imagination." Lexie said, rubbing her arms. "Is this a first for you? Digging in the middle of the night?"

Jackson frowned for a moment. "Actually, no. It's not even my second." Jackson tossed some dirt up onto the top of the growing pile.

"Should I even ask?" Lexie raised her brow.

"Probably best you don't," Jackson admitted. The hole was getting larger and larger and Jackson could tell Lexie was starting to get disappointed. He was not so easily deterred; if there was the slightest chance they would find the evidence Lexie's mother referred to, he would dig up the entire yard.

When Jackson's shovel met resistance, he immediately began to uncover something that looked like a box. Lexie leaned down to get a closer look as Jackson cleared away the dirt.

"Oh my god," Lexie said, looking at the box.

Jackson grabbed hold of it and pulled it free. Finding the box was like a weight being lifted off his shoulders. It was a plastic container about the size of a milk crate and didn't weigh much. He hoped whatever was inside would be something that would give them the weight they needed to make John Stodden's reign crumble beneath his feet.

Jackson stepped out of the hole and dropped it in front of Lexie. He pried the cover off and looked inside. Lexie held her phone up to shine a light inside. Jackson picked up the contents that were sealed in a plastic bag and heavily taped. It looked to be dry and Jackson was hopeful whatever was inside would be in good condition.

The sound of a branch snapping alerted them both. Lexie shoved her phone in her pocket to hide the light. They both listened for any other noise but their surroundings were suddenly too quiet and Jackson did not like the uneasy feeling that suddenly crawled up his spine.

"Let's get inside," Jackson suggested as he grabbed Lexie's hand. "I'll fix this in the morning."

Once inside, Jackson closed the door and turned the lock. He pushed the curtain aside on the small window to make sure it was clear before he joined Lexie at the kitchen table.

"Do you think someone is out there?" Lexie asked, looking nervously at the door.

"We're good." Jackson tried to ease her concern but the truth was he wasn't sure.

Lexie grabbed a pair of scissors from the kitchen and began cutting the tape. Jackson walked up beside her and watched as she opened the bag and pulled out files and a handful of floppy disks.

"How are we supposed to find out what's on these?" Lexie looked at the stack of disks.

"Teddy got a bunch of info off some of these my dad had stored away," Jackson said, turning his attention toward the files.

"I don't know what any of this means," Lexie confessed.

"I do," Jackson said, taking the file as Lexie passed it to him. "This one is business transactions." Jackson flipped open the other files. "Contacts; it looks like John had background checks on everyone he dealt with...bank account information...holy shit, no wonder John wanted these back. It may be only pieces of the bigger picture and out of date, but there is no way he can avoid prosecution with this evidence presented against him." Jackson picked up the file with the contacts in it and skimmed through the names. He didn't stop until he found the name he was looking for—Mark Rosh.

"Son of a bitch," Jackson cursed. He knew Rosh was guilty, but seeing his name in print was still painful. Jackson dropped the file on the table. "Who knows what's on those disks, but whatever it is, it will only make this case stronger. I have to call Haffey," Jackson said as he took pictures of the papers with his phone.

"The cop?" Lexie asked with a frown.

"I promised her I would keep her informed. It was the only way to keep her from reporting me and using you and Stephanie as witnesses. She knows I can get closer to Stodden than she can. Not to mention that I may have told her we had this…" Jackson waved his hands to the files. "It may have been the convincing factor," Jackson admitted.

"I know this is none of my business, but were you and this detective ever a thing?" Lexie asked with a slight crease forming between her brows.

"A thing?" Jackson asked with a raised brow. He could see the color crawling up Lexie's neck.

"I'm just curious. The past is the past, but it's just…" Lexie trailed off uncomfortably. "Never mind."

"I slept with her, once, before you. It was a mistake, but other than that, our relationship is strictly business," Jackson confessed truthfully. He didn't want to keep any secrets from Lexie. He hoped that because she asked, she was ready for the truth. He wasn't quite sure how she would feel about knowing.

Lexie shook her head and blew out a breath. "The idiot was right."

"What idiot?" Jackson questioned.

Jackson barely had the words formed when they both heard a loud bang on the front step. Jackson pulled his gun out and headed toward the window. "Stay back," he told Lexie as he pushed the curtain aside to look on onto the porch. He didn't see anyone there, but the rocking chair on the front step was knocked over; it now lay haphazardly against the house. Jackson opened the door and slipped outside. Holding up his gun, he surveyed the front yard for any sign of anyone.

Jackson stepped back inside. "Stay here, I'm gonna look around outside."

Lexie jumped and grabbed for the pair of scissors on the table when she heard the door handle of the rear door rattle. Jackson darted into the kitchen. Lexie was gripping the scissors so tightly her fingers were white as he motioned for her to step back into the kitchen and away from the door.

Jackson used the barrel of his gun to push the back door curtain aside to see who was on the back step. Mike was standing on the other side and began hitting his fist against the door. "I know she's here," Mike called out.

Jackson opened the door enough that Mike could see him. "What the fuck do you want?"

"I know Stephanie's here. She hasn't been home. She's with *him*, isn't she?" Mike said accusingly.

"She's not here," Jackson said sternly. He could tell Mike was drunk, his bloodshot eyes were glazed over and his shirt was torn. There was even dried blood on his lip and Jackson suspected he had gotten into a bar fight before wandering this way.

"Let him in." Lexie relaxed her hand with the scissors but still held onto them. "This is the idiot," Lexie said with a shake of her head.

Jackson looked at Mike and wondered how the hell this drunken piece of work came up with the fact that he had slept with Detective Haffey. Him mentioning it to Lexie only succeeded in making him dislike him more.

Mike pushed his way past Jackson and stumbled into the kitchen.

"She's not here, Mike." Lexie stepped in front of his path.

"Her parents went back home…said she was staying with you," Mike said angrily. "I need to talk to her."

"She needed to get away for a while. She's not here. Go home, Mike." Lexie raised her hands and Mike slapped them away.

Jackson grabbed him by the back of the shirt and hauled him backward. "She said to fucking leave." Jackson shoved Mike back against the wall and pressed his gun under his chin.

"Jackson," Lexie said, clearly uncomfortable with the situation.

"Oh Christ, what's happening here?" Cherry walked out into the main living area as she pulled the strings of her robe tighter.

"Mike was just leaving," Jackson insisted.

"I'm not leaving until I speak to Stephanie," Mike bit off. He was clearly too drunk to register the threat of Jackson's gun. Mike began to struggle, giving Jackson no option but to knock him out. Lexie gasped when Jackson delivered the blow and Mike's body collapsed against the wall and slid down to the floor.

"You just knocked him out!" Lexie gasped in surprise.

"Should I call the cops?" Cherry asked with a raised brow.

"No," Lexie answered. "He just needs to sleep this off. He gets irrational when he's drunk. Did you notice if Evan was awake? We might need him to take Mike home."

"I gave him some sleeping pills. He's out like a baby until morning," Cherry said.

"I'll take him home," Jackson suggested. "You two call me if anything—even the wind—sounds funny." Jackson watched Cherry walk closer to Lexie and wrap her arm around her.

"We'll be fine," Lexie insisted. "Thanks, Jackson."

"Take this." Jackson held out his gun toward Lexie. She wrapped her fingers around the hilt. "Don't take any chances and don't open the doors. I won't be long." Jackson grabbed Mike's heavy body and hauled him up to his feet. Mike was dead weight and difficult to maneuver, but he managed to get him over his shoulder and outside. He reeked like stale beer and smoke, and Jackson prayed he could hold his liquor, because the last thing he wanted was to have Mike lose the contents of his stomach in his car.

Jackson opened his truck and dropped Mike inside. He gave a slight moan of complaint but he didn't rouse. He wasn't taking the risk of having him wake up when he was driving. Mike was obviously out of control, and the last thing he wanted was to give him the opportunity to do something stupid. Jackson closed the trunk and jumped into the driver's seat. He didn't want to be gone any longer than necessary.

CHAPTER TWENTY

Lexie

"Should I ask why you smell like a garden and look like you were playing in the dirt? Or is this some kinky shit you and Duke have going on?" Cherry asked playfully.

Lexie looked down at her hands and shook her head. She had soil caked under her nails and her clothes were in need of a wash. "We found the evidence Mom had on Stodden. She buried it in the garden." Lexie walked back over to the table and began straightening everything into a neat pile. Having the very evidence that Stodden was willing to kill for spread out on top of her table made her very nervous. An irrational part of her was terrified he knew they had it and it would only be a matter of time before he came to collect it.

"This is all the shit that mad man has been after, huh?" Cherry said, picking up one of the floppy disk and examining it with a frown.

"Yeah." Lexie walked into the living room and

opened a closet her mother used for storage. Lexie grabbed a box off the top shelf and opened it up. It was mostly empty other than a few old photo albums. Setting the box on the table, Lexie removed the albums and placed the files and disks inside the box.

"Look at you," Cherry said, opening one of the albums. "You looked like candy come to life." Cherry smiled at the photographs as she flipped through the pages. Lexie knew the album well. She was five and six years old in most of the pictures.

She remembered the outfit Cherry was referring to, it had been her favorite.

"Mom let me pick out my own clothes," Lexie explained the mismatched colors and patterns that made up her unusual outfit.

"I think it was very fashion forward of you," Cherry mused.

Lexie laughed. "It was something, that's for sure." Lexie took the album from Cherry's hands and ran her fingers over the picture of her sitting on her mother's lap. They were at the annual community picnic. She could remember the day very clearly in her mind.

"The other kids told me I looked like a cupcake that day. The name stuck for a while. I was called "Princess Cupcake" for a few weeks after that. At first it made me angry until my mother told me it was my superhero name. She even made me a cape to go with the outfit and baked a whole bunch of cupcakes that I decorated with my "magic" sprinkles." Lexie flipped further into the book until she came to the picture of her running around the front yard in the same outfit with a bright pink cape."

"You're mother sounds like she was quite the woman," Cherry said as she patted Lexie on the shoulder.

"She was," Lexie responded as she wiped her eyes.

"I'm gonna make some tea before I head back to sleep. Do you want some?" Cherry asked, walking into the kitchen to fill up the kettle.

"I would, but I have to get in the shower and get this dirt off me," Lexie said as she set the albums on top of the files and closed the box. She tucked the box into the closet and walked back toward the table where she had set Jackson's gun.

"Take it with you, you'll feel safer. Trust me. I have slept with a gun under my pillow for years."

Lexie nodded and picked it up. "Goodnight, Cherry,"

"Goodnight, Princess Cupcake," Cherry called after her as Lexie started up the stairs.

When Lexie walked into the bathroom, she closed the door and turned the lock. She looked at her reflection and tried to pick out all the characteristics of herself that reminded her of her mother; the shape of her eyes, her cheekbones, her blonde hair, and her lips. These were the parts of her that she would cherish. Every time she looked in the mirror she could see the part of her mother that was still alive in her. Lexie didn't let herself think about what she shared with her father because it terrified her. She was scared to admit that a part of her was made up of evil. She desperately hoped she was strong enough to overcome it.

Lexie turned on the shower and waited for the steam to start filling the room. Now that they had found the evidence John was looking for, she hoped it gave them the power to finish this. She wanted to be free of the shackles John had bound her with. She wanted to leave everything to do with him in the past and move on.

Lexie showered quickly. She suddenly felt exhausted and wanted to crawl in bed and wait for Jackson to return. Lexie wrapped herself in her mother's favorite robe that was still hanging on the back of the bathroom door. It still smelled like her as Lexie held the fabric to her nose and breathed in the scent. She towel dried her hair and ran her fingers through it before heading to bed.

Lexie smiled when she walked into her room and saw a hot cup of chamomile tea sitting on the nightstand next to her bed. "Thank you, Cherry," she whispered as she picked it up to take a sip of the warm, comforting liquid. Lexie pulled on a pair of her favorite sleeping shorts and a tank top and hung her mother's robe up on the hook next to her closet. She ran her fingers over the silky floral material. "I love you, Mom," Lexie whispered.

Lexie checked her phone for messages before she picked up the gun she had left on her dresser. Lexie slid it under her pillow before crawling into bed. Cherry was right, she did feel better knowing it was close. Lexie wrapped her fingers around the hot mug and savored the stillness around her.

Lexie looked around her room. Her mother had kept all of her photos up on the walls. Lexie's room was still the same as when she lived here other than the fact that it didn't have all of her things cluttering the surfaces of the furniture. It was familiar and strange all in one, like a ghost from her past.

Lexie set her tea down and noticed the framed picture on her nightstand looked different. Frowning, she picked it up to get a closer look. Lexie could feel her stomach curl into a ball of lead as realization dawned on her. A picture was tucked inside the frame. It was a still of security camera footage. It was from the hotel room that Stodden had kept her in. She must have missed one of the cameras when she had searched. The picture was of her and Flint the night she had taken his phone, it made her stomach roll with nausea.

Lexie covered her mouth and threw the picture across the room. It hit the wall and the glass shattered. Lexie grabbed the gun and stood up in a panic. The room spun as she stumbled, grabbing for the side of the bed. Her feet suddenly wouldn't obey her and she slid to the floor. The gun felt heavy as she struggled to hold it up. Lexie willed her body to get up but it was no use. The floor felt uneven and swayed like it was fluid as she pushed against the floor.

Lexie heard footsteps coming up the stairs and panic burned her throat. "Cher…" Lexie tried to call out but her tongue felt swollen and too large for her mouth. She couldn't get her words to pass. Lexie heard the footsteps come to a stop at the entrance of her door. She could feel her fear fill the entire room until it was suffocating.

Flint filled the door frame. "Did you miss me?"

His cold voice crawled over her skin.

Lexie managed to raise the gun enough to aim. She pulled the trigger but only an empty click sounded from the gun.

"Looking for these?" Flint raised his fist and opened his hand. Bullets dropped from his open palm and scattered over the floor. Lexie gasped in despair.

Flint shook his head with a click of his tongue. "After what we shared, you're so quick to pull the trigger. I'm disappointed."

"Don't..." Lexie managed to push through her numbing lips.

"Don't what?" He tilted his head.

Lexie had no more strength as whatever drug he had put in the tea took all her strength and her ability to move. Lexie had no choice but to submit as she laid her head against her bed. She watched in horror as Flint knelt down beside her.

"You're much more vicious than you look, Lexie. So soft." He ran his fingers over her cheek and down her neck. Lexie wanted to scream and pull away but her body was no longer her own. "You betrayed me. I'm not a man that forgives easily."

Lexie wished she could respond to his repulsive words. She wanted to tell him what she thought, instead she had to submit to the torture of letting Flint do whatever he wished.

"I can see in your eyes that you have so much to say; always such a fighter. It took me a while to perfect this concoction. Don't worry, you'll stay conscious the entire time. I wouldn't want you to

175

miss out on any of the fun. There's something very appealing about being able to do whatever I want with someone while they watch helplessly locked away in here." Flint pressed his finger against her forehead. "I'm looking forward to our time together."

Lexie wanted to shove him away when he leaned in to place a kiss on her lips but she couldn't move. Her hands remained lifelessly in her lap, allowing him to kiss her and dip his tongue into her mouth, tasting her as he moaned. She still had enough sensation lingering in her skin to feel his touch and she wanted to claw his eyes out.

"You telling John about our time together was a very bad thing. You better hope he believes me over you. Your father is not a merciful man. Lucky for you, you found me a little bargaining chip that will make my proposition more appealing." Flint wrapped his fingers around her neck. "If that doesn't work, I want to make sure I enjoy what time I have left, and that includes making you suffer." Flint pressed his face into her neck and took a deep breath. "And I will enjoy every moment of it."

She felt the floor disappear from underneath her as he picked her up and swung her over his shoulder. Lexie caught a glimpse of her mother's open door and then his black shoes as he descended the stairs. She wanted to reach out and grab the railing and struggle against him. It was so close but her hands wouldn't cooperate.

Lexie tried to scream when she saw Cherry on the floor at the bottom of the stairs. She was so still and blood dripped down her face from a gash on her head. Her inner voice screamed as fear exploded inside her. She tried to allow her anger to burn through the fog that was calling her to sleep. She needed to help Cherry. She wanted to fight Flint and make him stop, but all she could do was be swallowed by the nightmare of being paralyzed. She was completely helpless.

CHAPTER TWENTY-ONE

Jackson

When Jackson came to a stop in front of Mike's parents' house, there were no lights on, nor any house on the entire street. It was a quaint little street with white picket fences and well-manicured lawns. It looked more like a scene from a movie than the reality that he had known as a neighborhood growing up. Even the stars seemed to shine brighter over this town. They were all blissfully asleep, and that was exactly what Jackson wished to be doing as he hauled Mike out of the trunk. Low moans escaped him as Jackson heaved him up on his shoulder and walked toward the front steps. Jackson noted the porch swing and decided to let Mike sleep it off on the front step rather than disturb his parents.

Jackson set Mike down on the wooden seat as gracefully as he could manage and headed back toward his car. He was anxious to get back to Lexie. He didn't like leaving her without his protection. It was easy to fall under the illusion of safety when the danger was not currently on your doorstep.

Teddy and Dane had to head back to Westford to help Giles and he was left without another option for taking Mike home. For some reason, Lexie wanted to spare him the embarrassment of involving the local authorities, and he felt he should respect that, despite the fact that he despised Mike. He knew exactly the type of man he was. The only reason he felt comfortable enough to leave was because he knew Stodden was still in Belhaven. He had been in touch with Max, who had given him as much information he could. It wasn't much, but enough to allow him to believe they still had time.

Before Jackson could grab the handle of his door, he heard a loud thud. He turned around and noticed Mike was lying face-first on the porch below the swing. It was only a matter of seconds before a light turned on inside the house. Jackson slid into the car and drove away. He did not want to face Mike's parents too; he didn't have the patience for it.

Jackson was barely off the street when his phone lit up the dark interior of the car.

"Hello?" Jackson answered.

"Jackson, there's a change of plans," Haffey said.

Jackson knew immediately that something terrible had happened by the tone of her voice. She sounded defeated, something he thought he would never hear from the woman who was an unstoppable spit-fire from the moment they met.

"What happened?" Jackson questioned.

"Stodden has my brother…" Haffey trailed off. He could hear her try to conceal the fact that she was close to tears. "I have no way to prove it's him. I received an untraceable video that shows Carlos being tortured," Haffey gasped into the phone. "The bastard cut his fucking finger off. The man in the video was wearing a mask but I bet my life it was him. The threat is pretty clear. "

"Shit, Haffey." Jackson said. "Send the video to Teddy. He'll try and pull anything from it. What do you need from me?"

"If I make any move, Stodden will kill him. I have to back off, I don't have a choice. His men are watching me and it's probably best we don't talk from here on out."

"Understood," Jackson confirmed. He was fully aware how Stodden worked. Haffey was getting too close and this was his way to extinguish the threat. "Do you still want Stodden alive?"

"Honestly, I don't care what you do with that motherfucker as long as he's stopped," Haffey said. Her guard was down and she was desperate, Jackson could tell by the sound of her voice how broken she was. "Terence Masten was killed before I could get any information out of him. I can't prove it, but I know Stodden was making sure he didn't have the opportunity to talk. No matter what I do that god damn motherfucker is always two steps ahead of me."

"Sounds about right," Jackson agreed.

"Jackson?" Haffey asked.

"Yeah?"

"Get my brother back," Haffey said.

"I will," Jackson assured her before he ended the call. Jackson dropped his phone in the console and rubbed the side of his face. Jackson shook his head. He was always the cop that everyone labeled as the "bad cop," but as soon as the shit went down, everyone looked to him to clean it up.

Jackson had just received the green light to go after Stodden. There were no longer any lines drawn in the sand that he was forbidden to cross. Haffey had just released his ties and unofficially told him to burn Stodden to the ground and he had every intention to do so.

Jackson stepped on the gas. If Stodden now believed he was free of the barriers Haffey had placed around him, then it wouldn't be long before he made his move toward Lexie. Jackson tore through the quiet streets. It felt all too convenient that Jackson wasn't with Lexie right now. A sick feeling settled in his stomach as he drove like his life depended upon it.

When Jackson neared the street, he passed an unfamiliar car, a black Mercedes. Jackson took note of the model as he pulled onto Lexie's mother's street. There were only a few cars on the road this time of night in the small town and not many Mercedes, let alone on this street. He read a partial off the plate but the car turned before he could get a good look.

Jackson pulled into the driveway and jumped out of the car. He headed toward the back door and jogged up the steps. His stomach dropped and his fears were reinforced when he noticed the door wide open. Jackson barrelled in the door with his gun raised. He noticed Cherry on the floor as soon as he entered.

"Cherry," Jackson called to her. He scanned the room for anyone else. "Lexie!" Jackson hollered as he dropped down next to Cherry's body and felt for a pulse. As soon as Jackson felt the steady beat of her heart, he let out a sigh of relief. "Be right back, Cherry," Jackson said before he bolted up the stairs. "Lexie!" he hollered.

Jackson pushed her mother's door open and cleared the room before heading toward Lexie's room. He kicked something as he neared her door that rolled across the floor. Jackson bent down and picked up a bullet, a quick glance around and he saw the entire chamber of rounds were scattered on the floor.

When Jackson walked in, he noticed the gun sitting on the floor. Jackson raked his hand through his hair and kicked the nightstand. A cup of tea sitting on top tumbled to the floor and shattered. He knew he was too late. Jackson ran back down the stairs and into Evan's room down the hall and slammed the door against the wall. Evan jerked awake from the noise, squinting his eyes groggily.

"Get the fuck up!" Jackson hollered, pulling the pillow from beneath his head and throwing it across the room.

Evan pushed himself up and rubbed his face. "What...huh?" he yawned.

"Lexie was taken and Cherry is hurt. Get the fuck out of bed now!"

Evan tumbled out of bed and rushed to his feet behind Jackson as he returned to Cherry, who still hadn't moved.

Jackson dropped on his knees beside her. "Cherry," Jackson nudged her shoulder. "Wake up."

Cherry moaned and lifted her hand to her head. "What the fuck?" she said when she pulled her hand away and noticed the blood. "Oh Jesus." She tried to sit up but Jackson placed his hand on her shoulder.

"Just give yourself a moment or you'll pass out again. What happened?"

Evan ran into the kitchen and grabbed a dishtowel. "Here," he said, pressing it to her head.

Cherry looked at her shaking hand covered in blood. Tears filled her eyes. "I didn't see him come in, Jackson. I, ah…I turned around after pouring tea. I only got a glimpse of him before he hit me. Where's Lexie?" She looked up at him with fearful eyes. "Oh god. Where's Lexie?"

"He took her," Jackson said tightly. He clenched his jaw so tight his jaw ached. "Tell me everything you know."

Cherry closed her eyes. "Um…he wore a shirt…a white one and he had a closely trimmed beard with a bit of grey. I didn't see his eyes."

"Any tattoos?" Jackson asked.

Cherry shook her head slightly and cringed. "I didn't see any, but he had a long sleeved shirt on."

"I didn't hear anything, Jackson. I'm so fucking sorry," Evan said, completely terrified and confused as he ran his hands through his hair.

Jackson pushed to his feet. "Fuck, he must have

taken the files and shit too," Jackson said, noting the bare table. Jackson didn't blame Evan because he had screwed up too. He should never have left her. Now Lexie was gone and the evidence they needed against Stodden as well.

"What files?" Evan asked.

"We found the shit Stodden is after," Jackson answered, rubbing his neck in frustration.

"How long have I been asleep?" Evan blurted in confusion.

"Lexie tucked it all away in a box on the top shelf," Cherry said, pointing toward the closet in the living room.

Jackson walked over to the closet; the door was swung closed, but not latched. A few items rolled out when he opened it and Jackson knew the top shelf would be empty before he even laid eyes on it. Jackson slammed it closed with a curse. He had screwed up worse than he could ever forgive himself for. The two most important things he had in his possession he'd failed to keep safe.

He was already too far behind to try and track down the car he passed. Jackson pulled his phone out of his pocket and dialed Teddy's number.

"What's up, man?" Teddy answered with a yawn. Teddy was used to receiving calls at all hours from Jackson and probably didn't even consider it urgent.

"I need you to track a vehicle for me right now," Jackson said, giving him the details he knew.

"That's a nice fucking car," Teddy said, his voice much clearer now. "That was in Freyview? No wonder you're suspicious."

"They have her," Jackson confessed. "I left for fucking twenty minutes tops and he just strolled in and took her."

"I'll find the car, Jackson. Just give me a few minutes to tap into the satellites."

Jackson could hear rustling on the other end of the line. "I'll call you once I find it," Teddy said.

Jackson hung up and immediately dialed Giles.

"I was talking to Haffey," Giles said when he answered. "I've been waiting for your call."

"He took Lexie and the fucking files we found on him," Jackson said angrily as he paced back and forth. Evan had helped Cherry to her feet and she was now sitting on the sofa with a bag of frozen peas pressed against her forehead. "We had just found everything we fucking needed to crush that motherfucker and he took it." Jackson practically growled he was so angry.

"Guess I can't be surprised. What happened?" Giles asked.

"It doesn't matter. I'm gonna fix it. I took a few pictures of the files. There's enough there to get what we need on Rosh, but unfortunately that's only part of the story for Stodden..." Jackson trailed off. "I'm sorry, Giles. I had it all and I let him walk away with it."

"Do what you need to do, Jackson. Stodden has our hands tied right now with her brother taken hostage. Haffey won't let anyone make a move; not even our precinct. There's no way of knowing if Stodden has anyone else on the inside, so Haffey won't take any chances. I can't even place a warrant for Rosh because he's tied too closely to it all.

185

You'll be on your own."

"That's the way I like it, you know that," Jackson answered truthfully.

"I can send Teddy and Dane. Set you up with the proper equipment. We may not officially be able to make a move but we sure is hell aren't going to let Stodden win. Call me if you need anything."

"Thanks, Giles."

"Send me what you have. I need to see it with my own eyes."

"I will," Jackson confirmed.

"You'll be on your own until Haffey's brother is extracted."

"Understood." Jackson hit end.

Jackson looked at Evan and Cherry both sitting on the sofa. They were staring at him expectantly. "I need you to take Cherry to the hospital. She'll need stitches," Jackson said to Evan.

"I'm fine," Cherry insisted. "How're we gonna find Lexie?"

"*You* are going to the hospital. The best thing for you both to do is stay here. I'm waiting on Teddy to find me a location and then I'm leaving."

"You're just going after her yourself?" Evan asked. "Why don't you call in the entire police force to take Stodden down?"

"We need Stodden to think we're playing by his rules. He, unfortunately, still holds the winning hand," Jackson said, tapping his finger on the side of his phone, anxious for Teddy's call. "This is not a fucking game of cops and robbers."

"Just thought that after what happened last time you'd need all the help you can get," Evan said, pushing off the sofa.

"Well, sometimes you need to work with what you have," Jackson responded.

"What if—" Evan began.

"Don't even suggest you're coming. You are going to that fucking rehab place. You're no good to us like this." Jackson waved his hand. "As soon as you get within distance of any type of drug, you'll lose your fucking head and you know it."

Evan closed his mouth and stared at Jackson. "I fucking hate standing on the sidelines being helpless."

"Good, maybe it will be enough to keep you clean so you're not dead weight," Jackson spat angrily and he immediately regretted it. Jackson raked his hands down his face. "Fuck, sorry. I'm just angry as shit right now."

"Don't apologize. We all know it's true," Evan confessed.

Jackson had to admit he had a lot of respect for Evan. He had only known him a short while and he had gone through two rounds of withdrawal and stayed determined through it all despite the torture. He knew the strength it took to accomplish what he had. Jackson had seen many men waste away from drugs, unable to face what it took to curb it.

Cherry took Evan's hand and squeezed tightly, offering comfort.

"Just say you'll bring Lexie home," Evan demanded.

"I will," Jackson said. "I will bring her home and end this. I won't let Stodden win."

"Good, that's the one thing I like about you is

the fact that you do what you'll say you'll do," Evan admitted.

"I haven't figured out what I like about you yet," Jackson said without conviction.

Evan smirked and shook his head. "You can't just walk away when this is over anymore, you know that, right?" Evan said.

"I know," Jackson acknowledged.

Jackson's phone barely started ringing before he accepted the call. "What do you have for me?"

"I found it," Teddy said.

CHAPTER TWENTY-TWO

Nate

"Are you sure you're ready for this? We have time," Nate asked as he pulled to a stop in front of the address Officer Jordan Carlton had given them. Stephanie had her hands balled in her lap, her fingers completely white from clasping them so tightly. She stared up at the blue house with white shutters. A perfectly manicured garden lined the front of the house with white and violet flowers. A lone pink bicycle with training wheels was parked on the grass. The tassels on the end of the handles fluttered in the breeze.

"Are you sure this is the right place?" Stephanie asked, her gaze lingering on the bike.

"Positive," Nate assured her. "That's the right house number." He pointed toward the mailbox at the end of the driveway. Nate knew that seeing the bicycle had thrown her off. In all of their talks leading up to this moment there had never been any mention that the owner of the ring could have been a mother. The idea of children being involved made the terrible situation that much worse.

Stephanie took a deep breath but remained quiet. Nate didn't want to rush her. She was already fragile from the trauma that was still an open wound. He could see the pain she still suffered every time he looked into her soulful brown eyes. He didn't know the first thing about consoling people. He had spent his entire life trying to survive one day at a time, only trusting a select few people.

Since he and Stephanie discovered their connection through pain and loss, she had begun to desire his company. It was the first time in his life that someone turned to him or sought him out for emotional support. The feelings she invoked in him were almost painful as they swelled too big for him to contain. He knew pain well, rejection and loneliness were familiar to him from a past of people turning away from him. When Stephanie grabbed his hand for comfort and curled into his side, this was strange. He didn't know this language as he desperately tried to navigate through this unknown territory. He was suddenly terrified about letting her down. The only thing he knew for certain was he wanted to be something solid for her to hold onto when she needed him.

He didn't understand it but every moment with Stephanie felt like she was slowly chipping away at the walls he had built up over the years. He was terrified what would happen when those barriers finally gave. He had no idea what was waiting on the inside. He knew eventually he would have to face it.

"They wouldn't have said yes to this meeting if they didn't want you to come. I think knowing that something good came out of this situation might help them. I know it helped me," Nate admitted. "*You* helped me." It felt strange to admit it, but he needed her just as much as she needed him.

Stephanie gave him a sad smile. She reached for his hand, wrapping her fingers around his and squeezed tightly. He didn't understand how a simple touch could feel like it did, but he hoped she never let go. People like Stephanie normally didn't want to acknowledge people like him. He had spent his life doing things that terrified most people. It was the first time he wished he was something more. He wanted to be better for her so he could be the person she needed him to be. Instead he found himself being scared that she would eventually see exactly what he was and run from him like everyone else did. He was no more than a criminal that had nothing to show for his life.

"Okay, I think I'm ready," Stephanie said with a nod of her head.

Nate walked around the car and opened her door."

Maybe I'm not ready," she said nervously. Nate held her door open but she remained frozen in her seat, twisting the ring around her finger.

The front door of the house opened and an older gentleman with white hair gave them a small wave.

Nate held out his hand. "I won't leave your side," Nate promised.

Stephanie looked between him and the man awaiting them. "Okay." Stephanie slid her hand into his and stepped out of the car. Stephanie tucked herself into Nate's side as they began walking toward the house. "I think I'm gonna throw up," Stephanie whispered.

"Seriously?" Nate questioned, trying to be polite and offer a smile toward the man holding the door open for them. Stephanie darted from his arms back toward the curb and threw up on the side of the road, just missing the car.

"We'll just be a moment," Nate called to the man, who nodded and closed the door softly.

Stephanie was leaning on her knees with her eyes squeezed shut. "I'm so embarrassed," she whispered. "I don't know if I can do this."

Nate grabbed a few napkins that were tucked in the glovebox of his car. He passed them to her and placed his hand on her back gently. "Do you want me to go in and talk to them for you?" he offered.

Stephanie shook her head and took a long slow breath. "No. I want to do this…I do," she said.

The door opened again and Nate turned to see the man had returned with a glass of water in his hand. He walked down the front steps and approached them slowly.

He wore a short sleeve button up shirt with khaki shorts. His gray hair was brushed back neatly and he had a sense of peace about his presence. The tension visibly drained from Stephanie as she faced him.

"I thought you could use a glass of water," the man said as he offered it. Stephanie accepted it with a shaky hand. The man smiled at the both of them. "I'm Mark, Brianna's father." His smile didn't reach his eyes when he mentioned his daughter.

"Nice to meet you, Mark." Nate shook his hand.

"Yes, nice to meet you," Stephanie said as she took a sip of the water. "I'm so sorry about…"

The man waved his hand in dismissal toward the street. "Don't worry about it, my dear. Come inside and have a seat. We can make you some coffee or tea, whichever you prefer."

"That would be lovely. Thank you."

They followed Mark inside. The house was in an older section of Belhaven, where the houses had lots of character from age. This particular house was impressively well-maintained. Thick moldings framed the walls and rich paint colors paired with accent wallpaper complimented its age, but also brought it into the present.

Mark led them into the main sitting area just off the foyer. A man in his early forties and a white-haired woman stood inside the room. Their conversation hushed as soon as they saw Nate and Stephanie walk in behind Mark.

The woman's face lit up immediately. "Hello and welcome," the woman said.

"Millie and Alden, this is Stephanie and Nate," Mark introduced everyone.

"Very nice to meet you both." Millie stepped forward and shook Nate's hand before she took both of Stephanie's hands in hers. "I know the strength it must take to come here. We appreciate it." The woman's eyes filled with tears. "Brianna was our only child…" The woman covered her mouth with her hand and then placed it on her chest once she collected herself. "Please forgive me." She guided Stephanie toward the sofa. "Let me get us something to drink. Do you prefer tea or coffee?" Millie asked.

"Tea would be wonderful. Thank you, Millie," Stephanie managed quietly as she sat down.

"Yes, please," Nate added when Millie looked to him. Truth was he didn't drink either. Nate couldn't even recall ever having tea, but since the option of liquor wasn't suggested, he would take what he could get.

"Thank you for coming today," Alden said once his mother-in-law slipped out into the hall with Mark.

Nate's instincts had immediately perked up when he entered the room and set eyes on Alden. While Brianna's parents were sweet and welcoming, this man was something altogether different. Nate had lived among criminals his entire life and could tell when someone was corrupt. He knew the feeling well because he was infected with the same twisted disease. He could feel it inside of him, taunting him since he crossed the line so many years ago. No matter how many times you may wash your hands, you can never remove the blood; it stained for the duration of your life.

Alden sat down in an armchair facing Stephanie and Nate. "When Officer Carlton contacted me to inform me that you wanted to meet, you can imagine my surprise." Alden's gaze traveled to Nate and his eyes narrowed just enough for Nate to pick up on. Nate knew that Alden was trying to get a read on him because it's exactly what he was trying to do to him.

"Yes, I suppose it would be a bit of a shock. I know how painful this is for you..." Stephanie began.

"On the contrary, having you here might mean that we finally have our answers to what happened to Brianna. The officers have been very vague," Alden said as he leaned back in his chair. "Until recently, we believed that Brianna abandoned us."

Mark and Millie walked in to the room, catching the conversation, and their faces fell.

"Brianna's behavior became erratic the last few months she was with us. We were still holding out hope that she would return, until of course, when the officers showed up at our door after Terence Masten was arrested. Brianna's body was identified as one of his victims." Alden placed his hand over his mouth in a show of emotional distress.

Nate studied Alden, trying to find holes in his story.

"The whole thing has been hard to understand," Millie added.

Mark set the tray down on the coffee table and Millie picked up two dainty cups and passed them to Nate and Stephanie before she walked over and placed her hand on Alden's shoulder.

Nate looked down at the cup. The handle seemed too small for his fingers. The size was more of a large shot glass as he decided to just set the base into the palm of his hand.

"It was truly a miracle that you survived. Knowing that some good has come out of this tragedy gives us solace," Mark said, sitting down in the chair next to Alden's.

Stephanie took a sip of her tea and held it in her lap. "I know there's nothing I can say that will make you feel better. I wish I could tell you what you want to know..." Stephanie trailed off when tears filled her eyes.

Millie passed her some tissues. "She is with the Lord now," Millie said, wiping her own eyes. "She's not suffering anymore. We have that at least."

"No matter how hard I try to make sense of what happened, I know I can never understand. I will carry the scars with me for the rest of my life. I wish I could have known Brianna, but finding her ring meant so much to me. I want you to know that. Your daughter helped me more than I could ever put into words."

Millie sat down on the other side of Stephanie and pulled her into her arms. "Brianna would have loved knowing she helped you. She was so kind-hearted."

Stephanie wrapped her fingers around the ring on her finger, twisting it one last time before she slipped it off her finger and passed it to Millie. Millie took it in her hand and ran her finger over the band. "I wanted to return it. That's why I'm here today," Stephanie said.

"As soon as we saw the picture the officer sent we knew it was hers," Millie said thoughtfully. "She had it made. It's one of a kind."

"I want you to have it so it can also bring you comfort when you need it."

Everyone turned toward the hallway when they heard shuffling. A small girl appeared in the doorway that looked no more than four years old. Her dark brown hair was pulled up in hair ties and she wore a blue dress with tiny flowers scattered over the material.

"Nanna?" she called into the room. She was holding a doll by its leg as it hung upside down from her hand.

"Yes, precious." Millie walked over to the girl.

"I'm hungry," she said as Millie picked her up in her arms.

"Nanna will get you something. Let's go to the kitchen. Did you want to say hello to our company?" Millie spun her around to see Stephanie and Nate. Her tiny hand gave them a small wave before they headed down the hallway.

"Brianna's parents moved in not long after she disappeared. It's impossible to take care of Paige by myself with my hectic work schedule. They have been a blessing," Alden said.

"We're happy to help," Mark said with a sad smile. "Paige reminds us so much of Brianna."

"She doesn't remember her mother," Alden said. "Paige was only a baby at the time her mother was taken."

Every minute in the company of Alden, made Nate more restless. He seemed to be the only one picking up on his intensity toward Stephanie and his poor show of sadness. This man was not mourning his wife. Nate would bet his life that the man before him was a heartless man with no real connection to the family that still remained beside him. Nate

197

wanted nothing more than to get Stephanie far away from him. He felt very protective of her and right now his instincts were screaming for him to get Stephanie out of there.

"I'm so sorry," Stephanie said.

"Yes, but in some ways it's for the best that she doesn't." Alden offered them a reserved smile. "Are you staying close by while you're in town?" Alden changed the subject.

"Yes, we are. We're—" Stephanie began but Nate felt the need to jump in. The less Alden knew about where they were staying or how long they would be in town, the better.

"We should get going, Stephanie. We promised Officer Carlton we would stop by the precinct to go over a few things."

Stephanie looked at him questioningly before nodding. "Yes, I'm sure we've taken enough of your time." Stephanie set her cup on the tray and stood up.

"You're welcome to stay as long as you wish," Alden offered.

"You are too kind, really, but Nate is right...we must be heading off," Stephanie said kindly. "It was nice to meet you, Mark and Alden. Please tell Millie and Paige goodbye for us."

"Yes, of course." Mark led them to the door.

Nate threw Alden one last glance as he left the room, which only reinforced his feelings toward the man. This was no family man, he knew his type well.

Nate ushered Stephanie out the door and placed his arm on the small of her back to quicken her step.

"Do you want to tell me why you practically ran us out of there?" Stephanie asked as they approached their car.

"I don't trust Alden. My bullshit meter was going fucking haywire," Nate answered as he rounded the car and opened his door. He looked over the roof of the car to Stephanie.

"What are you saying?" Stephanie asked.

Nate looked toward the front window of the house where Alden was standing in the open curtains with a phone to his ear. He raised his hand in a stiff wave toward Nate.

"I don't know. Let's just get out of here."

CHAPTER TWENTY-THREE

Lexie

A bright light flooded the room when the curtains were wrenched open. Lexie turned her face away from the overly bright glare that pulled her from a very unsettled sleep. She tried to move her hands only to be reminded that she was cuffed. The movement caused pain to flare up the lengths of her arms.

Lexie opened her eyes and looked at her raw wrists that were bound to the old radiator in the room. She had slept on a thin mattress that had been tossed on the floor of the old house she had been brought to the night before.

Lexie scanned the room. The walls were cracked and stained in the light of day. A stale smell filled her nose as she took a deep breath. A few boxes sat in the corner of the room. The cardboard had grown soft and the contents rounded the sides. The entire room was coated in dust as if it hadn't been used in years.

Someone cleared her throat and Lexie turned to see a woman leaning against the wall next to the window with a severe scowl painted across her face. Her dark hair was pulled back in a ponytail and harsh eyeliner circled her eyes, giving her a very hard edge.

"Who are you?" Lexie asked. She tried to push herself up into a sitting position so she didn't feel so vulnerable. Her mouth felt dry and her head throbbed from whatever Flint had given her.

"I'm the bitch that's gonna make your life a living hell," she answered, crossing her arms over her chest.

"Where's Flint?" Lexie asked in confusion. She gave up trying to find a comfortable position and stared at the woman looming over her. Lexie didn't have time to react when the woman lunged at her. She grabbed Lexie by the throat and smashed her head into the wall behind her. Lexie gasped as the pain radiated down her back and made her eyes water. Lexie tensed her body, unsure of what would follow as she cringed from the pain. She was defenseless.

Lexie snapped her eyes open when she heard the woman's laughter, her breath hot on Lexie's cheek.

"My brother told me what you did." She ran her fingernail down Lexie's cheek, hard enough to leave a stinging sensation along her skin.

"I didn't do anything." Lexie pulled away and rattled the handcuff in annoyance. "I'm the victim here."

201

"Hardly. I know your type. You manipulate to get what you want by batting your pretty little eyes. You're not getting away with putting a target on my brother's back. You better hope his plan works."

"Your brother has a target on his back because he's crazy, and apparently it runs in the family," Lexie spat angrily.

The woman wound up her fist and hit Lexie in the face. The coppery taste of blood filled her mouth and pain throbbed in her lip. Lexie looked down and noticed blood dripping on her tank top but she refused to let the woman know how much it hurt as she glared furiously. She needed to stop aggravating her because she was unable to defend herself, but Lexie was angry that she was back in this position again. She hated feeling like a caged animal...at least this time her cage seemed more likely to have weak spots. This woman staring back at her was filled with rage so thick it blackened her eyes. People like this made mistakes, and Lexie would be ready to take advantage.

"Sabine," a man's voice called from the hallway outside the door.

"In here," she answered.

The footsteps grew louder until they stopped at the entrance of the room. His shadow darkened the doorway before he stepped into the room. The man's dark, curious eyes landed on Sabine before they swung to Lexie. His unkempt black hair hung loose against his shoulders. Piercing brows hung heavy over eyes that carried dark shadows.

"So this is Stodden's girl," he said as he strolled into the room, his eyes never leaving Lexie as he drank in her entire presence. Lexie tried not to recoil from his cold, raking glare. She didn't want to show fear despite the fact that she didn't feel so comfortable being outnumbered and at a serious disadvantage.

He ran his hand through his hair and walked closer to Sabine. "What are we going to do with her?" he asked in a tone that gave Lexie chills.

"Nothing, for now. Flint said not to touch her while he's gone," Sabine responded despondently.

"It looks like you didn't listen." He smirked as he stepped closer to Lexie. She pulled away when he reached for her face.

"Don't touch me." Lexie pulled back as far as she could manage.

He watched her like she was a fascinating piece of art and he was trying to determine its meaning.

"How long is she staying here?" He looked back at Sabine.

"God knows what my foolish brother has in mind."

The man walked closer to Sabine. Stepping behind her, he ran his hand around her waist and pulled her tighter to him. He leaned in to bite her shoulder before he continued up the curve of her neck, caressing her skin with his lips and teeth. Sabine welcomed the touch as she submitted to him. A satisfied moan escaped her as his hand ran up the inside of her leg and under her skirt. "Maybe we can have a little fun with her while we wait," he suggested in Sabine's ear.

Lexie's eyes widened in fear and she pressed her back into the wall behind her. There was no way she would be taking in part in whatever he had in mind. Adrenaline began fueling her body in anticipation of what might take place.

Sabine's eyes snapped open and looked Lexie straight in the eye. A dark anger swirled beneath the surface as full and deep as Lexie's hatred for her. Sabine turned abruptly and shoved the man behind her. He stumbled backward with a shocked look on his face. "What the fuck, Sabine?"

"Not her," Sabine commanded. "You will never touch her and you will not think of her. Do you understand me?"

He nodded his head as his eyes flashed from Sabine and Lexie.

Sabine slapped him across the face with the back of her hand. "Do you understand me?" Sabine demanded.

"Yes." His eyes flared dark. Lexie only watched in disgust as these two danced some twisted game of foreplay. Despite the fact that this man was physically larger than Sabine, she exacted all the control. The harsher she became, the more willing and eager he was to please her.

"You want to make me happy, don't you?" Sabine cooed as she ran her fingernail along his chest.

"Always," he responded quickly.

"Then do what I say," Sabine said as she grabbed his chin roughly. Her nails looked like they were about to break his flesh as he looked down at her with exaggerated breath. His gaze dropped to her lips before he began to lean down toward her but she stopped him.

"Not now. I need to think," Sabine said, pushing him away.

The sound of a door closing on the lower floor claimed Sabine's attention. "Watch her." She pointed her talon-like nail toward Lexie as she stalked out of the room.

His eyes swung to Lexie and a subtle smile curled up the corners of his lips. Lexie didn't know what was worse, Sabine the aggressor, or her well-trained pet. They both gave Lexie the creeps. This entire situation did. They seemed unpredictable and danced on the boundary of insanity. This was nothing like being wrapped up in the carefully laid plans of John Stodden, whose moves were calculated and precise. This was like being thrown into a pit of fire when it was about to rain gasoline.

Lexie looked at her cuffs and gave them another tug. Her skin was aggravated from the chafing metal. She knew there was no way to be free of them on her terms. She pressed her head back against the wall and let out an exasperated breath. She could still feel the pain lingering from Sabine's welcoming embrace.

Every time she closed her eyes, even for a brief moment, she saw Cherry on the floor with blood smeared across her face. She prayed with every corner of her soul that she was well. Lexie was tired of the people she loved being caught in the crossfire.

This time Lexie was filled with anger. There was no fear of the unknown as she found herself at the mercy of these people. She had already been introduced to this dark side of humanity and had lost her mother because of it. Now she wanted revenge.

She knew Jackson would come for her this time…there was no doubt in her mind, but part of her didn't want him to. That part of her needed him to know she could take care of herself, despite the odds stacked against her. There was also the very real fear that something would happen to him, and she couldn't lose him. She couldn't lose anyone else in her life.

Jackson was supposed to have been a safe bet, someone she knew she wouldn't fall for. She knew he was dangerous, unstable, and capable of things she could only imagine. It was merely scratching a sexual need, but she had been in denial from the start, and she knew that now. He was everything she thought she wouldn't want, and yet now he was the only one she could picture giving herself to. Lexie had always envisioned herself with someone safe and comforting like Alex, but Jackson had led her to discover more about herself then she ever thought possible.

Jackson fit her in ways she never imagined; on levels so deep it penetrated her core. It was terrifying and raw to the point that she knew she could never turn back. He was still very much a closed book, with dark secrets she knew should terrify her, but a piece of her now existed in him, just like a piece of her was buried with Alex.

Lexie looked up at the man across the room as he lit his cigarette. His dark eyes never left her as she was forced to remain in his company.

"What's your name?" Lexie asked.

"Why?" He narrowed his eyes as he took a long pull from his cigarette.

"I was just curious if you had a name or if I should just call you Sabine's little pet," Lexie said defiantly. She wanted to know exactly who she was dealing with, and pushing his buttons seemed like a good place to start.

"You should be careful or I'll show you how not so little I am," he ground out through his clenched teeth. "The name is Neil." He blew out the smoke and watched it curl in the air around him. "Remember it." A sly smile curled up the edges of his lips.

"Well, Neil, is kidnapping women the norm around here?" Lexie asked.

"Depends," he said with a tilt of his head.

"Am I at least allowed to use the washroom?" Lexie raised a brow.

Neil glanced toward the door and then back at Lexie. "Yeah, I guess." He threw his cigarette down on the floor and stepped on it before he walked over toward the window and grabbed a key off the ledge. Lexie hadn't even noticed it until he retrieved it. "Don't try anything stupid. There are armed men everywhere in this house and they were ordered to shoot first and ask questions later."

"Fair enough." Lexie had noticed the gun tucked into his pants when he had turned his back. She needed to be careful.

"So what's it like to have John Stodden as a father?" Neil asked as he grabbed her wrist to unlock the cuffs.

"Terrible," Lexie answered honestly.

"Daddy issues?" Neil smiled mischievously.

"You have no idea."

"Give me your other hand." Neil said. Lexie tentatively held out her hand and Neil closed the cuff over her other wrist, securing her hands together. "Okay, get up." Neil stepped back to allow her room to get to her feet. He withdrew his gun and aimed it at her.

Lexie tried not to show fear as he waved the gun toward the doorway. "It's at the end of the hall."

Lexie walked slowly down the hall. The only thing she could think about was the gun pointed at her back. It left little room for thoughts of escape.

When Lexie stepped inside the washroom and grabbed the door, she turned around and closed it in Neil's face unapologetically. She tried to turn the lock, only to discover it was broken. She could hear Neil's snicker on the other side of the door.

Lexie walked over toward the sink and turned the water on. Water sputtered out of the old tarnished faucet before it began to run smoothly over her hands. Filling her hands with water, she splashed her face with the cool, refreshing liquid. She needed to think and the first person who came to mind was Jackson. He was the most resourceful person she had ever known and she tried to think about what he would do in this situation.

Lexie turned off the water and grabbed the towel hanging on the towel bar. It looked relatively clean as she grabbed the end to dry her face. Voices floated up through the grate on the floor and she bent down to listen. She recognized Flint and Sabine's voice immediately.

"…you don't need him, Flint. He was just your puppeteer for fucking years. Let's get him to give us some money for his daughter. I'm sure he'll pay a shitload for his little bitch," Sabine said.

"He won't let me get away with that. I need to convince him that Lexie was telling lies. He'll see it my way when I deliver her and the files to him," Flint responded. His voice seemed strained as she listened.

"Why do you want that bastard's approval?" Sabine was losing her temper as the tone of her voice rang loud and clear. "Do you honestly think he values your loyalty? We both know he doesn't give a shit about anyone but himself. You need to forget about your history with Stodden and think about keeping yourself alive."

"I'm as good as dead if I turn my back on him."

"He can't kill you if he can't find you. I can find a buyer easy for the girl and the shit Stodden wants. Do you know how much people would pay to have that power over him? We can take the money and disappear."

A banging on the door startled Lexie and she jumped to her feet. "Just a second." Lexie flushed the toilet and barely had time to prepare herself before the door swung open.

"Hurry up. What do you think this is, a luxury hotel?" Neil complained.

"I'm done," Lexie said as she stepped out into the hallway.

CHAPTER TWENTY-FOUR

Jackson

The pizza was stale and tasted like the cardboard box it had been sitting in since the night before as Jackson managed to swallow a few bites before tossing it to the pigeons. A large flock of them were beginning to collect outside the motel room. He leaned against the railing and watched them fight over the scraps of food, their wings fluttering madly as they pecked at the tough crust.

Jackson's headphones were around his neck. He could barely hear the music, but it was enough to clear his head. For Lexie's sake, he needed a solid plan. He would not gamble with her life. His entire life he had been diving into danger head first, and if he was honest with himself, part of him wished that he would never surface from the dangers he tempted. The situation that stood before him would have once made his mouth water in anticipation, but now he was determined not to make the wrong move.

Dane sighed as he settled back in one of the flimsy plastic chairs that sat outside the motel. It groaned unpleasantly and Jackson was surprised it didn't collapse under the strain of Dane's size. Dane tipped a bottle of whiskey to his lips and took a long haul.

"Breakfast of champions," Jackson said with a smirk.

"It's better than stale pizza," Dane said, wiping his lips with the back of his hand.

"You might be right. How much are you drinking these days, anyway?" Jackson asked Dane, who'd been nursing a bottle since he rolled out of bed. Jackson knew his history well enough to know that it didn't take much for him to spiral out of control. Jackson was not much of a talker himself but Dane was worse. He also had a habit of keeping things bottled deep inside and they slowly carved away at him, piece by piece. It was only a matter of time until he couldn't stand it anymore. Jackson didn't fault him for trying to forget with a bottle. It was a coping technique they both used.

This time of year was particularly hard on Dane, and normally a bender would cause him to disappear without a word for days, sometimes weeks at a time. Jackson and Teddy never let on, but they always tracked his every movement on these occasions. They needed to make sure they were there to step in if Dane got himself into trouble. It only came to that one time and Dane was too inebriated to remember they'd come to his rescue. Jackson thought it was best he didn't remember they intervened. There was something that felt sacred about Dane's time away from his life, where he sought complete dullness of mind and let himself get lost. He was always a new man when he returned, like he had hit reset on the torment that haunted him. And the cycle would start again until the next year.

Jackson had known about Dane's history, but only what he had found on paper when he looked into Dane when they first met. The truth about Dane's demons was hidden deep inside him.

"What are you talking about? You drink me and Teddy under the table," Dane argued.

"I won't deny that, but you usually drink when the sun is setting, not rising." Jackson needed him to be with them for this to work. He hoped Dane understood how important he was in pulling this off. Dane looked down at the bottle in his hand thoughtfully before he tipped it up and poured the rest of the contents on the ground.

"I have an appointment with that shrink…" Dane said absently.

"Just make some shit up like you normally do," Jackson said dismissively, not really understanding what had Dane so distraught about meeting with this new psychiatrist.

"I can't. She's not like the others. She can see through my bullshit, and Giles said if I didn't meet her, he'd take my badge."

"Then talk. What harm can it do? Maybe it will even help," Jackson suggested.

Dane narrowed his eyes as he looked at Jackson.

"Tell me why Lexie has you all turned around. What is it about her that has got you seeing fucking stars?"

"See, you'll be fine. You got that deflection shit down to a science." Jackson turned around and leaned both elbows back on the railing. "Just talk circles around her until your hour is up."

"She's a professional and sees right through that shit, and I'm serious, man. I want to know why you let Lexie in. She's *his* daughter and the last person I would have thought could crack your shell. I've been your friend for years and you never let anyone in, and now all of a sudden we're picking up strays everywhere, and you're thinking through your actions and shit. She changed you."

"Is that what this is about? You have a crush on that shrink and you're scared she'll get inside and see all the dark shit you carry around with you?"

"Fuck, man, talk about deflection. We are a pair, aren't we?"

"I'm not going soft, if that's what you're worried about," Jackson said defensively.

"You can rest assured that no one can ever accuse you of being soft, but if you start sending me birthday cards and shit, I might have to shoot you." Dane chuckled.

"Please do."

"After this fucked up conversation I'm starting to regret pouring that good whiskey out." Dane looked down at the wet stain on the ground.

"Me too." Jackson frowned. "I'm feeling like a drink myself."

"Jacks?" Teddy called from inside their room.

Jackson locked eyes with Dane before pushing off the railing. "What do you have?" He walked into the room to see Teddy in the exact same place, parked in front of his multiple laptops spread out on the small round table in the corner of the room. The space was less than ideal, but Teddy never complained. He knew what needed to be done. Jackson was never one for technology, all the screens that were up looked like a completely different language to him.

"Just got a tip on a private bid; seems whoever took Lexie is trying to cash in," Teddy said, pointing toward his screen where he tapped into a private message board.

"That means we can rule out that Stodden has her." They had tracked Lexie's location to a residential property and took up position at the hotel that was just far enough to stop and get a handle on the situation before they moved in. Something about the scenario seemed off to Jackson and they were now discovering why.

"I've tracked the name of who took the bait. It's a man named Dillan Neumann."

"Who's that?" Jackson asked with a frown.

"On the surface he looks like a nobody. His record is clean as fuck, but I dug a little deeper and found out that he has connections with Marcel Quintano."

Jackson's confusion deepened when he heard the name. Marcel Quintano was a man he had been introduced to many years ago, even before he earned his badge and learned the man's criminal history. His name was practically a household name

214

in Belhaven. Marcel had spent most of his youth behind bars until he wised up to the system and managed to keep his hands clean enough to evade prosecution. He was now the president of a bike club that was located just outside Belhaven, the Heathens. Most of the city feared them with good reason, but fortunately for the police their matters did not interfere with the wellbeing of the general population. Jackson knew him better than either Teddy or Dane realized.

"Why the fuck would Quintano get involved with Stodden's shit?" Jackson rubbed the side of his face thoughtfully, trying to find the connection. Jackson knew for a fact that Quintano made it his personal mission to stay far away from anything with Stodden's prints on it. He wanted to know what changed that. "Find me the connection."

"Already working on it," Teddy replied.

"What are the chances that Stodden is already on to this lead?"

"This was kept on the low in a private group. We should have a good head start," Teddy said.

"How did you find it?" Jackson asked

"You aren't the only one with friends in dark places, and besides, I'm the shit," Teddy boasted.

"Whoever crossed Stodden will have probably left a trail, so we should move fast." Jackson mentally began to check the boxes of his plan, making sure everything was lined up to make their move.

"No one has left the property, but a car recently arrived," Teddy said, pointing toward the satellite view of the house where Lexie was.

215

"Dane and I have to go make our pick up. Call me with any change." Jackson looked up and noticed something on one of his other screens. "What's this? Is that a hallway in Max's apartment building?" Jackson recognized the sad looking interior of the building.

Teddy closed the screen on the computer in question and looked up at Jackson with a guilty look in his eye. "What? I'm just making sure that bastard doesn't sneak into her apartment again and put another camera in there."

"Fuck me." Jackson shook his head in disbelief as he looked at Teddy. "We'll be back soon, Stalker." Jackson smacked him on the back as he grabbed his keys of the nightstand.

"I'm just looking out for her." Teddy raised his hands in question. "There's something about her…"

"The fact that she has tits?" Jackson interrupted.

"Ha ha, you're so funny. I'm looking out for her because she seemed scared."

"Yeah, she's scared of *you,* and rightfully so," Dane said.

"Fuck you, guys." Teddy waved them off and began typing away as they slipped out the door.

Giles had arranged for a care package for them and they were going to need it. Though the orders were not official, Jackson knew that everyone was counting on him. Stodden's power had grown too great and he had contaminated even the people sworn to protect it. Jackson knew he was the last resort.

CHAPTER TWENTY-FIVE

Stephanie

Looking down at her bare finger, Stephanie sighed. She missed the ring more than she would ever admit, but it was back where it belonged, and that was what she would find comfort in now. Stephanie looked up and caught Nate looking at her from the driver's seat. He had concern in his eyes that she wished wasn't there. It only made her feel guilty.

"I'm fine. Stop looking at me like you have to hide all the sharp objects. Why are we stopped here, anyway?" Stephanie asked as she looked out the windshield to a small park with quaint wooden benches that overlooked a small lake. The sun set high in the sky and there was little breeze to break the intense heat. She was surprised there was no one around on such a beautiful day.

Nate leaned back in his seat. "I just want to make

sure we're not being followed."

"Why would we be followed?" Stephanie turned her head so she could watch the wheels turning behind his troubled eyes.

"There was something way off with that guy," he confessed.

"Alden? He only just found out his wife was abducted by a demented serial killer that was also very recently the mayor of his city, of course there would be something off," Stephanie suggested.

"No, it's not that." Nate's phone sounded from the console of the car. He picked it up and looked at the screen. His face looked like it paled as he read the screen.

"Who is it?" Stephanie asked nervously. She got a quick glance at the phone and recognized the name as one of the officers working on the Masten case.

"Hello?" Nate asked in a reserved tone. "That's me."

Stephanie could only watch helplessly from the passenger's seat as Nate listened to the other end of the line. Despite the heat of the sun, she could feel the temperature drop around him. Her imagination began to run wild as she listened to Nate's breathing. The only thing she knew for certain was the information he was receiving carved deep into him by the rigidness of his posture. Stephanie wanted to offer him comfort but she didn't know how. All she could do was wait.

Stephanie held her breath when Nate ended the call. "It's nice to know people with connections," Nate said, trying to be light, but it was unconvincing.

"What was it?" Stephanie blurted. "What happened?"

"They didn't find my mother buried with the others," Nate said as he locked eyes with her.

"Oh." Stephanie could tell her confusion was written on her face. "But I thought they already identified her?"

"She was there...they found her body stuffed in a freezer in the basement."

Stephanie didn't know how to respond as she stared at him with a heavy weight in her stomach.

"He kept her in there for all these years..."

Stephanie tentatively placed her hand on his arm, needing to know that she was doing something to relieve some of his pain.

"I saw that freezer when we were in that basement. When we came for you...do you remember when I opened those other doors? I can remember seeing it sitting in the corner."

Stephanie covered her mouth. "Oh god," she whispered.

"Because she was frozen, her remains were better preserved than the others. It looks like she died from complications of childbirth."

"Did they find a baby?" The question burst from her without any thought.

Nate looked at her, but all he could do was shake his head. They both remained quiet, lost in thought to what this meant; the horror of wondering if an innocent baby was killed or allowing the slightest hope that the child survived somehow. It was so overwhelming it was hard to digest. Stephanie could only watch Nate and wonder if the same thoughts were going through his head.

Nate spun around in his seat, startling Stephanie before he suddenly reached over her and opened his glove box. Stephanie watched wide-eyed as he grabbed a handgun. "Get down and stay down," Nate ordered.

Stephanie slid down in her seat, completely frozen with fear. She was too terrified to turn around and look but she knew a car had come to a stop behind them. Stephanie held her breath as she tried to make herself as small as possible.

Stephanie slapped her hands over her mouth to stop the scream that escaped her when the back window of their car exploded as gunshots rang out. Nate had opened his door and slipped out of the car. She had no idea where he was as she heard more gunshots and then the sound of struggling.

Something slammed against the side of the car and made her jump. She glanced back to see Nate fighting with Alden. This was not the same man she had only just met, who had welcomed her into his home. This man had fire in his eyes and was intent on killing Nate. Stephanie looked inside the open glove box to see a knife. She grabbed the handle and tore off the case with shaky hands.

Taking a deep breath to calm her nerves, she crawled over the console of the car to the driver's seat. Another bang against the car jolted her and she tumbled out of the car onto the ground. Her body trembled so badly she didn't know if she would be able to stand as she looked under the car to see Nate and Alden's feet still on the other side.

"Oh god, oh god..." Stephanie whispered as she ducked down low and moved toward the back of the car. She looked at the thick forest that was only just on the opposite side of the road. She knew she could probably make it if she ran and hid. Every part of her screamed to run but she couldn't leave Nate. She knew she would hate herself for it. Squeezing her eyes shut tight, she drew in a deep breath and looked up at the sky, praying for strength. She rounded the car but darted back as both men came barreling toward her, knocking into the side of the car, which caused it to painfully dig into her back.

Nausea raked through her as she cringed from the pain. The men fought for control of the gun and a bullet shot off mere feet from where she was huddled behind the car. She cried out as she pressed herself back into the car tighter. Adjusting her sweaty grip on the knife, she knew she needed to act before Alden turned the gun on them.

Stephanie grabbed hold of her survival instinct and acted. She lunged forward and jabbed the blade of the knife into Alden's calf muscle as Nate pressed him against the car.

Alden screamed out in pain as blood streamed down his leg. Stephanie scrambled backward, her eyes not leaving the knife. Nate knocked him backward and managed to wrestle the gun from his hand.

Stephanie watched as Nate pulled the trigger and a red hole appeared on Alden's stomach and his blood began to spread across his shirt. Alden looked down at his wound and placed his hand over it, watching the blood coat his fingers. He staggered on his feet before he looked back up at Nate.

"I know that you gave your wife to that sick bastard, but what I can't figure out is why?" Nate narrowed his eyes. "Why the fuck would you send the mother of your child to a man you know would torture and ultimately kill her?"

Alden smiled sadistically. "Fuck you," he said as he spit blood out on the ground.

Nate released another shot, again into his leg, and Alden cried out and dropped down on his knee.

"Tell me!" Nate screamed.

"She was a cheating whore. She deserved what she got. Every fucking second of it," Alden said cold-heartedly. Each second drew out longer than she thought possible as each bullet jolted his body until he dropped to the ground. Nate had released the entire round into him.

Stephanie couldn't take her eyes off him as she just watched his lifeless body. She wondered if this nightmare was ever going to end. The world didn't feel the same. The evil of the world had ripped her veil of happiness away and she didn't know what to think of it anymore.

"Thank you, Stephanie," Nate said, kneeling down beside her after an unidentifiable amount of time passed. She felt like she had been drifting for hours.

"Thank you for what? Stabbing someone?" Stephanie said in disbelief.

"It was him or us," Nate said, nudging her shoulder with his.

"It's not that simple." Stephanie shook her head.

"That little girl lost her mother and now her father is gone."

"She has her grandparents. She'll be fine. Trust me, that little girl is better off not knowing who her father really was," Nate said without remorse.

"How did you know?" Stephanie asked.

"I had a feeling. I know he's involved in this Stodden shit somehow. He was as ruthless as the rest of them. I just have to find out the how part."

"I don't even know what to say," Stephanie confessed as she leaned back against the car.

Nate stood up and walked around to the driver's side of the car and returned a few seconds later with his phone. Stephanie watched numbly as he dialed a number and placed the phone against his ear. "I need to speak with Detective Haffey."

Stephanie pushed off the car and barely stood up before she threw up all over the ground, barely missing Nate's feet.

CHAPTER TWENTY-SIX

Sabine

"You always were the soft one, brother," Sabine said as she picked up a bottle of red wine that sat next to a collection of empties and pulled the cork out. She brought it to her nose before she tipped it to her lips.

The kitchen was a ghost of what it had been. It would have once been standing proud as the cherished home of an upper class family. The fine details were still present under a thick layer of dust and grime. It was once a trophy of success but now remained abandoned after something horrific tainted it. The home must had once brought envy to the neighbors but now it stood as a reminder that nothing is what it seems.

People stayed away from this house, and that was exactly why Sabine decided it was the perfect place. The real estate agent jumped at the chance to rent it, and after she discussed terms, he agreed to let the paperwork slide. Sabine smiled to herself how easy it was to convince him to let her stay here unofficially.

Sex could make any man bend, it was almost too easy. Just like all the ones before him it didn't matter if he wore a ring, it didn't matter who was waiting at home. Men were weak creatures, and if it didn't serve her so well she would be disgusted by the fact that they swayed too easily from their morals. She enjoyed sex just as much as the next person, but it would never make her lose sight of her goal.

"Are you gonna drink the rest of the bottle?" Flint complained. He was standing with his back against the wall and his arms folded across his chest.

"I might save you a drop," Sabine teased as she watched him with a tilt of her head. She tapped her fingers on the side of the bottle as she revisited old memories. "Do you remember all those rodents and disgusting little insects you used to collect and keep in boxes in your room?"

"Where the fuck are you going with this, Sabine? I don't want to drag up old ghosts." Flint rubbed his forehead. The dark circles under his eyes showed his stress.

"I still remember the look on your face when you came home and saw the pile of boxes in the backyard. Dad was pouring lighter fluid all over them. You begged him to stop. You were crying and screaming," Sabine said thoughtfully. "And then whoosh." She waved her arms to mimic the fire. "Our fucking father lit up all those little bastards you loved so much." Sabine walked closer to her brother. He stared at her and she could feel his anger starting to bubble under his skin. Sabine pointed to the ceiling. "That little bitch upstairs is your pet and Stodden is our father. It's a cycle you can't seem to break. It's only a matter of time before he destroys you. Just like our father did. Every. Single. Day. Take my advice now and walk away. You give people too much power over you."

"I was ten years old," Flint said as he narrowed his eyes.

"What's your excuse now? You've been trying to win Stodden's approval for years just like you did with Father. It's pathetic."

"Shut the fuck up, Sabine. You don't know what you're talking about."

"Don't I?"

Sabine wasn't surprised when she felt the sting of her brother's hand across her face. She smiled and wiped the back of her hand across her lips and saw blood just as she began to taste the copper on her tongue.

She held up the bottle of wine and Flint grabbed it from her hand. He downed the rest before tossing the empty bottle across the room. They both watched it shatter against the wall and rain down on the floor.

"I'm the only one who really cares about you, Flint. If you're not gonna do what needs to be done, then I will. Just like I always have."

"What did you do?" Flint narrowed his eyes. His words sounded like poison as they dripped from his lips.

Sabine placed her hands on her hips and gave him a sly smile. She knew it was only a matter of time before her plan became obvious. The look on her brother's face would be priceless. "What the fuck did you do, Sabine? Answer me," Flint demanded as he grabbed for her shoulders. His grip dug painfully into her skin, but she would never let him know it. She would never show anyone weakness; not even to her brother, the only person she truly cared about. Sabine watched his eyes widen slightly before his hands slid down her arms, falling to his sides. He looked down at his uncooperative hands, trying to flex his fingers.

"Sabine…" Flint tried to force the words from his mouth but his tongue would no longer cooperate. He began to stumble and Sabine caught him under the arms before he dropped to the ground.

"It will be all right, Flint." Sabine helped guide him down to the floor and then propped him against the wall. "You were right, your little science experiments do come in handy." Sabine tapped him on the side of the face. "I didn't know how much to give you, so I may have gone overboard. You might have one hell of a headache when you come out of this, brother."

Sabine leaned back on her heels and looked at Flint leaning against the wall. She could tell by the look in his eyes he was livid. "You pushed me to it. I can't let you make this mistake." Sabine stood up and ran her hands over her face and then looked down at her fingers. "You know I can still feel his blood on my hands." A strangled laugh escaped her.

"Part of me hated you for constantly trying to impress Father. He didn't deserve it. He didn't deserve anything. That night...that night when he found out you had scratched his car. I stopped him. I knew he was angry. I did what I had to. You know that, right? That I did it for you." Sabine bit her tongue hard to stop any emotion from appearing. "When they released me all those years later I hated the fact that you had found another bastard to crawl in the shadow of. You have to get your shit together, Flint, so I don't have to keep coming to your rescue.

"Neil!" Sabine screamed. She grabbed a pack of smokes off the kitchen table and stalked toward the stairs. She pulled a smoke from the pack and placed it on her lips and lit it with the lighter that was shoved inside the pack. She pulled the smoke deep inside her lungs and let it calm her. "Neil!" she belted again as she started up the steps.

"Yes! What the fuck, Sabine?" Neil answered, coming out of the room they were keeping Lexie in as she neared the top of the steps.

"We're going ahead," she informed him as she walked into one of the other bedrooms at the top of the stairs.

"How'd you get Flint on board?" Neil asked, following her inside.

Sabine spun around. "I didn't, exactly."

"What did you do?" Neil asked with a cunning smile turning up his lips.

"What needed to be done." Sabine picked up her cell phone and began scrolling through the numbers

228

but paused when Neil dropped to his knees in front of her. "What are you up to?" Sabine asked with narrowed eyes.

Neil ran his fingers up the inside of her bare leg. "You're so sexy when you get like this. You know what it does to me," Neil said as he leaned in and kissed her thigh before he bit her skin, gently pulling with his teeth.

Sabine leaned back against the desk behind her and a sensual moan escaped her lips as he pushed up her skirt. His fingers dug into her flesh as he moved slowly up the inside of her legs. His exploration tugged directly on her sex. A sensual heat flamed deep in her core as he rubbed her center with rough fingers.

"Fuck, no panties. You are one hell of a woman."

"You know I hate that fucking word," Sabine gasped as she threw her head back.

"Panties." He chuckled before sliding his fingers deep inside of her until he filled her. Sabine grabbed him by the hair and pulled his head back. She could see excitement flare wildly in his eyes.

"Don't say that fucking word or I will cut you," Sabine threatened before shoving his face between her legs. "Now stop talking and make me come."

Neil thrust his fingers deep inside her, over and over, his warm mouth and tongue pulling at her sensitive flesh. She could feel the pleasure dripping from her, she could see her wetness on his lips and face as he eagerly gorged on her. It took a little guidance, but Neil was so pliable that it didn't take him long to know exactly how she like to be pleased.

The numbing heat began to flood her legs and soon she felt as if she were floating, completely unattached to the world for the brief moment until pleasure snapped through her. The haze immediately began to dissipate. She had always thought a good orgasm was like a reboot to a system. Her thoughts were clearer and her body was now recharged.

Sabine lifted her leg and placed her foot on his shoulder, pushing him back. He dropped back on his heels, looking up at her like a puppy waiting for a command. Her release was smeared across his face. If she had more time she would draw this out longer, but she knew time was limited. She needed to get in touch with her buyer and make sure the meeting was going ahead as planned.

Sabine stood up, straightened her skirt, and picked up her phone.

"What about me?" Neil asked, biting his lip seductively. His erection was straining against his pants. It wouldn't faze her to leave him unsatisfied but she wanted him to have a clear head.

"Touch yourself," Sabine demanded.

Neil hesitated for a moment before he grabbed the buckle of his belt and unfastened his pants. He shoved his jeans down his legs, releasing his throbbing erection. He wrapped his hand around his length and slowly worked his hand up and down the length. His mouth opened slightly, showing the pleasure that was reeling through him.

"Faster," Sabine ordered him.

His strokes began to quicken as his eyes stayed

locked on hers. Sabine grabbed his chin, shoving her thumb in his mouth and squeezed. "Faster."

She could feel his body tighten, every muscle constrict in anticipation as she gazed deep into his lust-filled eyes. He clamped his teeth down on her thumb and she could feel the vibration of his moan that worked its way up from his chest as he growled out in release, his cum spraying on the floor in front of him.

Sabine hit send on the phone and ran her hand down the front of her shirt, making sure her clothes were in order.

"Sabine," the voice answered on the other end of the line. "I was wondering when I'd hear from you."

"7:00 p.m. at the abandoned sawmill on Cumberland."

"I think we can make that work," he answered.

"If you're not there, the goods are going to the next buyer I have lined up," Sabine said dryly.

"Noted. See you soon, Sabine."

Sabine hit end and looked down at Neil, still lazily stroking himself. His head hung low with his eyes closed as he recovered.

"Clean that up," Sabine said as she stalked out of the room. "We need to get ready to leave."

CHAPTER TWENTY-SEVEN

Jackson

The unmarked cube van was parked just under the overpass, out of sight from the occasional car that could be heard passing overhead. The driver was slouched down in his seat, the glow from his phone highlighting his features in the dim light.

Jackson shook his head when he saw who had been sent to meet them. He pulled his car to a stop behind the truck and killed the engine.

"Fuck. It's Crisler," Jackson muttered.

"Do you want me to handle him?" Dane asked.

"Let's just get this over with." Jackson swung his door open and stepped out. He walked up to the back of the truck and hit the overhead door. The sound echoed around them from the concrete enclosure of the bridge. He was not looking forward to dealing with Tom Crisler. The man thought he was God's gift to the police force and had it in for

Jackson.

Jackson knew Crisler was always sniffing around, trying to find anything that indicated he stepped outside the lines. Trying to uncover Jackson's dirty secrets seemed to have become an obsession for the man. Little did he know that if he looked in the right places, he would find a jackpot of evidence to lock Jackson away for life. Jackson knew he was already living on borrowed time.

"Who'd you blow to get this little delivery?" Crisler said as he came around the back. An obnoxious grin was painted on his face as he crossed his arms and leaned against the back of the truck.

"Why? You looking for a promotion?" Jackson asked impatiently. He wanted the exchange to be over as quickly as possible.

"I don't swing that way. Though, I always knew you and Giles had some twisted thing going on."

Jackson stepped forward with his fists clenched tight. He could practically taste blood he was so angry. Dane grabbed him by the arm, stopping him.

"That's the only thing that makes sense with all the shit you get away with." Crisler continued to throw fuel on the fire.

"Why the fuck did Giles send you?" Dane asked.

"You should know that Giles hasn't been in the last few days since you are all so cozy. Glenshaw wants me to find out what's going on. We both smell the shit in the situation and want to know what's really going on here."

"The only shit I smell is you. Now, open the fucking truck," Jackson demanded.

"Tell Glenshaw not to get his hopes up. He won't be taking Giles' job anytime soon." Dane shook his head.

Crisler's obnoxious smile carved deeper into his face. "Why the fuck did Giles set you two up with a shitload of weapons, anyway?"

"Don't you wish you had the authority to know? Now open the fucking truck," Jackson demanded.

Crisler narrowed his eyes before he pulled a key out of his pocket to unlock the door. "When this all blows up in your face. I'll make sure I'm the one that gets the satisfaction of putting your asses behind bars." Crisler pushed the door open.

"Keep dreaming, Crisler," Jackson said as he jumped up in the back of the truck to examine the contents. His phone began to vibrate in his pocket. He pulled it out and saw Teddy's face on his screen. "Yeah."

"Marcel Quintano's son was just arrested for drug trafficking. The shit they have on him indicates he'll be locked up until he's a fucking old man."

Jackson looked over at Crisler, knowing he had to be careful what he said in his presence. "Is there a connection?"

"It's a bit unclear, but if I had to guess, Chase Quintano was a scapegoat for Stodden. The set up for the drugs was far more advanced than this kid with a record of petty break-ins and speeding tickets. This was a professional job, and every fucking corner was swept clean. Chase was handed to the police with a pretty fucking bow, and if you ask me, we only know one person capable of that."

"Good enough for me," Jackson replied as he unzipped one of the black bags sitting in the back of the truck.

"Haffey was involved in the case," Teddy added.

"It's my lucky day." Jackson hung up and passed the bag to Dane. Jackson jumped down from the back of the truck and grabbed the other bag, swinging it over his shoulder. "We'd invite you to the party, Crisler, but your ugly face scares all the girls away."

"Fuck you, Finley," Crisler bit off.

***

"What makes you think these guys won't just run us over? 'Cause I gotta tell you, I really like my face the way it is. I mean, look at me," Teddy said, rubbing his hand on the side of his face. "I'm fucking beautiful."

Jackson couldn't help but smile and shake his head. "If they don't stop, your face is the last thing you'll be worried about." They were standing in the middle of the old highway, leaning against Jackson's car that was parked across both lanes. It was mainly used by transport trucks and was the road of choice for the Heathens because it was less patrolled than the main roads that ran through Belhaven. Jackson knew they would use this road on the way to this particular meeting.

"But seriously, my face is my opening move, man. It draws the ladies in. If anything happens to it I'll have to start with my second move, and somehow I think it won't work as well without my first move to lead them into the situation."

"What's your second move?"

"My dick. It's a proven infallible move to lead with my face and then smoothly move into phase two, which works every time. If I have to start with my dick hanging out 'cause my face is all marred to shit, then I have a feeling it's not gonna have the same result. The ladies trust these dimples. I mean, my dick is pretty awesome, but ladies don't appreciate it if you whip it out too soon. It's a science that I've mastered."

Jackson turned when he heard Dane whistle from up the hill. He wanted a better vantage point to see them approach. Dane started jogging toward the open trunk of the car that held all his toys. Dane never liked to enter any situation without an arsenal at his disposal.

"I just hope you know what you're doing, Jackson," Teddy said, his tone growing more serious.

"Don't worry, I won't let anything happen to your pretty face." Jackson smiled.

The sound of a low rumble began to grow louder until the earth began to vibrate beneath their feet. Numerous motorcycles began to appear from around the curve of the road and line up as they slowed down when they noticed the unexpected road block.

Jackson raised his hands to show he was unarmed as the bikes came to a stop. One of the men dismounted his bike, and pulled his helmet off to reveal a thick head of grey hair. Jackson knew it was Marcel immediately. The others soon followed suit, turning their bikes off.

"Don't pull out a gun, Dane. Do not show a weapon unless they shoot first. I mean it. Unless they pull the trigger, do not flash your piece. Every one of them is armed to shit," Jackson insisted. Dane nodded with a clenched jaw.

Jackson began walking toward them, Teddy stayed close to his side as he approached. The group of them were as rough cut as you'd expect a group of bikers to be. They all looked like the road had chewed them up and spit them out.

"Aren't they the guys from that garage you got Evan's hit from?" Teddy asked when they were close enough to see the faces of the men.

"Yep."

Marcel stepped forward and pulled a gun out of his holster and pointed it toward Jackson's head. Jackson didn't move as he kept his hands up in the air. Every one of the men pulled out a weapon. The odds did not look good for them if Jackson didn't talk his way out of this.

"Quintano," Jackson acknowledged.

"Finley," Quintano replied. "I'd advise you to get the fuck out of our way."

"It's good to see you too," Jackson replied blandly. "I need to talk to you."

Quintano narrowed his eyes as he stared over the barrel of his gun. "Bang," he said before he broke out into a grin and lowered his gun. "I've got nothing to say, so move out of my way before I make you."

"I think you'll want to listen. It involves your son and Stodden." Jackson threw it out on a whim that they had come to the correct conclusion.

Quintano's tightened his lips as he stared at Jackson suspiciously.

"What of my son?"

"It involves him getting out of that jail cell and back on his bike."

"Let's find a better place for this conversation," Quintano said, tucking his gun away and heading back toward his bike. "Follow us."

Jackson nodded before turning around and heading back toward their car. Dane hadn't moved since they left him, his eyes still remained on the men behind Jackson and Teddy.

"You have a lot of explaining to do, Jackson," Teddy said, looking back over his shoulder as he followed Jackson to their car.

"You have no idea."

CHAPTER TWENTY-EIGHT

Stephanie

The curtains were pulled closed in the hotel room, giving the illusion of a late hour. Stephanie sat on the edge of the bed, numbly flicking through the channels to find something to distract her thoughts. She pulled her robe tight around her and smoothed her wet hair away from her face. She anxiously awaited Nate as he showered. She was terrified to be alone. Every sound had her on edge.

They had come back here after they had talked to Detective Haffey about what had happened with Alden. Nate had filled her in on the connection he believed Alden had with his own wife's abduction, Masten, and the fact that it all led back to Stodden. The line he showed her was so clear no one could deny it.

Stephanie couldn't help but notice the dark circles under Detective Haffey's eyes. She looked fragile as she jotted down all the information Nate could give her. Stephanie didn't know her well because most of her dealings were with Officer Carlton, but she remembered the normally fierce Detective. Stephanie and couldn't help but wonder what this meant.

Stephanie hadn't been able to get a hold of Lexie, but Nate assured her that Jackson was keeping him up to date and there was nothing to worry about. She wanted to believe him, but there was something in his eyes that terrified her.

Stephanie didn't want to think of about any of it but she didn't know how to shut it off. If she closed her eyes she could still see Alden's body lying on the street, surrounded by blood. Her chest still felt too tight as she concentrated on taking deep breaths.

Stephanie's eyes flashed open when a familiar name was spoken on the television. The remote fell out of her hand when she saw Masten's picture displayed on the screen. Those eyes bored right into her as he stared back at her. Stephanie pulled her legs up against her chest and wrapped her arms around herself.

"We just got word that Terrance Masten has died today. He was being held at Rosewater Penitentiary while authorities prepared for his sentencing. The once beloved Mayor of Belhaven had recently become one of the most hated men in the community when the truth of his nature was revealed. No official statements have been released from Rosewater but rumor has it that he was involved in an altercation with other inmates. More

details are to come once we know more..."

Stephanie turned around when she heard a noise behind her. Nate was standing in the doorway of the washroom watching the screen. He had heard it all; she could see it on his face.

"I wanted him dead. I thought about it so much because I thought it would make me feel happy, but I don't know what I feel. There is too much mess inside me to know anything anymore." Stephanie reached for the remote and turned the television off.

Nate pushed off the doorframe and sat down next to her on the bed, his weight caused her to lean toward him. She didn't even try to stop as she collapsed against him. He wrapped his arm around her and held her close. He had jogging pants on but his chest was still bare and damp from the shower. He felt safe and warm and she didn't want to let go. "Pain from something like that never goes away. It becomes a part of you and you have to learn how to find happiness despite it. It will take time. At least you can find comfort in knowing that he won't hurt anyone else." The vibrations of his voice through his chest were comforting and she closed her eyes.

"I'm so tired of being scared."

"You and me both," Nate confessed with a sad smile.

"There is so much in my head. I need it all to go away even just for a minute so I can breathe," Stephanie whispered. She ran her hand over Nate's stomach. His entire body stiffened as she placed her hand on his lap and grabbed hold of him. She could feel him harden in her hold.

"Don't, Stephanie. This isn't going to help." Nate placed his hand over hers.

"I need to feel something good." Stephanie pulled her hand from under his and stood in front of him. Her knees were pressed into his as he watched her.

Stephanie untied her robe and let it fall away until she was completely exposed. Nate closed his eyes and took a deep breath as she climbed on his lap and shoved his pants down. His erection sprung free and Stephanie grabbed him firmly and slid him inside her. She was acting without thought and felt detached.

It was uncomfortable as Nate slid inside her because her body refused to become aroused, refused to fill her with need. She could feel the tears begin to surface as she shoved Nate back and pressed his shoulders into the bed. She couldn't look him in the eye or she would fall apart. She just needed to ignite a part of her that would remind her she was still alive.

She thrust her hips hard and fast in search of pleasure but her body remained numb and it terrified her. This was not natural, she was not natural anymore. She was frantic for the pleasure that eluded her. This side of her was a stranger, she didn't understand this version of herself but she had no will to fight it, either.

Nate tightened his grip on her thighs. "Steph?" he said in a pained voice. "Stop. Please stop."

She looked into his concerned eyes. The tears sprung to life and poured from her eyes. He pulled her toward him and she let herself fall against his body. He held onto her while her hot tears soaked his chest.

Stephanie wasn't sure how much time had passed when he rolled her onto her side and pulled the blanket over her. He stayed with her and she was so grateful. She didn't even know what to say to him. She felt so exhausted and embarrassed about her behavior.

They both remained quiet for what felt like hours as Nate brushed her hair gently with his fingers. He seemed to be just as lost in thought as she was.

"I'm sorry." Stephanie finally broke the silence when she found the strength.

"For what? Giving me an enormous case of blue-balls?" Nate asked.

Stephanie moaned and turned her face into his shoulder. "I shouldn't have done that."

Nate took a long, deep breath. "I wish I could make your pain go away, Stephanie. Trying to drown it out with sex or anything else doesn't work. I know better than anyone. It's what I did for years." Nate rubbed his hand down his face. He grew quiet for a few minutes. "I was in a bad place and it's not far enough behind me to risk it. I wanted to give up. I did give up. I put a gun in my mouth and pulled the trigger."

"What?" Stephanie gasped. She stared at him in the dim light.

"I wouldn't be here right now if Jackson hadn't taken the bullets. I need things in my life to mean something. I've spent my whole life chasing after meaningless things in an effort to find happiness. I can't do that anymore. I can't be that for you,

243

knowing I'm a frantic effort to feel something other than despair. It would just add to this giant mess we're in."

"You're right. Everything is such a huge mess and I'm the biggest of all." Stephanie placed her hands on her face. "I didn't mean to hurt you. I wasn't thinking."

Nate reached for her hand and gave it a gentle squeeze. She didn't want him to ever let go. "You didn't hurt me...emotionally, at least."

"Oh god, I'm sorry."

"I'm just joking," Nate assured her.

"I'm so glad Jackson stopped you," Stephanie confessed. "You're one of the best things that happened to me."

"I'm glad he did too, because I feel the same about you."

"Can we forget what I did?" Stephanie asked.

"Not a fucking chance." Nate's smile radiated through his words.

Stephanie moaned in embarrassment again. "At least don't tell anyone."

"By anyone, do you mean..." Nate began but Stephanie gave him a playful shove and he broke out into laughter. It was her new favorite sound. In this moment she couldn't think of anything more beautiful.

Nate's phone began to ring across the room. His laughter died away as he pushed himself off the bed. Stephanie watched him check the caller ID before he answered the call quickly.

"Jacks," he answered.

Stephanie didn't move as she watched him

listening on the phone. Panic bubbled up in her throat as she watched his face for any sign that something horrible happened, but he gave nothing away.

"I'll be there as soon as I can," Nate replied before ending the call and looking at Stephanie.

"What is it? Is Lexie all right?" Stephanie sat up and pulled the blanket up to her neck.

"Jackson needs my help. I need you to stay here. I'm gonna call Officer Carlton and get you some protection. I will be back as soon as I can," Nate said. He grabbed his clothes off the back of the chair and headed toward the bathroom.

"Is everything okay?" Stephanie asked.

"Define okay," Nate asked with a raised brow.

Stephanie shook her head sadly.

"Let's just say all players are still accounted for, and considering the circumstances, it's as good as it gets." Nate shut the door to the bathroom. Stephanie released her breath and collapsed back on the bed. She stared up at the ceiling and silently prayed that Lexie would be safe. She prayed they would all be safe.

CHAPTER TWENTY-NINE

Sabine

The moon hung lazily in the sky, casting little light on the dark grounds of the abandoned sawmill. It was situated in an older part of the city that was left for Mother Nature to slowly reclaim. The horrific accident that caused the closing of the company ten years ago still haunted the community. Fifteen of its workers died in a fire. Rather than rebuild the structure, the company shut its doors and walked away. The pain was carved too deep to ever recover, especially since the owner of the company also perished in the fire.

Sabine pulled their van to a stop at the rear of the building. They were early for the meeting but Sabine wanted to arrive on the grounds first. She didn't trust the Heathens to any degree. These men had spent more time behind bars than they had been free men. She saw them as barbarians with

246

matching jackets and was amazed their little bike club was able to survive after all these years with so much internal drama tearing down their structure of power. It was only by a miracle they were standing in her eyes.

The only thing Sabine cared about was the fact that they seemed to have mutual feelings toward John Stodden, and right now that opportunity was too great to pass up. She needed cash for her plan to get her and her brother away from Belhaven and Stodden's shadow. This town had never been good to either one of them, and she was determined to make her brother see it.

"Keep the girl out of sight until I say," Sabine said to Neil, who was in the passenger's seat. He pulled a long drag from his cigarette before he smiled at her.

"Whatever you say, boss." He reached over and squeezed her leg, pushing her skirt up at the same time.

"Hands off," Sabine barked. She opened the door and jumped out of the van. Neil rounded the other side and pulled the door open for her. Lexie was leaning against the side of the interior. Her hands and feet were tied and a bag placed over her head. "Don't worry. I'm sure those bikers are gonna take real good care of you."

"Screw you." Lexie kicked her legs out.

Sabine laughed and grabbed the box of files and slammed the door. She banged her fist against the rusted metal door on the large brick building.

The door opened immediately and Frank looked out at her. He had soot smeared across his face and looked a little skittish. "What took you so long? This place gives me the fucking creeps," Frank complained.

He backed out of the way as Sabine grabbed the door and wrenched it from his grasp. "Stop complaining, you fucking baby. Did you clear the whole building?"

"Yeah, we're the only ones here, but there's lots of strange sounds," Frank said nervously as his eyes travelled up with the sound of creaking above his head.

"It's an old building that is falling down, what do you expect?" Sabine said impatiently.

"Are you sure it's safe to be here?"

"Get out of my face and watch for any approaching vehicles," Sabine snapped as she grabbed the flashlight out of his hand. "I don't have time for your bloody tears." Sabine couldn't wait to be rid of some of her current company. For now they were a necessary annoyance.

Frank pushed the door open and slipped outside without another word. Sabine headed down the hall, where she could see a dim light stretching eerily down the walls. Most of the damage was in the north side of the building. The loading area had virtually been left untouched by damage.

Several lights had been set up around the large warehouse. Two of her other men were leaning against a pallet of wood that was left abandoned with the property, never to serve a purpose but to collect dust. She placed the box on top of the pile and clenched her teeth in irritation.

"Put those joints out. I need you focused so you

don't get us all killed. This is not some goddam meet and greet," Sabine said irritably as she grabbed the joint out of the hand of the nearest man, Roman. She dropped it on the ground and stomped on it. "Do I seriously have to babysit you stupid assholes every minute? The Heathens will be arriving any time now. I need you to be ready to shoot if any of them so much as reaches for their weapons. Do you hear me?"

Neither Roman nor his brother, Nicolaus, responded as they narrowed their eyes and pushed off the wood pile. They weren't as pliable as some of the others she had promised a cut to, but she needed their ruthlessness. They weren't fans of being bossed around, and Sabine knew she shouldn't push her luck. Patience was not a characteristic of her personality and she couldn't seem to find the energy to care about pissing them off.

"If you want your money, make sure we all survive long enough," Sabine leaned in to accentuate her point.

"Loud and clear, honey," Roman said. He had dark, menacing eyes with a tattoo that covered his neck and stretched up onto his right cheek. Sabine knew the pair of them were brothers. a fact she discovered while running a background check on them. She never relied on trust when it came to anything, especially business. There was nothing these two didn't do for money and that was the type of men she needed right now.

"You'll soon discover the word *honey* does not apply to me."

The rumble of bikes in the distance caught her attention.

"Fuck, they're early. Open the overhead doors and have your guns concealed but ready."

Nicolaus grabbed the manual rope to pull the main cargo door open. A loud shrill sound echoed through the hollow interior but was soon drowned out by the approaching bikes, that sounded like continuous thunder vibrating the earth.

Sabine was familiar enough with the Heathens to know who Marcel Quintano was. She watched him pull his helmet off his head and hang it off his handlebars. He had four other riders with him. Most of them looked to be at least twenty years younger, but all were as rough looking as she imagined they would be. They all embodied the motorcycle club persona. They were used to intimidating people purely by appearance alone, but Sabine wasn't so easily fooled. She had known dangerous men her whole life and they no longer stirred fear in her. A van pulled up behind the bikes, but no one made any move to exit the vehicle.

Sabine crossed her arms and waited for Quintano to approach. He walked into the interior with three of the bikers by his side. Their eyes scanned the entire perimeter, they were expecting danger.

"Does Stodden know you have his shit?" Quintano asked as he stopped about fifteen feet from Sabine.

"By the time he finds out I had anything to do with this he won't be able to find me," Sabine said confidently. "Did you bring the cash?"

Quintano nodded to the men at his side. All three

of them pulled bags off their backs and dropped them on the ground. They knelt down and unzipped them to show the stacks of cash packed inside.

"Good." Sabine grabbed the box and dropped it at her feet. She placed her foot on top. "This contains all the files, just as we discussed."

"And the girl?" Quintano asked causally, like he was ordering a cup of coffee. Sabine wanted this exchange to be over as quickly as possible. Something about the look in Quintano's eye bothered her.

Sabine pulled out her phone and dialed Neil. "Bring in the girl." Sabine tucked her phone back in her pocket and looked up at the men standing before her. The one on the end that had a scar running down his cheek blew her a kiss. She rolled her eyes and shook her head.

Sabine turned around when she heard footsteps approach behind. Neil walked around the corner empty handed. "What the fuck, Neil?" Sabine bit off.

"I…" Neil started but stumbled forward. It was then that Sabine saw Lexie behind him holding a gun to his back.

"Jesus Christ, Neil." Sabine rubbed her temple angrily. "How the fuck did you manage this?"

Neil just shook his head.

"What the fuck do you plan on doing?" Sabine asked Lexie in disbelief. "You're surrounded by fucking guns."

"Oh, I wasn't expecting to get away. There was just something I needed to do first," Lexie said before she shoved Neil and dove for Sabine.

251

Sabine tried to grab her own gun but Lexie collided with her too fast, knocking her off her feet. Blinding pain radiated down her face with the impact of Lexie's fist. "Fuck," Sabine screamed out as she scrambled backward.

"It doesn't feel so nice, does it?" Lexie yelled as she grabbed Sabine by the neck and slammed her head down on the ground. Sabine managed to pull her leg up and kick Lexie backward. It was enough to twist around and grab her gun that was tucked in the back of her pants.

"Someone get this bitch off me," Sabine screamed as she tried to aim her gun toward Lexie as she was being pinned to the ground.

Lexie grabbed hold of her arm and twisted hard but Sabine refused to loosen her grip as they both struggled. Sabine knew she couldn't shoot Lexie or the deal would be off and she wouldn't risk it. She wound up and forced the heel of her hand into Lexie's jaw, momentarily stunning her.

Sabine managed to kick off the ground and spin Lexie around to pin her down. Lexie's knee came up to catch Sabine in the stomach enough to force her breath from her. Lexie's fist swung across Sabine's face and the sting made her eyes water. The gun was knocked from her hand as she struggled but she managed to get her hands around Lexie's neck. "What are you gonna do now, you stupid little bitch?" Sabine breathed fire. "Neil!" Sabine called over her shoulder.

Sabine looked down when she felt something hard pressed firmly against her stomach. Lexie had her gun aimed and ready to fire. Sabine narrowed her eyes—she was furious she lost the upper hand.

Someone grabbed her around the waist and hauled her off Lexie. Sabine tried to struggle, but the scene unfolding around her made her freeze. The Heathens were retreating. The bags of cash were gone. Their engines roared to life as their wheels kicked up the loose dirt, filling the air with a cloud of dust. Dread settled deep in Sabine's stomach. Her ticket out of this black hole of a town was slipping through her fingers.

Her men were lined up on their knees at gunpoint by men she didn't recognize. "What the fuck is going on here?" Sabine demanded as she was tossed to the ground next to Neil. She tried to scramble to her feet but a gun was pointed in her face.

She looked up at the bluest eyes she had ever seen and ground her teeth. "Are you Stodden's men?"

Blue eyes raised a brow as he looked down at her. "Fuck no."

"Is anyone else here as turned on as I am?" the blond-haired man standing across the room asked. "Nothing gets the blood flowing like a good girl fight."

"Shut up, Ted," the dark-haired one said with a shake of his head as he helped Lexie to her feet.

"Who the fuck are you then?" Sabine demanded.

Her eyes travelled between all three men before settling on the one next to Lexie. His hands lingering on her body, the relief in his eyes, the way she leaned toward him as he whispered close to her ear, it was obvious they were lovers. Sabine shook her head in disbelief and rubbed her hands over her face.

The blue-eyed man with the gun pointed at her face reached in his pocket and pulled out a badge. Sabine looked at in confusion. She was trying to file all the pieces in place.

"Stodden's daughter is fucking a cop?" Sabine laughed deep and rich. "This is priceless. What does good old Daddy think of that?"

Lexie crossed her arms over her chest and glared at Sabine. "I couldn't care less about what he thinks."

"Well, that's one thing we can agree on," Sabine admitted. She looked around at the small group that had them at gunpoint. "You want Stodden? Is this what this is about? I will gladly tell you everything I know about that fucking piece of shit..." Sabine trailed off when she felt a dull snap against her forehead. Her focus blurred and strange words filled her mouth and then vanished. She felt like she was suddenly tossed into a disturbing dream. She touched her face with a numb hand. Her eyes filled with hot, red liquid...then the world was swallowed in blackness.

CHAPTER THIRTY

Lexie

"Get down!" Jackson screamed as he pushed Lexie to the ground. She couldn't pull her eyes away from Sabine. Lexie didn't know if she had actually screamed or if her mouth was too paralyzed and the sound was trapped inside her head. Sabine's body crumpled to the ground. Neil fell next, hard and fast. The impact hit him in the chest as he tried to run away from the onslaught of bullets. Lexie's heartbeat exploded in a frenzy of panic, thinking they would be next. Her body thrummed with energy as her flee response hit overdrive. Bullets sprayed into the warehouse, hitting the walls and stirring up dust.

"Move," Jackson screamed out as Dane began firing through the overhead doors at a target Lexie couldn't see. She didn't waste any time as she scrambled to her feet and headed toward the entrance to the hallway. Jackson was on her heels. He placed his hand on her back and forced her to keep moving when she glanced behind her.

When Lexie neared the end of the dark narrow hall she slowed down. Teddy and Dane had followed behind them, holding off whoever was attacking.

"Stay here until I tell you it's clear," Jackson said as he passed her a gun. Lexie took it from him and nodded. She couldn't find any words to speak. Her head felt like it was filled with cotton. Jackson pulled the door open and leaned out to see what was waiting outside before he slipped out.

"Jackson," Lexie called but he was gone and she was left grasping at air. Seconds stretched into minutes as she kept glancing between the door and the hallway where Dane and Teddy were blocking their pursuers.

"You all right, Lex?" Teddy asked as he bumped her shoulder.

She tried to smile but she was terrified that Jackson wouldn't return.

"Don't worry about Jackson, that bastard has proved over and over that he's invincible," Teddy said as he slid a new clip in his gun. He stepped back in line with Dane as they held position.

Lexie jumped when the door opened unexpectedly. "Let's go." Jackson waved them out. Lexie's body swam in relief with his return. She quickly slipped through the door, wanting to get out of the building as quickly as possible. Teddy and Dane were close behind her.

Jackson pulled a large barrel toward the door and Dane helped him position it so whoever might try to follow would be blocked.

Lexie spun around to look around them. "How do you know its safe out here? Seems a bit strange that they wouldn't have the building surrounded, isn't it?"

"They wanted to drive us out of the building while they eliminated the others. They have all the road access blocked off." Jackson frowned thoughtfully. "This was planned."

"It sounds like they might want a little chat," Teddy said, looking at Jackson and then Lexie.

"Load up, boys, let's go find out what they have to say," Jackson said as he reloaded his guns.

"What about Lexie?" Dane asked with a nod.

"I'm a part of this too…" Lexie began.

"You're going to hang back out of sight," Jackson insisted.

"What?" Lexie frowned.

"You hanging back might be the only reason they don't shoot us down as soon as we step foot around the building," Jackson placed his hand on her arm and pulled her closer to him. It was too dark to see the look in his eye but she knew it well. It still reached deep inside her and stirred everything up.

Lexie could feel her eyes widen in panic as she grabbed hold of his shirt, balling the material in her tight fists. This moment felt like they were awaiting inevitable doom that loomed overhead, waiting to be unleashed. There was no way to know they would survive what was waiting for them. Lexie didn't care that they had an audience, she pulled him closer and he melted against her without resistance.

She was fueled with many emotions, all driving her toward Jackson. His lips met hers and her fingers twisted in his hair and pulled at his shoulders. Fear that this was the last time she would hold Jackson and taste him drove her to madness. She wanted to take a piece of him wherever she was meant to go.

"I'd say get a room, but our current circumstances make that a bit impossible." Teddy chuckled.

They all quieted as they heard a whistle pierce the air. Lexie pulled away to catch her breath. She still did not relinquish her hold; she wasn't ready to let him go.

"Come out, come out, wherever you are," a male voice floated through the air. Lexie didn't know who was speaking, but his voice sent chills through her blood.

"It will be okay," Jackson assured her. Placing his hands on either side of her face, he gave her one last kiss. "Stay back, Lexie, I mean it."

She nodded as she watched the three of them approach the side of the building and disappear around the corner. Lexie pressed herself against the wall but she couldn't see anything from where she was. She needed to know what was happening, she hated hiding in the shadows.

Taking a deep breath, she pushed off the wall and neared the back of a dumpster that was situated on the side of the building. She ducked down low to try and see who was waiting out front.

"Always a pleasure, Jackson."

"Get the fuck on with it, Rosh," Jackson said

irritably. They stood before a van with three men. The headlights from another vehicle shone upon them, lighting up the area. Two of them looked familiar to Lexie from her captivity with Stodden. The other, who Jackson called Rosh, she didn't recognize, but she knew the name. She knew he was the man who had been at the hospital the night her mother died. He was the same man who killed Jackson's father.

She covered her mouth for a moment, trying to calm her emotions and think about the right course of action. She held the gun firmly in her hand. Looking down, she wondered if she could hit him from where she was standing.

Lexie held the gun out in front of her, peering over the barrel at the face of the man named Rosh as he spoke with Jackson. Her finger shook on the trigger. Her whole body thrummed with emotion. She didn't know if she was capable of pulling the trigger and ending his life despite what he had done. There was an internal struggle warring her insides.

"You know I really didn't want it to come to this, but you didn't know when to leave things alone. You're so much like your father."

"Maybe, but there's a huge difference between us," Jackson responded with venom dripping from his words.

"Oh yeah, what's that?" Rosh pursed his lips.

"I know you're a lying piece of shit," Jackson seethed.

Rosh laughed and shook his head. "Your father knew exactly who I was. It was his fault for thinking he could change me. I'll tell you what, let's make a little exchange." Rosh waved to the door of the van. One of the men standing with him opened it. Lexie couldn't make out what they were looking at, but she could see Jackson's entire body stiffen. A man stepped out with a gun before pulling someone out behind him. The man was bound and gagged as he tumbled to the ground. The man holding the gun hauled him to his feet and that's when Lexie finally got a clear view of his face. It was Giles. Lexie knew that Jackson was being made to choose between her and the man that represented the only family he had after his parents died.

"You look surprised?" Rosh said with a sinister smile. "Hand over the girl and I won't shoot his fucking brains out." Rosh held up the gun toward Giles' head.

"Don't..." Giles began but the man next to him hit him in the stomach with the butt of his gun. Giles doubled over in pain before he was hauled back to his feet and shoved up against the van.

"Last chance," Rosh announced.

Something caught Lexie's eye, a slight movement in the darkness. She couldn't quite make out what it was until the light caught his features just enough. Nate opened the door of one of the parked trucks and slipped inside. She needed to buy him some time and cause a distraction. She didn't know what he had planned, but she hoped it was enough.

Not knowing what else to do, she jumped up. "I'm here!" she screamed, coming out from the shadows with her gun raised. "Don't hurt anyone! I'll come." She only knew she needed everyone to look in her direction and hope she bought the time Nate needed.

"How many times is she gonna fall for that trick?" Teddy complained.

"That's a good girl. I'm glad one of you is smart enough move this shit along," Rosh said.

Lexie locked eyes with Jackson.

"Why don't you put that gun down before you hurt yourself?" Rosh raised a brow.

"You said this was an exchange, so let Giles go and I will come with you. Wasn't that the deal?"

Rosh narrowed his eyes slightly before a plastic smile curled his lips. "Of course." Rosh stepped closer to Lexie. "Release him." Rosh waved toward his men.

The man who had been in the van with Giles shoved him toward Jackson. He stumbled and fell to his knees before climbing back up.

"Though, as Jackson pointed out...I'm a liar." Rosh announced sinisterly.

"Lexie!" Jackson called out just as someone knocked the gun from her hand and grabbed her from behind. She struggled against her attacker but he had too much size on her. She watched the gun slide to a stop in the dirt, too far out of reach.

"Kill them all," Rosh called out over the commotion. Lexie tried to scream but a hand was clamped over her mouth.

An engine roared to life and tires squealed just as bullets began to tear through the air. The truck Nate had climbed into came barrelling through the action and slammed into the van Rosh's men were standing in front of. The sound of metal scraping

261

rang out as the side crumpled from the impact.

Lexie lost track of everyone as she tried to break free from her assailant.

"Get down, Lexie!" Jackson called to her. Lexie immediately dropped her body in a dead weight and the man's hold was compromised. She could feel herself slip through his fingers. Just as Lexie felt the ground beneath her fingers, the man's head whipped backward from the force of a bullet. Lexie immediately grabbed at the ground and tried to move away from him as his body began to fall. When he hit the ground, he barely missed her legs.

The angles of the headlights made it hard to see, as she tried to keep low. She had no idea what was happening. She felt completely disoriented as she spun around looking for Jackson. The shower of bullets faded away and a strange silence started to settle.

Lexie grabbed for her gun that was sitting in the dirt and brushed the hair out of her eyes. She couldn't see anyone in the darkness. She headed in the direction she knew Jackson was last. She could make out a shadow and noticed someone was slumped on the ground near the building. A wave of panic hit her in the chest as she neared. "Jackson?"

She moved closer to see who it was. It was Giles, still bound and gagged. She grabbed for the tie around his mouth and loosened it.

"Are you hurt?" Lexie asked, trying to do a quick assessment in the dark.

"Yeah, my side," he gasped.

Lexie reached for his side and felt his wet shirt. He flinched in pain. "Sorry," Lexie apologized.

Lexie jumped when someone knelt down beside her. She went to grab for her gun she had set on the ground by her feet.

"Don't even think about shooting me, Lex," Teddy said as he placed his hand on her back. Lexie was awash with relief and threw her arms around him.

"Jackson?" she asked quickly. "Where's Jackson?"

"He's fine." Teddy pulled out a flashlight and lit up Giles' side to show his gunshot wound. Lexie flinched at the sight. There was so much blood.

"It could be worse," Teddy said, completely unfazed by the sight of blood.

"Don't you dare tell me to shake it off, Teddy," Giles said through clenched teeth. "I'll fire you. I swear I will."

Teddy laughed as he pressed something against his side. Giles groaned in pain. "This is why you sit behind a fancy desk. You're supposed to leave this shit to us," Teddy said as he pulled a knife from his pocket and began cutting his ties.

Lexie stood up and glanced around for Jackson. "Stay here, Lex," Teddy said distractedly.

"I'm not going far," Lexie assured him. She just needed to lay eyes on Jackson. To see for herself that he was well. Lexie rounded the wreckage from the vehicles, nervous there were still dangers lurking in the corners. Dust danced in the light of the headlights as she passed the front of the car.

She blinked her eyes to adjust them as she stepped out of the light. Jackson was standing over a man with his gun aimed at his head. As she approached she could make out the conversation.

"…all those years you pretended like you gave a fuck. Did you get a kick out of stringing along my mother and I? And all that shit you told me," Jackson's voice cracked as he dug the barrel of his gun into the side of Rosh's head.

Lexie looked down at something on the ground as she continued to approach slowly. Her eyes widened when she realized it was a dead body. She tried to shake it from her thoughts as she circled around it before drawing closer. Dane was standing next to Jackson with a gun in each hand. He was eerily still as he stood by Jackson's side. Lexie was still surprised by the relationship between Jackson, Dane, and Teddy. They had unspoken communication and understanding of each other that fascinated her. It was an energy they all shared, it was thick and invigorating. She couldn't help but respect it when she saw them in action.

Jackson's emotions were pouring out on the ground around him. Rosh had left a deep gash on Jackson's soul and now he was confronting the demon.

"You don't think I would have wanted things to turn out differently? I cared for you, like a—" Rosh admitted.

"Don't. Don't you fucking say it. Don't you ever fucking say it! You fucking piece of shit." Jackson fired the gun. Lexie couldn't help but gasp in surprise. Rosh screamed out and grabbed his leg as he doubled over with a curse.

Both Jackson and Dane looked at her. "Get her out of here," Jackson said to Dane. Jackson was possessed with rage to the point that it caused goosebumps to break out across her skin. She wasn't scared of this version of him. She understood it because that same raged lived deep inside her. If she could control it, she would let it out, but she was scared to find out what it was capable of.

"No," Lexie demanded. "I'm not going anywhere."

Dane came closer but Lexie was determined to stand her ground. "You don't want to see this, Lexie. Trust me, some things can't be unseen."

"I have seen enough to know what I'm asking," Lexie looked up into Dane's eyes as he tucked his gun away and placed his hand on her shoulder. He gave her a slight nod before wrapping his large arm around her shoulder and pulling her close.

She looked up at Jackson, who was watching her quietly before he turned back toward Rosh when he started pleading with Jackson. "I'm sure we can work something out. I have information…"

Jackson raised his gun and fired. Rosh's words were stopped immediately as his body fell to the ground. Lexie watched Jackson's shoulders drop as he stared at the man that had betrayed his father. She wondered if he felt relief that he had his revenge. Lexie wanted to feel better knowing he was gone, but nothing would change the fact that she would never be able to wrap her arms around her mother again. The weight was still on her shoulders. The only consolation she had was that he could no longer hurt anyone else.

Lexie ran toward Jackson. She wrapped her arms

around his waist and held him tight. She didn't breathe until he accepted her in his arms.

"Well, we have the girl, but those bastards took off with the evidence," Dane broke the silence. Lexie looked up at Dane.

"Come on, guys. Have a little faith. You don't think I would just run a car into a gunfight without a plan?" Nate said as he limped toward them with a box stuffed under his arm. He dropped the box at Dane's feet.

"Plans are really your style, Nate," Jackson shook his head with quiet relief.

"Yeah, well, It was actually just dumb luck," Nate admitted with a laugh. "Let's get the fuck out of here. My ankle is killing me."

CHAPTER THIRTY-ONE

Flint

The floor of the truck was covered in scraps of metal and other debris. Every bump of the uneven road caused the sharp objects to dig into his skin. The pain was becoming unbearable as he lay helpless, still under the influence of the drug.

When he realized what his sister had done he was beyond furious, trapped in a body that was completely immobile while his brain raced in anger. He was left to stare at the dirtied floor while Sabine went against his wishes and doomed them both. His screams were trapped in his head as he tried to force his body to move. Without knowing how much she had given him, he had no idea how long the effects would last.

All he could do was wait for what was coming as he sat on the kitchen floor. When the front door opened and he heard footsteps echo through the empty house, he knew his time was up. Familiar black shoes stepped into view. His eyes were so dry it was hard to focus but he knew exactly who it was. He could taste his own demise on his tongue when Jacobs leaned down in his line of sight.

"Tsk tsk." Jacobs smiled. "This is too easy. What the fuck is wrong with you, anyway? Testing out your drug shit on yourself?" Jacobs laughed as he smacked Flint on the side of the face. "Let's get you back to John."

Jacobs had thrown him in the back of his truck, leaving him there for the extent of the drive. Flint knew exactly what was waiting for him at the end of this ride. He had taken too many people himself to John for this exact same fate. He was desperate to force his body into action but no matter how hard he tried, he couldn't so much as twitch a finger or move his parched lips. The only hope he had was that feeling was beginning to return.

He needed to reason with John to save himself. Surely John would not forget the years of loyalty he had given him. The reason he was in this situation was because of Lexie. She had cursed him to this fate. John must know how much turmoil that girl had caused them since she came into the picture. She was the real problem that needed to be eliminated; he needed to show John this truth. Maybe now that Mary was gone John's obsession with her ghost would subside and he would realize that Lexie was just a reminder of something he could never have again. He would have to remind John how vital he was to the operation. For years he had thought of John as his family. They understood and trusted each other. He needed to believe John would grant him the opportunity to explain himself.

Frigid water slapped him in the face and Flint gasped for air. He hadn't realized he had fallen asleep until his harsh awakening. He was tied to a chair in the dark interrogation room in the basement of Bitter Sweet. He never thought he would be the one in the chair. He gripped the armrests. He realized he was regaining control of his body. He ran his sluggish tongue over his lips and swallowed.

"There you are," Jacobs said as he leaned in. "Looks like your drug is wearing off. It will make this more fun if you squirm." Jacobs laughed.

"Whe…" Flint tried to force words through his throat. "Where…"

Jacobs raised a brow as he looked at him, waiting him to finish his words.

"John," Flint finished. His words were barely recognizable but he knew Jacobs would understand.

"He's on his way, but he said we could start without him," Jacobs said as he walked over to the table. "Oh, and by the way, you pissed yourself. I think we can both agree this is not one of your finer moments." Jacobs frowned casually.

"You…don't need…to do…this," Flint pleaded.

"Oh, but I do," Jacobs said as he ran his finger along a knife blade he had picked up off the table. "I do because you know better than anyone what happens when you cross John."

Flint squeezed his eyes shut, desperate to think through the cloud of fear that was muddying his thoughts. "I was bringing…her back. I had her," Flint explained.

"You think John is going to believe that?" Jacobs took a roll of duct tape and pulled the tape free. The sound echoed in the room and a small whimper tried to escape the back of Flint's throat. Jacobs wrapped the tape around his hand, pinning it down so he could not move his fingers.

"Don't do this," Flint pleaded as Jacobs positioned the blade against his index fingertip. The sharp point of the blade dug into his skin. His entire body clenched as Jacobs hit the end of the handle with a hammer, driving the blade into his finger.

A scream tore through Flint's throat so raw as his entire body jolted in pain. The chair scraped along the concrete floor as tears streamed down his face. "Stop…stop," he mumbled as he gasped in pain. "Please…" It didn't stop Jacobs from moving to his next finger and the next until he felt his consciousness slipping from the assault.

More water cold water was thrown in his face. He awoke with a gasp and immediately remembered the hell he was enduring. Blood covered his mangled fingers and dripped down to the floor. He forced his head to look up as the door opened and John walked in.

"John…stop this, please. It's me," Flint whispered through his swollen throat.

"It is you," John said as he approached him.

"I was trying to get her back for you. I never intended…"

"Enough!" John demanded he stop. Flint looked up into John's stone cold gaze. "I'm not a forgiving man, Flint, but we have known each other for a long time."

270

"Yes...yes," Flint agreed, desperate for him to show mercy.

"I may be willing to come to an agreement if you do something for me," John said. His cigar smoke made the room appear cloudy.

"Anything," Flint agreed.

John pulled his cigar out of his mouth and studied it before his eyes returned to Flint. "Tell me the truth and we can put this behind us. Did you touch her?"

Flint stared at him. He wasn't sure how to answer the question. Knowing John, he already knew the truth and he was testing him. "She tried to seduce me...I had every intention of telling you. She planned it. I would never have fucked her without your permission."

John placed the cigar against his lips and drew the smoke into his mouth. It slowly escaped to join the cloud gathering in the room that smelled of spice. It made the air feel drier as Flint breathed it in.

"Pull his pants down," John ordered Jacobs.

"What? John? I didn't fuck her..." Flint struggled against Jacobs, who unbuttoned his pants and yanked them down. He tried to resist but he was bound to the chair. "I didn't fuck her!" he screamed as he tried to loosen his ties.

"And you never will," John said coldly as he removed his jacket and rolled up his sleeves.

"Don't do this, John. Please don't fucking do this!" Flint screamed.

John stepped toward him with the bloodied blade in his hand that Jacobs handed him. The white hot pain was blinding as John made the cut. Flint screamed and fought against the ties that cut into his flesh but it was futile. He looked down at the remains of his manhood before he was swallowed in nothingness. He hoped he never woke.

CHAPTER THIRTY-TWO

Lexie

Lexie didn't realize she was bouncing her knee until Jackson placed his hand on it and gave it a gentle squeeze. She looked up from her folded hands in her lap into his deep brown eyes.

"Sorry, I'm not a big fan of hospitals anymore," Lexie admitted.

"Don't be sorry," Jackson said with a smile. He took her hand in his and wound their fingers. His skin felt so warm against hers and she savored the feel of him. It calmed her despite the chaos in her heart, knowing she was in the last place her mother was alive. The place she lost her.

Lexie looked across the waiting room to see Dane asleep with his feet up on the table, that deep line between his brows still prominent in his sleep. She wondered if she would ever get to know what was beneath all his layers. Those impossible blue eyes were always so haunted.

Teddy was captivated by his phone and he clicked away at whatever he was up to. He sipped on the cold coffee he had been nursing for the last hour. Lexie could barely stomach it while it was hot. He was a closed book as well, never letting anyone see deeper than what he presented them. They were both puzzles she hoped one day she would understand.

Both Giles and Nate were admitted when they arrived. Nate could barely walk by the time they arrived at the hospital. The doctor suspected he broke some bones in his foot and he was whisked away to be x-rayed.

Giles' skin was a few shades of grey when they placed him on a gurney. He had still been conscious and able to laugh at Teddy's ridiculous antics, but it was obvious he was in extreme pain. The doctor seemed to be optimistic when he updated them on his condition. They wanted to admit him for a few days but said they expected he would make a full recovery. They were lucky it was all the injuries that they sustained, considering what they had been through.

"Can we get out of here for a little bit?" Lexie asked. "I need some air."

"Sure," Jackson said before he stood up. "Call me with any updates," he called out to Teddy before he followed Lexie's lead. She needed to get out of the building, take a deep breath of fresh air, and calm her nerves.

"Where to?" Jackson asked when they stepped outside the front doors of the hospital. Lexie

274

immediately felt some of the tension melt away.

"I need some caffeine that doesn't taste like it could kill me," Lexie admitted as she wrapped her arms around herself.

"I have an idea," Jackson said reassuringly as he placed his arm around her shoulder and pulled her into his side.

"Good, 'cause I'm too exhausted to think."

***

Lexie wrapped her hands around her hot cup of tea as Jackson pulled off the road. She looked around, unsure of where they were. It was an old winding road that appeared to take them nowhere. She had fallen into a comfortable silence and hadn't asked where he was driving, but now that he pulled off the main road onto a narrow dirt drive, her curiosity couldn't be contained.

"Where are we?" Lexie sat up further in her seat to check out their surroundings.

Jackson turned his head and looked at her with a sly smile. "It's where I used to come when I still lived here. It was where I came to clear my head," Jackson said as the trees began to open up and Jackson pulled the car to a stop. Lexie opened her door to get a better look. She stepped out into the cool evening air. Taking a deep breath, she could smell the earth and foliage that surrounded them. It reminded her of home.

Lexie closed her door and spun around before stopping to see Jackson watching her.

"Come here." He held his hand out for her to

take. "I want you to see something."

He led her to the edge where they could see the entire city below. The lights of Belhaven looked like a work of art from their vantage point.

"Wow, it's beautiful," Lexie said. "You can't see the ugly from here."

"No, you can't," Jackson agreed thoughtfully. "I spent a lot of time here after my mother died. I got on my bike one day and just kept peddling, further and further from the city until eventually it was too dark to see anymore and I was here. I don't even know how I found this place, but I did. I slept right here on the ground that night, under the stars, wondering why my life was so shitty when the world looked so beautiful."

"It's all an illusion," Lexie said. They both looked at the lights below.

"I thought so too at first, for most of my life, actually, but all the darkness is what makes all the lights look so bright. That was when I found you. I've never seen a light so bright, and it made me want to crawl out of the darkness."

Lexie didn't know how to respond to that. His words plucked chords deep inside her and she thrummed with heat.

Jackson turned toward her. "Too cheesy?" He raised his brow.

Lexie laughed. "Maybe a little." She held her fingers to animate her answer.

"I'm trying my hardest to get in your pants," Jackson admitted lightly.

"All you had to do was ask, but I do appreciate the sweet talk." Lexie smiled, feeling elation wash away all the heavy emotions that had been weighing her down.

Jackson brought her hands up so they were around his neck and lifted her body against his. "You know what's better than a thinking place?" Jackson asked with a mischievous smile in between kisses along her jaw and grazing her lips. Her mind was losing the ability to process anything but his lips on her skin and the tingling heat they stirred.

"What's that?" She giggled as he nipped her neck.

"A make-out place," Jackson said against her skin. Goosebumps flashed over her sensitized flesh.

Lexie gasped in surprise when Jackson placed her on the hood of his car. He placed his hands on either side of her, flattening his palms on the car as he looked down at her. Their relationship had been a beautiful disaster since the moment it began. Jackson had found a way to wrap himself around her fragile heart and she embraced it. When she thought of her future, he was in every scenario.

"I love you, Jackson Finley," Lexie whispered. He stayed still, completely unmoving to the point where it started to scare her. She waited for his response but it didn't come. "Jackson?"

"I didn't hear you, what did you say?" he finally said.

Lexie slapped his arm playfully. "You heard me, you liar."

"Just say it again. Louder this time, so I know for sure," he asked, still leaning over her.

Lexie shook her head before she screamed as loud as she could. "I love you, Jackson Finley!" Her voice echoed in the distance. "Did you hear me that time?" Lexie laughed.

Jackson leaned down and took her lips in his, devouring her as he pressed his body against hers. Lexie pulled him closer to deepen their kiss. She noticed his cheeks felt wet to the touch.

"Jackson, what's wrong?"

He pulled back and rubbed his hands down his face. "Nothing, I'm good. I'm better than good." He pressed his lips against hers.

"Why the tears?" Lexie took his face in her hands and held him close.

"You noticed that, huh? Would you believe I had something in my eye?"

"Not a chance," Lexie said as she ran her fingers through his hair.

"You were the first person to ever tell me that. Those words coming from your lips sound too good to be true. You are too good to be true, Lexie Wilder," Jackson confessed.

Lexie grabbed his shirt and pulled it up until Jackson reached over his shoulder and pulled it over his head. He was just as quick to remove her shirt, pulling the material away so they would have no barriers. The feel of having his skin against hers was intoxicating, she felt completely drunk on lust.

Lexie felt a sense of freedom now that she admitted her feelings to Jackson. She wanted to explore their connection in every way and discover all his secrets. For now, she would settle for the pleasure they could give each other as they connected on a primal level…one of the things they did very well together.

When Jackson tossed the rest of her clothes aside, Lexie pushed herself off the car. Placing her hand against his chest, she pushed him back a few steps before turning around. She rubbed the curve of her behind against him, eliciting a groan of approval. Jackson wrapped his arms around her, cupping her breasts as Lexie placed her knee on the car. His hand slid down her side and around the curve of her hip before his fingers began to tease her sensitive flesh. His lips grazed her shoulder as his erection throbbed against her backside.

The slight chill to the air was invigorating as it seemed to heighten her senses. Standing naked outdoors, with the breeze caressing her nipples and Jackson's expert touch had her delirious with want. Arching her back, she could feel his excitement dripping on her skin. He wanted inside her as much as she did.

Taking him in her hand, she guided him to her entrance. He slid in painfully slow while still milking her pleasure. His other hand grabbed her breast and squeezed as he filled her.

"Harder," Lexie demanded.

Jackson slid himself out slowly before thrusting back in hard enough that she had to brace herself on the car. "I thought gentle was for love. You just confessed your love for me. Shouldn't we take this slow?"

"God no, I'll go insane," Lexie gasped. "Now that we established our feelings, it's all in the name of love."

"Good," Jackson said as he thrust deep into her core. Grasping her breasts, he made sure to pay

279

attention to all her pleasure points. His deep, hard thrusts were sparking intense bliss that was set to ignite. She lost sensation of the ground beneath her feet and the cool metal of the car, as her body became a slave to the desire of release that Jackson was leading her toward, fast and furiously.

The gasp of pleasure resonated from somewhere deep inside of her as her release spread like wildfire through her entire body. Lexie melted like hot wax as Jackson held her. He followed with a few more deep pushes before pulling her close. His entire body stiffened and he growled into the curve of her neck before his teeth grazed the flesh of she shoulder, making her shudder.

Jackson wrapped both arms around her and held her tight, placing a kiss on her head. "I love you, Lex."

"Me too."

CHAPTER THIRTY-THREE

Jackson

"How long has this pizza been sitting here?" Stephanie asked, looking down at the remains in the box.

"I wouldn't risk it. Let's just order a new one," Lexie said with a look of disgust.

"Why waste perfectly good food?" Dane leaned in, grabbed a cold slice, and took a big bite.

Stephanie shook her head and closed the box. "We are definitely getting a new one. Besides, it would probably do you guys some good to get one with vegetables on it."

"What are vegetables?" Dane asked as he took another bite.

Lexie and Stephanie both looked at each other and shook their heads. As soon as Nate was released they brought him back to the hotel where Jackson had been staying. They all managed a few hours of sleep before the sun rose. The short rest would be all they could manage because they needed to regroup after what happened. Stodden's men failed to get their hands on either of the things they had been sent for and that meant they would be seeing him again soon.

Jackson drained his glass of whiskey and set it down on the table. He pulled a few bills out of his wallet and held them toward Lexie.

"Why don't you go grab us some food?" Jackson suggested.

"Not a chance. I'll order in. I know what you're doing. You're trying to get me out of here so you can make plans without me. I'm in this, Jackson. I'm not gonna wait around until someone tries to kidnap me again. It's getting old." Lexie crossed her arms and narrowed her eyes. Jackson tried not to notice how the position of her arms accentuated her cleavage. She looked so beautiful with her stern features and tousled hair. He knew he would never have enough of her to satisfy the need that continued to build in intensity. His gaze lingered on her full, pink lips that he could still feel against his. He couldn't help the smile that began to curve his lips.

She had changed so much since she first came into his life. She used to be nervous, terrified, and sad, but now she was strong and confident. She no longer twisted the edge of her shirt between her fingers or shook in the face of fear. She amazed him how she came to own what life had thrown at her. She was a survivor like him. He was thrilled that he was able to call her his. He wanted to shout it out to the world but first he needed to make sure he eliminated the one thing that threatened her, that threatened them, and could take it all away.

"You are so stubborn," Jackson said, shaking his head. He tucked the money in her pants and nipped her bottom lip.

"I'm already in enough pain, don't make me watch you two fucking make-out," Nate teased.

"Well, I'm super fine with sitting this one out. I've already had too much excitement." Stephanie raised her hands. "If I never see a gun again it will be too soon."

Lexie turned to her friend and wrapped her arms around her. "This will be behind us soon."

"I hope you're right, Lex. I missing boring," Stephanie confessed.

Lexie smiled. "Me too."

"Why don't you pour me a whiskey?" Nate was sitting on one of the two beds, his cast propped up with pillows.

"Doc said no drinking with your pain meds. Nice try, though," Jackson said before tossing him a bottle of water that was sitting on the table.

Nate caught it and looked at it with an unamused expression. "Since when do I start doing what I'm told?"

"Since now," Stephanie added. "No whiskey." She pointed at him in warning.

Nate sighed before setting the water on the nightstand.

Jackson pulled up a chair beside Teddy to see if he was making any progress. They knew the private opening for Bitter Sweet was this evening and

Stodden's attendance was guaranteed. He was never one to miss the opportunity to flaunt himself to admirers. Now they just needed to figure out a plan to get inside the private function undetected and kill the man of the hour.

"Give me something, Teddy," Jackson said, running his hand through his hair.

"I'm in the computer of Brian Crothers. While you guys were sleeping, I looked into Stodden's partner. He's owned various successful bars in Belhaven in the last twelve years but this is the first time he's joined forces with a risky partner like Stodden. Looks like Stodden made him an offer he couldn't refuse."

"How'd you get in?" Jackson asked. He was trying to keep up with all the info Teddy was pulling up on the screen.

"His password was his fucking birthday, took me all of two seconds. People are as predictable as shit."

"This is exactly why I stay off these things," Jackson replied. "What did you find?"

"He has a bit of a porn addiction," Teddy dished.

"Don't we all?" Dane joked. He shoved the rest of the piece of pizza in his mouth and leaned back on the bed.

"They're pulling all the stops for security. I found some corresponding emails about taking no chances when it comes to securing the property."

"Are they using a legit company?" Jackson asked with a frown.

"Fuck no, they're using their armed goons, but it looks like they tripled their numbers for tonight, seems they have a lot of high profile clients attending." Teddy pulled up a list of names on his screen.

"What the fuck? Some of these names…" Jackson said, scanning the list. Some of the names stood out as men in the public eye, politicians, there was even some business owners that were well known. "How does he expect some these men to show?"

"Apparently every one of them received a mask with their personal invite. The whole evening is to be anonymous. Even the staff and entertainment will be wearing masks to hide their identity based on these invoices. They even have a car service picking up the invites at various locations. His plan is to win these men over, and apparently it's working."

Jackson rubbed his hand over his face thoughtfully. "Yeah, I guess the promise of sex to old stuffy men will do that. I'm assuming these men will be offered more than a little peep show."

"Yeah, with their invites they were sent blood tests of all the girls to confirm they were all clean. I imagine a lot of shit will be going down."

"Where are the girls coming from?" Jackson asked.

"All over, some are local, though." Teddy pulled up the file with all the profiles of the women they were bringing in for tonight's entertainment.

Dane sat up to get a better look at the computer screen as Teddy shuffled through the different girls.

"Stop," Dane said. "Go back."

"Which one?" Teddy asked, flicking back

slowly.

"That one," Dane said, pointing toward the screen. "I know her."

"I bet you do," Teddy teased. The pretty blonde stared back at them from the screen. "Crystal Corr," Teddy read her name out loud. Based on her profile, she was twenty-four and lived in Belhaven.

"So let's come up with a plan with all this information that was so kindly provided by Crothers. Pull up the blueprints of the building." Jackson tried to get them back on course.

Teddy turned around in his seat and looked at Lexie before turning back to the picture of Crystal. Jackson watched the wheels turning in Teddy's head.

"What the fuck are you doing, Ted?"

"I think I have a plan that will work," Teddy looked up at him. "But you're not gonna like it."

Jackson looked at the picture of Crystal and narrowed his eyes. "No fucking way."

CHAPTER THIRTY-FOUR

Dane

"It's a good fucking plan and you know it," Dane said to Jackson. He turned his head to see Jackson fuming behind the wheel of his car. He still hadn't calmed down since Teddy had told him the plan. He had been ready to shut it all down when Lexie stepped in and insisted she was in. Lexie reached up from the backseat and squeezed Jackson's shoulder.

"I want to do this, Jacks," Lexie insisted.

Jackson grabbed her hand and turned around to look her in the eye. "You keep that microphone on. If you feel threatened at all, you just say the trigger word and I'll pull you out of there."

Lexie nodded. "I'm ready," Lexie said, looking up at Dane.

Dane opened his door and stepped onto the sidewalk. "See you soon."

"You sure this girl is gonna cooperate?"

287

"It'll work. Don't worry." Dane shut the door, grabbed his bag from the trunk, and led Lexie into the apartment building. Crystal may have been a prostitute, but she knew how to work the system to build a very comfortable life for herself. Dane had known her for years and their relationship extended beyond the typical client would have. She trusted Dane and he knew how hard that was to accomplish. The apartment building was in an upscale area of the city, which spoke of her success.

"How well do you know her?" Lexie whispered when the elevator doors closed.

Dane looked at her with a raised brow. "Are you asking if I paid her for sex?"

"Just curious what we're walking into," Lexie responded with a hint of red staining her cheeks.

"The answer is yes," Dane admitted casually. "Trust me when I tell you this is the easy part of the evening."

Lexie sighed as the doors opened. "Here we go."

Dane smiled and led her down the hallway toward Crystal's door. He pulled out his phone.

Dane: Outside your door.

"Why don't you just knock?" Lexie asked with a frown. "We're standing right here." Lexie waved toward the dark stained wooden door.

"When you work in her industry, you don't just open doors without knowing who's behind them," Dane explained as he tucked his phone away. He knew just how troublesome things had been for Crystal before she had earned respect. They were

288

two people with twisted pasts that found comfort knowing they were not alone. "Trust me, if I didn't text her, she wouldn't come to the door."

Dane heard footsteps approach the door before he heard the chain lock release. The door swung open and Crystal stood before them in a pink silk robe and curlers in her hair. Her bright red lipstick was already applied and glitter surrounded her dark, painted eyes.

"Dane, come in." She waved them both in and closed the door, sliding the lock in place. "I was surprised to hear from you today." Crystal led them into her posh apartment that was tailored to her lavish taste. One would never know standing in her place that she was homeless five years ago.

Crystal was good at reading people and she used this to her advantage. Her clients were wealthy business men who didn't have time to date or had lost interest in their wives. She gave them what they wanted, and in return she was able to obtain a substantial fortune. Dane didn't fall into her requirements, but she had developed a soft spot for him along the way. Maybe because he was the only one who knew who she really was behind the fancy clothes.

"I knew how much you were missing me," Dane said, straight-faced.

Crystal shook her head and her red lips turned up into a full grin. "Of course I missed you." She leaned up on her toes and planted a kiss on his cheek.

Dane immediately wiped his face. "Did you get that red shit on me?"

"You love it." Crystal laughed. "And who might you be?" Crystal held out her hand.

"I'm—" Lexie began but Dane cut her off.

"She's going to be *you* for the rest of the evening," Dane didn't even try to break the news kindly. He thought it was best to jump right into the thick of it. Time was not a luxury they had.

Crystal's hand fell to her side "What the fuck?" She raised her eyebrows at Dane, looking for an explanation. "Please don't tell me you're dragging me into one of your insane schemes?"

"Trust me, you'll thank me later," Dane insisted. "And I'm not dragging you into it because you're not going."

"I'm getting paid a lot of money to go to that opening." Crystal narrowed her eyes.

"Considering we're planning to kill the man that's gonna sign your paycheck, it's safe to say you're never going to receive it." Dane watched Crystal's eyes widen.

"Well, this is fucking great. I just had one of my biggest clients tell me he can no longer do business with me because he's gonna work on his shit marriage, and now this," Crystal said dramatically. "I need a drink, and if you're going to be me, then you need one too." Crystal grabbed Lexie by the arm and led her into the kitchen.

"A drink sounds really good right now. I'm Lexie, by the way."

"Nice to meet you, Lexie," Crystal said.

Dane followed the girls into the kitchen, where Crystal poured two glasses of red wine from her impressive collection.

"So how is this gonna happen?" Crystal eyed Dane and Lexie over the rim of her glass.

"I'm assuming you received a costume for tonight's masked theme?" Dane asked as he leaned against the counter.

"Oh, that I did, I was actually looking forward to slipping that little number on. What a pity." Crystal frowned.

Dane dropped his bag on the counter and clapped his hands together. "Well, considering what time it is, I need you to make Lexie look like you so we can get this show on the road."

"What's that?" Crystal asked, eyeing the bag.

"Toys that Teddy gave us to pull this off."

An unamused expression crossed Crystal's face. "You are gonna owe me big time," she warned Dane. She drained her glass and set it down on the counter.

"I've heard that before," Dane said, unconcerned.

"At least you keep my life interesting." Crystal turned toward Lexie. "He's really something, isn't he?"

"I haven't quite figured him out yet." Lexie tilted her head. "Dane's a bit of a mystery."

Crystal threw her head back and laughed. "Honey, you've figured out as much as I have and I've known him for a long time. Let's get you ready. I was planning on leaving in an hour." Crystal ushered Lexie out of the kitchen. She turned back around before disappearing down the hall. "You better not get me in trouble, Dane. I know who Stodden is, and if you don't succeed in this little plan, I want to make sure he doesn't come after me."

"You'll be safe, I promise."

Crystal shook her head with a sigh before continuing down the hall.

CHAPTER
THIRTY-FIVE

Lexie

"Take a deep breath, Lexie. In and out," Teddy's voice soothed her from the tiny communicator that was tucked in her ear. Lexie squeezed the steering wheel so tight her hands began to hurt as she looked through the windshield at the large black building that filled her entire windshield. She was parked in the back, where Crystal informed her she was instructed to when she arrived for the evening. She didn't realize how nervous she was until she dropped off Dane.

Lexie was terrified she would be recognized despite the mask that covered the majority of her face. She angled the rear view mirror so she could see her reflection. When she confirmed everything was as it should be, she pulled a deep breath into her tight chest. "I can't believe you guys do this for a living. I feel like my heart is about to explode."

"Well, we don't actually do what you're about to do. Although, I'm sure Dane would look hilarious in sparkly lingerie," Teddy joked.

"You know what I mean," Lexie said with a small semblance of a laugh.

"We won't be far behind you. Once you get a location on Stodden, we'll move in. Just look like you know what you're doing and you should be able to buy enough time."

"I don't see you guys." Lexie looked around the parking lot.

"That's the point. The important thing is that we can see you, and you really need to move that pretty butt before you start to look suspicious," Teddy said calmly.

"Yeah, yeah." Lexie took another deep breath. "Please, god, let the thin straps of this ridiculously small outfit hold."

Teddy laughter erupted in the earpiece. "I think everyone will be praying for the opposite. Shit. Jackson...I was fucking joking...give that back." Teddy sounded like he was struggling. "That hurt."

"Don't listen to that piece of fuck. Be safe, baby. I'll be in there before you know it," Jackson said reassuringly. Just the sound of his voice instantly calmed her down. "Do you have the piece for the door?"

"Yeah." Lexie reached into the cup holder and pulled out the small device that she was instructed to fit onto the door latch. She wrapped her fingers around it tightly.

"Yep, I'm heading in. I'll see you soon," Lexie said, opening her door, knowing from here on in she couldn't talk anymore but listening to him would help keep her focused. The distraction from her racing heart and sweating palms was much needed.

"Be with you soon," Jackson replied. "Keep the target in mind."

Lexie looked around as she walked toward the back door.

"Relax, you don't want to look guilty, babe," Jackson suggested.

Lexie grabbed hold of the railing and walked up the steps. She knocked like she was instructed to do and the door immediately swung open. A bald-headed man that Lexie recognized from when Stodden held her captive stood before her, and for a moment she forgot she was wearing a mask.

"Well, get the fuck in here. You're late," the man barked at her.

"Sorry…" Lexie began.

"Don't apologize. Just tell him to fuck off," Jackson said in her ear.

"…but I'm here now." Lexie tried to force arrogance in her voice.

He clenched his jaw and waved impatiently for her to enter. Lexie grabbed the edge of the door and pulled it out of his grasp, making sure she kept his eyes distracted as she tried to pull off a dramatic display. "You try to fit into this little outfit and be on time," Lexie said, pulling open the tie of her jacket. His eyes wandered down the length of her body as Lexie shoved the device over the door latch. She hoped she placed it correctly, because she couldn't watch what she was doing without drawing his attention. She knew it was how they were

295

planning on getting into the building. This step was important and she couldn't mess it up.

She stepped inside the hallway and tried to focus on what she needed to do. She ran through the checklist Crystal had drilled into her head before leaving. She needed to check in with Ronnie, who had initially interviewed all the women who were entertaining this evening.

Lexie walked up to the third door down the hallway, pretending she was familiar with the building and knew exactly where she was going. Luckily, most of the bodies that were passing her seemed preoccupied.

Lexie knocked on the wooden door while placing her other hand against the wall. She needed to feel a solid wall against her shaking hand.

"Come in," a male voice called out from the other side.

Lexie opened the door. A man was sitting behind the desk with papers spread out in a cluttered mess. He looked up at her and shook his head. "The masks make it impossible to know who I'm fucking talking to all evening."

"Crystal Corr," Lexie offered. She placed her hands on her hips and tried to exude the same confidence she noted in Crystal.

He gave her outfit a once over before his eyes came back to hers. "I was starting to wonder about you. You're late." Ronnie raised an unamused brow. Ronnie held up a key for her and waved toward the hallway. "Head to the dressing room with the other girls while I deal with this last minute shit. This key is for your locker. The guests should start arriving soon. I'll be there in a few minutes to give everyone the low down."

Lexie nodded and headed out of the room, closing the door behind her. She had no idea where the dressing room was. She started down the hall, glancing in the different rooms along the way.

"Last on the left," Jackson whispered. "Just head straight there."

She picked up her pace and passed the shady looking characters standing in the hall having a hushed conversation. They paused and glared at her as she passed. She tried not to look affected as she continued at her pace, averting her eyes. She wanted to pull her coat closer around her but she knew that would make her look nervous.

"Just keep going," Jackson encouraged. "Ignore them." The interior of the building still smelled of fresh paint and Lexie was impressed by the art displayed on the walls. A lot of thought was put into the décor. It was definitely not the typical strip bar from what Lexie could tell. This reminded her of an old world building with ornate moldings and rich colors.

She was relieved when she stepped into the dressing room. It was filled with women all in different outfits, all just as flashy and tiny as the others. Lexie placed her hand against her chest. Her heart was refusing to slow down.

"Be careful of the camera, Lex," Jackson said quietly.

She pulled her hand away and looked down at the flowers that were covering the cup of her bra-like top. She had forgotten for a moment about the little trinket that was so small it could be concealed on her clothes.

Lexie slipped her jacket off and opened the locker that was marked with the same number as her key. Tucking it inside, she turned around and looked down at her outfit, wondering where the hell she was going to stick the key.

"There's a small, concealed pocket inside your bra to put your key," one of the girls mentioned when she noticed Lexie's dilemma.

Lexie looked up to see the girl sitting on a chair beside her. She had a friendly smile that was painted with magenta lipstick. Her bleached blonde hair was curled and piled on the top of her head. She had a very relaxed demeanour as she sipped a glass of wine.

"Oh, thank you. I didn't notice it when I got dressed." Lexie tried to delicately look for it without disrupting the camera.

"You have to take it off to find it. I'll show you," she offered as she set her wine glass down. She reached behind her and unsnapped her top, sliding it off her shoulders.

"Yesss…" She could hear Teddy's voice in the background. "This is fucking awesome."

Lexie tried to ignore him as she placed her hand over where she knew the camera was. They did not need to spy on the women to do their job.

"Oh come on," Teddy complained. She ignored Teddy's pleas as she watched the girl show her the small pocket tucked inside the bottom of the cup. This woman was completely unfazed by being nude in public as she stood in front of Lexie without returning her shirt.

"Just don't throw your bra when you take if off or you might lose it. I'm Sarah," she introduced herself.

"Hi Sarah. I'm Crystal." Lexie smiled warmly.

"Crystal Corr?" Sarah asked with a twist of her mouth.

"Yeah." Lexie's heartbeat starting thrumming again. Crystal didn't say she knew any of the girls here.

"I've heard about you. I thought you'd be a bitch, no offense," Sarah said.

"None taken," Lexie assured her. Sarah's eyes raked Lexie's entire body. Lexie resisted the urge to narrow her eyes as this woman's judging eyes sized her up.

Sarah sat back down in her seat and grabbed her glass of wine. She was in no hurry to put her top back on. "Help yourself to the wine. It's good shit."

"Thanks, I will," Lexie said as she headed toward the serving cart that held rows of wine glasses and several bottles of wine. She discreetly tucked her key under her bra. She was comfortable taking off her clothes in the comfort of her home and delightfully in front of Jackson, but she had no plans to reveal anything more than she already was in this place.

Lexie hoped she looked confident as she strutted around half-naked, because many eyes followed her around the room. Suddenly Lexie felt like she was in some competition. Lexie didn't have the head space for the mind games. These were all beautiful women that swallowed a whole lot of ugly. It dripped from their painted lips and she couldn't stand the energy of the room as they whispered and glared.

The heels were already beginning to hurt her feet. The wine was something she would not pass on because she needed to forget about her throbbing feet. She poured a glass and downed the entire contents just as Ronnie walked into the room.

"Okay ladies, let's get this show started. Some of you have been assigned certain guests for the evening, while others will be on stage. Just line up in front of me and I will direct you. Dancers first please, and then we'll figure out where the rest of you need to be." Ronnie looked down at his clipboard as the girls all filed in line. Lexie set her glass down reluctantly and headed toward the back of the line.

The dancers were taken to another room to get ready for their performance, leaving a little more than half to be assigned. Lexie was glad she was in the back of the line because it meant she had more time to mentally prepare herself.

"You're doing great, Lex." Lexie resisted touching her ear in an effort to feel closer to Jackson. Instead she grasped her hands in front of her. She stepped up to Ronnie as the girl in front of her headed out of the room.

Ronnie looked up from his list and smiled. "Ah, yes, Miss Corr," Ronnie said with a creepy smile. "*You,* my dear, can come with me." Ronnie smiled as he held out an arm for her and tucked the clipboard under the other.

"May I ask what my assignment is?" Lexie asked

curiously. All the other women were told before they were whisked away, while she was left to look at Ronnie's big smile that was hiding the information she wanted. Lexie slid her arm through his.

"There's a reason why John is paying you the big money. You're the star of the show tonight," Ronnie announced.

"What the fuck does that mean, Dane?" she heard Jackson ask.

"She didn't say anything about it. They didn't tell her anything about what she was doing," Dane responded in a muffled voice.

Lexie's throat squeezed tight like a rope was just pulled taut around it. She had no idea what that meant and she was terrified to find out. His arm tightened his hold on her like he had read her thoughts.

"Any sign of trouble and I'm heading in," Jackson said. She wasn't sure if he was talking to her or the guys, but it sounded good to her.

Lexie allowed Ronnie to lead her down the hallway. She hoped Jackson was getting all the information he needed. From what she could tell, there was an alarming number of security guards. Ronnie led her down another hallway and through a set of double doors that led into very dramatic lighting.

The music playing was very enchanting and set a very seductive pace that played into the atmosphere. Many wine colored booths where clustered throughout the area, most angled toward the various stages. The seating was designed for comfort as she noticed the customers looking relaxed and already sipping on their drinks and taking advantage of the cocaine that was presented in the middle of the tables.

The dress code of formal attire and masks added to the grandness of the event. These men could have been anything at all in the public eye but here they were free to submit to their desires without prosecution. Stodden was going out of his way to win over these powerful men and it was scary how easy it seemed to be.

The men were already growing comfortable with the women. She spotted Sarah sitting on a man's lap as he fondled her and she laughed playfully. Lexie didn't want to think about what the girls would endure this evening. She only hoped they knew what they signed up for. Lexie had witnessed Stodden's parties before and she knew where this was leading. Her only shred of hope was that these were not the criminals that normally attended Stodden's functions, these were men of stature. Surely they had the decency to be respectful.

She stayed close to Ronnie's side as he led her toward a winding staircase that led up to a balcony. The area was dressed to entertain a small group. Two small dance areas with brass poles flanked three large booths that were positioned in a large half circle set to overlook the entire bar below. Two women were dancing against the poles, trying to seduce the men with their playful smiles and alluring flesh. Six men sat in the oversized seats, all wearing masks, but she knew immediately who Stodden was. Not only was his mask more ornate than the others, but she could tell strictly by his mannerisms, the way he tapped his glass with his finger and observed the room. Anger boiled hot in her stomach but she refused to let it show. She would not give him a reason to suspect her.

"Got him," Jackson said in her ear. "We're coming."

CHAPTER THIRTY-SIX

Jackson

"How'd you get the masks so fast?" Dane asked, adjusting his on his face.

"Sent an email from Crothers' computer saying they needed a rush order for a few defective masks. They were very accommodating and seemed terrified. I also gave his computer a little virus. I'd love to see his face next time he turns on his computer."

"The camera's taken care of?" Jackson asked impatiently as he tapped his fingers on the door.

"Just a second...now," Teddy announced. "Let's go."

Jackson swung the back of the van open and jumped out onto the pavement. He headed for the rear door. He knew there were three men standing on the other side of the door that would need to be taken care of discreetly. He knocked and leaned casually against the wall.

The door swung open and the security guard looked at all three of them dressed in suits and masks. "Why the fuck are you out here?"

"We…ah…we started the party a bit early and missed our car service." Jackson stumbled backwards down the steps and bumped into Teddy.

"Hey, what the fuck, man?" Teddy shoved him into Dane.

"Fuck you," Dane hollered as they began to throw punches. The security officer waved the others to join him outside and they pulled out their guns.

"That's enough," the one who opened the door hollered with his gun drawn. "There will be no trouble here."

"Good to know," Jackson said as he grabbed the gun and twisted the man's arms, causing him to lose grip on his weapon. He brought his elbow up into the man's neck, knocking him back into the wall. Dane and Teddy addressed the other two that threw themselves into the fight. Jackson pulled out his gun and aimed for the man's head just as he pushed off the wall and dove for his own gun. Jackson pulled the trigger and the man dropped instantly, landing at his feet.

Teddy kicked a body of one of the men aside and pulled out his phone. Jackson grabbed hold of the door handle and waited for Teddy's nod. He could hear the click as the lock released. He pulled the door open and walked inside with Teddy and Dane behind him, guns drawn.

CHAPTER THIRTY-SEVEN

Lexie

"What a magnificent creature," the man sitting close to Stodden said as he observed Lexie like she was a bottle of wine being served.

"Tonight is about pleasure, Roman. This is my gift to you." Stodden waved toward Lexie.

"Go sit next to our guest," Ronnie whispered in her ear. "Make sure he's happy." Lexie walked slowly toward him. She could feel Stodden's eyes on her as she approached but she didn't once glance his way. She neared the man as he patted the seat beside him. Her tiny outfit seemed even smaller now that she was on display. She wanted to keep her distance but she had no choice. She knew she was surrounded by ruthless men.

Lexie sat down on the edge of the seat and smiled at the man named Roman. She could tell by his mouth he was a younger man, but his features were obscured by his mask. His name wasn't familiar, nor was the slight accent that he still carried with his words.

"You're a shy one," Roman said slyly. Lexie let out a surprised gasp when he grabbed her and pulled her closer. "I like it."

He ran his fingers along the swell of her breasts and Lexie had to consciously work at not squirming in discomfort. It took everything she had to keep the smile upon her lips.

"Take off your mask so I can get a better look at you," he said as he tilted her chin up.

Lexie leaned in closer so John wouldn't be able to recognize her voice. "I thought tonight was all about secrets," she whispered against his ear.

"Yes, but I want to know your secrets," Roman said as he placed his finger upon her lip and pressed it into her mouth. Lexie had no choice but to play along with his lead. She gently sucked as he slowly pulled his finger out. He grabbed her hand and placed it on his erection straining against his pants. His pulled on the strap holding her top and she panicked. Lexie immediately pulled away. She knew she blew her cover but there was no way she was going that far.

Roman grabbed her by the neck and pulled her closer. "Who the fuck do you think you are?" he growled. She didn't have time to stop him before he ripped the mask from her face.

Her eyes flashed toward Stodden, who was looking at her with a dark expression. There was no way she was getting out of this situation. She grabbed for Roman's gun, tucked inside his jacket, and she managed to pull it free.

She aimed it in Stodden's direction and pulled the trigger without hesitation. She didn't know if she would ever have a chance again. Stodden jolted from the impact of the bullet. Lexie was in shock that she actually pulled the trigger as she stared down at the weapon in her hands.

Three men reached the top of the stairs with their guns drawn. It took her a moment to realize it was Jackson, Teddy, and Dane in disguise. The dancers were screaming and trying to find a place to hide.

Roman knocked into Lexie, shoving her into the railing. A sharp pain radiated through her hip from the impact.

"Don't move," Jackson shouted at Roman in warning but Roman threw himself over the railing. Lexie watched him land on a table below. Gunfire was going off around her as she spun back to look at John, who was no longer in his seat. He hauled one of the women off the floor and held his gun to her head. The woman had mascara mixed tears streaming down her face as she shook in his hold.

"Please let me go," she begged.

"Drop the gun, Stodden, and let the girl go," Jackson demanded.

"And why would I do that?" Stodden asked, pulling the girl tighter against him.

Teddy and Dane were holding off the men on the stairs. Bodies littered the ground around them, shot down just as quickly as they came to Stodden's rescue, but no one was managing to get through their defenses.

Lexie noticed John shirt under his jacket was

stained red. She looked down and noticed that it was beginning to drip on the floor by his feet. She just needed to stall him long enough for him to weaken. The amount of blood she was seeing had to mean the injury was grave.

"Why did you kill my mother?" Lexie demanded, still holding the gun.

"It was an accident," John insisted. He pulled the mask off his face.

"Was it an accident when you sent Rosh to finish her off?" Lexie asked angrily.

"I assure you I didn't send anyone to finish her off." Stodden looked surprised by her accusation. It was not the reaction she was expecting. She could see beads of sweat form on his forehead and his normally hard edge was blurred with a look of exhaustion.

"Then maybe you should ask Mark Rosh why he did…oh right, you can't because he's *dead*," Lexie confessed.

"Then I should thank you," Stodden replied. "I assure you I would've made him suffer, had I known."

"The person who deserves to suffer is you," Lexie demanded. She could feel herself fraying at the edges.

"So much anger, dear Lexie. Are you sure you're directing it at the right person? Did you know Jackson set fire to a home and killed three innocent young children?" Stodden held tight to the distraught woman, whose eyes pleaded with someone to save her. The gun pressed into the side of her head. "At least I have never hurt a child."

"Shut the fuck up, Stodden," Jackson screamed. Lexie looked over at Jackson, who looked visibly shaken.

"And you think I'm the monster." Stodden smiled sinisterly as he watched Jackson. He turned his attention back toward Lexie. "I'm your own flesh and blood, Lexie. Do you really want to kill me?"

"No." Lexie lowered her gun. "I can't deny that I'm alive because of you and now I'll spare yours to make us even," Lexie said.

"Lexie?" Jackson asked in confusion.

"What the fuck is going on here?" Teddy asked as his gaze flickered to Lexie.

Stodden looked confused by her surrender when she had the upper hand in the situation.

"But Jackson owes you nothing." Lexie raised her brow. "And you killed his father and destroyed his family." Stodden made a move to raise his gun toward Jackson but Dane was too quick. His bullet lodged in Stodden's right shoulder, causing him to drop his gun.

"Fuck," Stodden hollered as he grabbed at the table for support. The girl ran screaming from him and stumbled down the stairs. The blood saturating his shirt was in plain sight as he swayed on his feet.

"Jacobs...Rayner..." Stodden called for his men. He had lost but he refused to submit.

"Sorry, Stodden, but your men are dead," Jackson announced. "Tell me where Haffey's brother is."

"I'll tell you if you lower your gun," Stodden demanded with his one last remaining bargaining chip. "You let me walk out of here and I will give you the information you need." Stodden grimaced through the pain. Lexie searched for any sign of humanity in his eyes, but the only thing she saw when she looked at him was a monster.

"Nah, I don't think so. Besides, I bet your little buddy knows where he is." Jackson nodded toward Brian Crothers, who was cowering against the wall as Dane held him at gunpoint. His mask was pulled down around his neck and a look of desperation was painted on his features.

"Where is he? Dane asked, pushing his gun into Crothers' cheek.

"Don't fucking talk, Brian," Stodden demanded, but the threat of the gun apparently took precedence.

"I'm sorry...don't kill me. He's...he's being kept at um..." Crothers' glanced over at Stodden but Dane twisted the barrel of the gun harder into his flesh. "Okay, okay, as far as I know he's at a man's house named Trent Baker," Crothers confessed.

"Now that I have that little piece of information I don't need your piece of shit ass."

"Think about what you're doing, Jackson. It was Rosh that killed your father and you know it. I'm just a fellow man who doesn't like to pass up on good opportunities. Nothing more."

"Fuck you, Stodden," Jackson seethed.

Lexie knew Jackson had been envisioning this moment his entire life.

"You sentenced my father to death and this is my retribution," Jackson raged as he pulled the trigger.

311

The bullet hit Stodden in the other shoulder, causing him to stumble backward. Stodden lunged toward Lexie in on last desperate attempt. He never made it to her because the spray of bullets stopped him in his tracks. One by one his body jerked with the impact as he backed into the railing next to Lexie. She was frozen in place as he gave her a last fleeting look, reaching for her with a bloodied hand. Lexie covered her mouth with a gasp.

The momentum of his fall caused him to topple over the railing, his lifeless body dropped to the ground below with a sickening thud. Lexie looked at Stodden's dead body with wide-eyes. It was over. It was all over. She looked up and met Jackson's gaze. She was waiting for the feeling of joy to wash over her but instead tears filled her eyes. She wasn't sure what she was feeling, she was too high on adrenaline to register what emotion was fighting for center stage. Jackson wrapped his jacket around her and gathered her in his arms.

"Everyone cleared out in a hurry," Teddy said, looking at the empty club.

"Bullets do that," Dane answered.

"And I would imagine from the guest list it would be bad for those men to be here when the cops pull in," Teddy added.

Jackson held her against his side, placing a kiss on her forehead. She could feel his body shaking next to hers, or maybe it was her own, she couldn't tell.

"Call Haffey and give her the good news," Jackson said.

"On it," Teddy said, pulling out his phone.

312

Dane still had Brian Crothers against the wall at gunpoint. "What should I do with him?" Dane asked as the man whimpered. Apparently Stodden's partner didn't have a stomach for violence.

"Lock him in one of the offices downstairs. Haffey can deal with him. Let's get out of here," Jackson said to Lexie as he guided her toward the stairs. Lexie wrapped her arm around his waist and felt a warm, wet heat.

"Jackson?" Lexie pulled her hand away and saw the blood on her fingers. "You're hurt!"

"I'm fine," Jackson tried to dismiss her but Lexie wouldn't let it go. She pulled up his shirt to look for the wound. "I like where this is going."

Lexie looked up at him from under her lashes. "You're impossible," Lexie said with a shake of her head. "Dane?" Lexie called to him.

Dane looked at Crothers' for a moment before he hit him with the butt of his gun and he dropped unconscious on the floor. "I couldn't leave him. I don't trust the bastard after seeing the shit on his computer."

"I'll be fine," Jackson insisted. "The bullet just grazed me."

"Let's see," Dane said examining the wound. "Fuck, that looks like it hurts. We'll get you fixed up," Dane assured him.

"That's a lot of blood for a graze."

"He'll be all right. He's been shot more than any of us," Dane said dismissively.

"That doesn't make me feel any better." Lexie sighed. "Let's just get out of here."

By the time they made it outside the sound of

sirens could be heard in the distance and it was music to her ears. She had never felt so good to walk through a door in her entire life. She never wanted to step back into that place again.

"I could use a drink right now," Jackson said.

"Me too, but let's hold off the celebration until we get you stitched up," Lexie insisted. Jackson gave her a smile and leaned in close.

"About what Stodden said…"

"Don't worry about that right now. Let's just have this moment." Lexie grabbed his cheeks and pressed her lips against his. "It's over," she whispered against his lips.

"It's over," he repeated with a relieved smile.

CHAPTER THIRTY-EIGHT

Haffey

The street was quiet in the late night hour as they drove by the rows of houses, all similar in size and style. The street looked very unassuming and the very last place Haffey would have considered looking for her brother. Though, she was not surprised. Stodden had found a way to penetrate every layer of the city.

Trent Baker was a typical family man. He owned and operated his own auto painting company for the last twenty years. He was also known to take on odd jobs when business was down. He had a wife and two children in high school; his oldest set to graduate in the spring. Nothing on paper stood out about this man that would raise any flags. Haffey didn't think about it much, she knew the dots could be connected later. The only thing that drove her was finding her brother, and time was of the

315

essence.

When they neared the address located at the end of the street, they pulled onto a long driveway with a sign indicating, Baker's Auto Painting. The house was set off the road in a cluster of trees. The headlights illuminated the dark house as they pulled to a stop. The large garage behind the house was cast aglow in light that streamed through the windows along the side of the building. Music could be heard radiating from the interior as they pulled to a stop.

The three cruisers behind Haffey's vehicle pulled in, blocking off the driveway. The officers filed out of their cars with their weapons readied, awaiting her orders.

"Peters and Sanchez," Haffey motioned toward the dark house. "Clear the house. The rest of you follow me."

Haffey glanced at Sieks, who closed in by her side as they headed toward the garage. The music was the perfect cover to keep their approach quiet as she neared the side door. She could hear someone making noise from inside. Haffey motioned toward the others to ready themselves as she approached the door. They had no idea what to expect upon entry of the building. Haffey leaned away from the glass upper portion of the door to stay out of view from the interior and grabbed the handle. It wasn't locked.

He nodded toward Sieks as she pushed the door in. She and Sieks stepped in with their weapons raised. She could see Baker across the shop, he was wearing white overalls covered in paint, with a mask covering most of his face, but she knew it was him. "Put your hands up, Trent Baker."

The man looked terrified as she stayed frozen in place, watching the men file in his shop with guns pointed toward him.

"Put your hands up!" Haffey demanded.

Baker dropped his spray gun and made a grab for something on his work bench. "Don't fucking move!" Sieks screamed, circling the car that sat in the center of the room. The room reeked of paint fumes and it made Haffey lightheaded.

Haffey noticed what he was grabbing for. A pistol was sitting among his tools. "Put the weapon down, Mr. Baker. Surrender and you won't get hurt."

He pulled the mask off his face and looked at Haffey. "I'm sorry," he mumbled before lifting the gun to his head. Haffey made a lunge for him but she wasn't quick enough. He pulled the trigger and she watched the side of his head explode.

"No!" Haffey screamed but it was too late. Blood sprayed all over the freshly painted car. "Oh god." She covered her mouth as she took in the horrific scene. She pulled her hand away and noticed some of the blood splatter had gotten on her face. She frantically wiped it away.

Sieks walked up beside her and placed his hand on her shoulder. "Here." He passed her a cloth to help clean the blood.

Sieks addressed the others still in the room. "Search the property and see if we can find any sign of Haffey's brother."

Sieks guided her away from the scene and led

her out of the garage. "Take a moment," he said when they were alone.

"I don't need a moment. I need to find my brother," She passed Sieks back the bloodied cloth. She knew she needed to focus on finding her brother. That was the most important thing. She would worry about Trent Baker later.

They searched the house from top to bottom, leaving nothing untouched, and Haffey was growing increasingly restless. He had to be here, they were out of options.

"I found something!" one of the officers called from the doorway of the garage. Haffey immediately ran into the building. She ignored the bloody mess as she passed by into the office space, off the back of the garage. The mat was pulled up off the floor and a latch was opened to reveal a descending staircase.

Haffey used her phone as a flashlight and pulled out her gun as she started down the steep stairway without hesitation. Sieks was quick to follow her; she could feel him against her back.

"There's a light," Sieks said, pointing to a chain hanging down from the ceiling at the bottom of the stairs. She pulled it and the small enclosed space was illuminated. They were looking at a wooden wall and door that led into another area.

Haffey grabbed the door latch and slowly pulled it open. Holding her gun, she stepped inside. She could make out wooden crates piled up against the wall. She heard a small sound from inside, but the sound of footsteps coming down behind her drowned out any other noise.

"Be quiet," Haffey whispered. Sieks turned around and motioned for them to stop making noise. She froze in place, listening. It was a soft moaning sound coming from inside the dark room.

"Carlos?" Haffey called out as she stepped inside.

The moaning stopped and she heard movement, a bucket being knocked over, and the sound of a chain rattling.

"Carlos?" she called out again, this time louder.

"Belisa." Her name brought a rush of excitement. Her brother was still alive. Her worst fear was lifted from her shoulders and she gasped with relief.

"I'm coming," she said as she shone her light up and walked further. The boxes opened up into an empty area where she could see her brother chained in the corner of the basement. He was badly injured from what she could tell in the dim light. The sight of him brought tears to her eyes, both of horror and relief.

Haffey dropped to her knees and threw her arms around him before placing her hands on either side of his face. The light from Sieks' flashlight illuminated his swollen features but she could see her brother behind the damage.

"Get something to cut these chains," she called out to no one in particular. She wanted to get her brother out of this horrible place and bring him home.

***

Haffey pulled the blanket tighter around Carlos'

shoulders as he sat in the back of the ambulance. The paramedic was examining him and bandaging his open wounds.

Haffey looked up and saw Sieks and another officer approach. Sieks nodded for her to join them.

"I'll be back in a second, Carlos," Haffey said, giving his shoulder a gentle pat.

He nodded quietly. She could see the tortured look in his eyes and knew that he was suffering more than physical wounds.

Haffey jumped out of the back of the vehicle. "What's going on?" she asked.

"Peters spoke with some of the neighbors. They said that a about a week ago his wife and kids packed up and left late one night. It took everyone by surprise because the family looked like they were doing well before things took a turn. Darlene Baker was driving a brand new BMW and lots of delivery trucks had been arriving the last few months. By the looks of the interior of the house, they bought a whole lot of brand new shit lately."

"A little unlikely for a small auto painting company to make that much profit in a short period of time." Haffey pursed her lips.

"Maybe Darlene found out where the money was coming from and took off," Peters added.

"Seems likely. Track her down and call me as soon as you do. I'm heading to the hospital with Carlos," Haffey informed them.

"Sure thing," Sieks said. He looked at Carlos, who was still being examined. "I'll be by the hospital as soon as I clean things up here."

"Thanks, Sieks." Haffey offered a small smile.

"Of course. Now go take care of your brother and leave the rest to me."

"I don't deserve you," Haffey said as she walked backward toward the ambulance.

"You're right." Sieks winked at her.

CHAPTER THIRTY-NINE

Jackson

"No gun slinging for a few weeks." The doctor secured the bandage on Jackson's side. "Although by the look of that shoulder, I'd say you don't listen well." The doctor examined the recently healed wound. Jackson had forgotten about.

"Yeah, I've never been much of a listener," Jackson confirmed with a frown.

"Well, surprisingly, it's healing nicely," the doctor said as he pulled off his gloves and tossed them into the garbage can by the door. "I've had the pleasure of meeting that lovely young lady waiting outside your door, and if you have any sense at all, I'd say you'd better start," the doctor said with an amused shake of his head.

"Thanks, Doc," Jackson said.

"Of course." The doctor gave him a nod as he slipped through the door.

"He's all yours," Jackson heard him announce to Lexie as he walked out into the hall.

Lexie's beautiful face appeared in the doorway and Jackson felt the smile immediately capture his mouth. Every time he looked at her it was like seeing the rising sun after a long, cold night.

Jackson grabbed his shirt off the examination table.

"I vote for leaving your shirt off," Lexie said playfully as she approached him.

"Come here." Jackson held his hand out for her. She placed hers in his and he pulled her into him, wrapping his arms around her. It always felt so wonderful to hold onto her. Her fingers traced the edge of the bandage as she leaned into him.

"Does it hurt?" she asked, pulling away to look up at him.

"Nah." Jackson brushed the hair from her face and pressed his lips to hers. He felt like he was home. The haunted part of him that couldn't rest until Stodden was stopped was finally quiet. All the noise in his head was suddenly muted and he was left staring into the most beautiful eyes in world. He was never one to believe in luck, but in this moment it was hard not to. Though, his momentary bliss was short lived when reality started to shake its ugly head. Stodden's words echoed in the back of his mind, reminding him of his true colors.

"Where is everyone?" Jackson asked.

"Waiting for you in Giles' room."

"Let's go see the old man," Jackson said, taking Lexie's hand.

Nate was leaning on his crutches next to Teddy

as they looked over papers that were scattered over Giles' feet as he lay in his bed. Stephanie was sitting in the chair tucked in the corner with a cup of coffee in her hand. She looked completely enthralled in the conversation between Teddy and Nate. Dane was standing against the walls with his arms crossed, watching over the entire room.

"There he is," Dane said when he noticed Jackson.

Everyone turned around to see Jackson and Lexie walk into the room.

"So you made it. Teddy and Dane were arguing who should get your job if you didn't," Giles joked. He was looking much better since the last time he had seen him. Jackson walked up to the side of his bed. "It's good to see you, Jackson," Giles said.

"You too," Jackson replied.

"Giles is just being nice. What we were actually arguing about was who gets to console Lexie," Teddy teased.

Jackson just shook his head in disbelief. "You are unbelievable." He smiled. "What's all this?" Jackson pointed toward the files.

"Nate had me look into something for him," Teddy explained.

"My mother was pregnant when she was taken and the autopsy revealed that she had given birth just before her death," Nate said in a rush.

"I'm sorry, man." Jackson placed his hand on Nate's shoulder.

"I think my brother is still alive, Jackson," Nate confessed.

Jackson looked into Nate's hopeful expression.

"Brother? What'd you find?" Jackson asked, glancing between Nate and Teddy.

"Six months after Nate's mother was taken, the Mastens adopted a baby boy," Teddy informed him.

"What makes you think he's Nate's brother?" Jackson asked.

Teddy picked up a photograph of Terence Masten and his wife next to their son on his graduation. "This picture is a few years old, but it speaks for itself." He passed it to Jackson.

Jackson looked at the young man in the picture. "Holy fuck." He looked up at Nate. The resemblance was remarkable.

"It's enough to convince me to look into it," Nate said with a nod of his head.

Jackson grabbed Nate by the back of the neck and pulled him in for a hug. "You let me know if you need my help." Jackson patted him on the back.

"Thanks, man," Nate said.

"I have some more good news," Giles said. "The doctors said I'm free to leave this place, so one of you is taking me home."

"Dane and I will take you. We're heading back to Westford anyway," Teddy offered.

Jackson wrapped his arm around Lexie's shoulder. "We're heading out, ladies," Jackson teased. "We're going back to the hotel to grab a few hours of sleep and then I need to get this girl home."

"Are you coming, Stephanie?" Lexie asked.

"No, I'm gonna stay with Nate. I already broke the news to my parents, so I might as well wait out their wrath," Stephanie said as she walked around the bed to give Lexie a parting hug.

"Mike's mom called me. He's been missing for a few days. Do you think we should be worried?" A line creased Stephanie's brows.

"He'll show up eventually. It's not the first time. Did they check the clubs?" Lexie asked dismissively.

"Yeah, no sign of him. He was so angry. You don't think he would do anything stupid, do you?" Stephanie asked worriedly.

"It's Mike we're talking about."

"Oh shit." Stephanie looked wide-eyed at Lexie.

"Listen, Steph. Stay here and help Nate. When I get home I'll track him down. He's been known to disappear on occasion."

"Okay, you're right. I'll be home soon. We'll figure it out, and don't forget we have lots of boring to catch up on." Stephanie smiled.

"Yes we do."

CHAPTER FORTY

Lexie

When Lexie opened the door to her mother's house she was met with Cherry's beaming face.

"There's my beauty," Cherry gushed and threw her arms around Lexie before she even made it through the door. It felt so good to be home as she squeezed Cherry back.

"You look well, darling." Cherry stepped back to get a good look at her.

"I am," Lexie said. "How are you?"

"Fantastic, now that you're back. All this worrying you guys were making me do was threatening to give me wrinkles." Cherry patted the skin beneath her eyes in a dramatic display.

Lexie laughed as she walked into the kitchen. "I missed you, Cherry." She took a deep breath, dropped her purse on the kitchen table, and collapsed into the chair.

"Where's your hot piece of ass boyfriend?" Cherry asked, setting a wine glass in front of Lexie.

"He was making a phone call. He'll be in any minute," Lexie said as she sat her chin in her hands and leaned on the table. "I feel like I could sleep for days."

"I'd join you for a glass but I have to get this hot butt to the diner. They can't survive without me," Cherry said with a wink. "I really like this small town. Everyone loves my twist on the famous pies and *you know* my mystery meat really fascinates the locals."

"I bet it does," Lexie said, grabbing Cherry's hand and giving it a squeeze. "Thanks for holding the fort."

"Any time," Cherry said. "I love that little diner."

"Did you hear from Evan?" Lexie asked hopefully.

"Not since he left, but he said as soon as he was allowed visitors he would demand we all come."

"Good, he better," Lexie replied.

"So glad you're back." Cherry kissed her on the forehead and grabbed her keys off the table.

"Cherry?" Lexie called after her.

"Yeah, sweetness?"

"I'm so glad you're here." Lexie smiled. "You know, we might never let you leave."

"I hope not." Cherry blew her a kiss before opening the door and slipping outside.

Lexie took a sip of her wine and noticed the bottle of nail polish in her bag. She picked it up and looked at it with a sad smile.

She pushed herself to her feet and walked into the living room, toward the fireplace. Her mother

328

had a collection of some of her favorite things lined up on the mantle. Lexie looked at her mother's favorite tea cup, pictures, books, candles, and the quirky little wood carving. All the memories of her mother washed over her with full-bodied emotion as she felt tears run down her cheeks. She missed her mother so much and the pain was still so fresh.

The door opened and Jackson walked in. "Cherry just slapped my ass," Jackson said, shaking his head.

Lexie tried to smile but she couldn't hide the sadness that was radiating from her. Jackson's face fell when he noticed. "What's wrong?"

Jackson looked up at the framed picture of Lexie and her mother and understanding dawned over his face. He wrapped his arm around her and rubbed her shoulder.

"I'm all right. I just miss her. I will always miss her," Lexie admitted. "And just glad to be home."

"I wish I could tell you the pain goes away," Jackson said sadly.

"I know. It helps if I think about the good things. Like you. I'm glad you're here with me," Lexie confessed, leaning into him.

Jackson dropped his arm from Lexie, she immediately missed his touch. "I have to tell you something." Jackson seemed nervous as he scratched his chin. "It's about what Stodden said about the fire. He was telling the truth," Jackson admitted.

"I know," Lexie said, meeting his gaze. "I saw the look on your face when he said it."

"I've done a lot of bad shit in my life, Lexie. A

lot of shit I can't undo, and that still haunts me. That night is one of many."

"You can tell me when you're ready," Lexie suggested, knowing how difficult this conversation was for him.

"No, I need to tell you. You deserve to know what I've done." Jackson searched her eyes and Lexie offered him encouragement.

"It was the day before I was arrested for the final time. Giles pulled me off the street the next day, but it wasn't soon enough. I was still working for Black at the time as his fucking puppet. He told me what to do and I did it, no questions asked. He sent us to burn down a house. I didn't think much about it. Black had always used extreme measures to send a message to anyone who didn't obey him. He told us no one was home." Jackson paused to take a deep, calming breath. "I sat in my car and watched the guys pour gasoline all around the house and douse the front step. I thought I saw movement in the window upstairs. I watched it for a moment but believed it was just my imagination." Lexie could see Jackson's eyes glisten as he looked at nothing in particular. He was lost in the haunting memory. "I still can still see the match light and then the flames completely engulf the house. I can still feel the heat on my face as I watched it burn." Jackson closed his eyes. "I didn't know there was a family in there until I read the fucking paper in the police station a few days later. "It hate myself for it. I hate myself for all the terrible shit I've done. I should have checked the house." Jackson opened his eyes again and what Lexie saw scared her.

"Jackson, look at me." Lexie grabbed his arm and turned him toward her. "Those deaths are on Black. If you weren't there that night, he would have sent someone else. It was a horrible thing that happened, but you didn't know. You didn't knowingly hurt them."

"I might as well have," Jackson confessed.

"No, you can't think like that. It will destroy you," Lexie insisted. "We need to learn from our mistakes and make better decisions. You're not that person anymore."

"When Stodden was still alive it was easy to convince myself to stay, but ever since we walked out of that club, the reasons that I should go are piling up," Jackson admitted. "If I walk away you can have a fresh start without the reminders of the terrible things that have happened. With me you will never truly be safe. My job puts me in danger every day."

"Stop it, Jackson. Don't you dare say another word," Lexie demanded. "I was stuck in the past before all this happened. I didn't really have a future because I couldn't stop looking behind me." Lexie held up the nail polish. "Alex bought this color for me. He painted it on my toes the morning before he was killed." Lexie looked into Jackson's eyes. He was quiet as he waited for her to continue. "After it happened, I would paint my toes whenever the color would begin to chip away, because in some way that made it seem like he was still with me. I lived in this bubble, surviving one day to the next until the bottle ran out. I was terrified what it meant. I just wanted to stay close to him the only way I knew how. I searched everywhere for that color until I found it that day with you." Lexie paused to take a deep, calming breath. "But I haven't been able to bring myself to put it on because I know I don't want to live in the past anymore. I want to remember, but now I want a future. You made me realize there is more for me in the world than what I have already lived. I'm not scared of danger, Jackson. I'm not scared of what you've done. The only thing I'm scared of was the girl I was. You are part of my life now whether you agree with it or not. I will not let you walk away from me. I'll take you however you come because I'm in love with you."

"Remember when you asked me if beautiful things can come from horrible beginnings?" Jackson asked.

"Yeah."

"They can," Jackson said. His smile felt so warm and bright it melted away all the sadness.

Lexie set the nail polish on the mantle and ran her fingers over it. "To remembering those we have loved and lost, and also to remind us that we owe it to them to live."

Jackson reached in his jacket pocket and pulled out the Walkman he still carried with him. He looked at it for a moment thoughtfully before placing it beside the nail polish.

"Your father would be proud of you, Jackson."

"He would've loved you," Jackson confessed. She could feel the tension draining from him as he placed his hands on either side of her face and leaned in close. "God, I know I do," Jackson whispered against her mouth before claiming it.

Lexie moaned in appreciation "Mmm...I'm looking forward to the future because it tastes absolutely delicious," Lexie said delightfully.

Jackson pulled away with a devious glimmer in his eye. "Delicious, you say?"

Lexie screamed as he grabbed her and threw her over his shoulder. "Be careful! You're injured."

"You're not the only one that likes a little pain with their pleasure, baby."

To be continued...

ACKNOWLEDGEMENTS

A huge thank you to:

My family, who are always my biggest fans.
Limitless Publishing, for giving me the opportunity to share this series with the world.
Toni Rakestraw, my fabulous editor, who has to fix all of my annoying writing habits.
Dawn Canfield, Hot Pressed Books, for her great advice.
My reader group, Aimee's Amazing Aces, who are endlessly lovely and supportive!
Readers, these were only words upon the pages until you brought them to life.

ABOUT THE AUTHOR

Aimee McNeil was born and raised in Nova Scotia, Canada, where she continues to live today with her husband and three children. She is a stay-at-home mother that loves every colorful moment with her family.

Aimee spends most of her free time indulging in her love of writing. You can also find her lost in the pages of a good book, or making a mess with her paints. Aimee loves to explore anything that promotes creativity. It is one of the many reason she enjoys writing.

Facebook:
https://www.facebook.com/aimeemcneilswriting

Twitter:
https://twitter.com/aimeeswriting

Website:
http://www.aimeemcneil.com/